A FRIENDLY DECEIT

JOHNS HOPKINS: POETRY AND FICTION

John T. Irwin, General Editor

A Friendly Deceit

SHORT STORIES
BY

Greg Johnson

The
Johns Hopkins
University Press

BALTIMORE *&* LONDON

This book has been brought to publication with
the generous assistance of the G. Harry Pouder Fund.

Printed in the United States of America
on acid-free paper

The Johns Hopkins University Press
701 West 40th Street
Baltimore, Maryland 21211-2190
The Johns Hopkins Press Ltd., London

Library of Congress Cataloging-in-Publication Data

Johnson, Greg, 1953–
A friendly deceit / Greg Johnson.
p.   cm. — (Johns Hopkins, poetry and fiction)
ISBN 0-8018-4406-1 (hc). — ISBN 0-8018-4407-X (pbk).
I. Title.   II. Series.
PS3560.03775F7   1992
813'.54—dc20   91-44218

DESIGNED BY LAURY A. EGAN

—*for* Joyce and Ray Smith

So it is more useful to watch a man in times of peril, and in adversity to discern what kind of man he is; for then at last words of truth are drawn from the depths of his heart, and when the mask is torn off, reality remains.
—Lucretius, *De Rerum Natura*

There is a smile of love,
And there is a smile of deceit,
And there is a smile of smiles
In which these two smiles meet.
—William Blake, "The Smile"

CONTENTS

A FRIENDLY DECEIT

A Friendly Deceit

I

SHE TOLD him everything, finally. She had no choice.

When he was younger, he'd often ask about his father, but had to be content with her vague or minimal replies. *He* had no choice, then. During his tenderest years his mother conspired with her Aunt Agnes to create a Vietnam father, a twenty-year-old "Ramey Senior" complete with rugged idealism, a soldierly blondness, an airport kiss planted on his infant son's forehead. This gave him a respectable story to tell at school. Yet Ramey hadn't been bothered by his friends' jibes at his fatherless state, their crude interpretations of his mother's resolute singleness, or even his own schoolyard status as "little bastard," eventually shortened out of laziness or boredom to "L.B.," his nickname until he transferred to junior high; rather he was troubled by the chinks in his mother and great aunt's story, the frequent contradictions. (He'd learned to question them separately, in his carefully oblique manner, and their stories were seldom straight, his aunt's flowery and too detailed, like Agnes herself, and his mother's two-dimensional, impatient, offhand, as if she must invent his father afresh each time the boy asked.) However the women tried, "Ramey Senior" never assumed the ghostly resonance of space once occupied by flesh and blood.

And there were no photographs—strange. ("Your mother burned them," Aunt Agnes said, her eyes brimming, "on the night she heard the news; she couldn't bear reminders." "I lost them during one of our moves," his mother said.) And their surname was Martin, the same as Aunt Agnes's—stranger still. ("His last name?" Aunt Agnes said, flustered. "It was . . . Jones, but your mother went back to Martin; she didn't want to be reminded." His mother said, "Well, his last name was Martin, too. It's a common name, Ramey.") Yet he never confronted them. That wasn't his mother's style and did not become his.

By the time he was fourteen, the fiction of his war-veteran father had been abandoned, a tacit agreement among them. Ramey had become a quiet, intent, eerily self-possessed boy who knew better than to ask childish questions. His aunt, whom he saw less frequently now, surely felt a guilty relief, and Ramey supposed in rare moments of whimsy that his mother had forgotten the story entirely. "What? A soldier?" she might respond if he raised the question suddenly, after these several years (which were a small lifetime to him), "a soldier in Vietnam . . . ?" But he didn't ask, of course. When his friends at the new school would ask, he responded curtly: "He died. I never knew him." That usually ended the matter. By the time he was sixteen or seventeen and began to have steady girlfriends, he faced an occasional inquisition on the subject, but they were neither as subtle nor as studied as his own had been, years ago; such queries were easy to deflect or dismiss. Yet he never lied, and after dating several girls he earned a reputation for cruelty. He pondered the irony of this, for he had learned everything except truthfulness from his mother, who was known for her "compassion" although she seldom spoke the truth to anyone.

Or because she didn't, maybe. His mother was a nurse; while her son was a toddler, she'd begun putting herself through school. She worked in hospitals for a while—some of his earliest memories were the odor of disinfectant soap on her hands and arms when she came home, and the pleasantly clinical smell of her white rubber shoes— but got tired, she said, of "dealing with the bureaucracy," and became a critical-care nurse. She stayed in the homes of patients, most of them terminally ill, some of them wealthy, and without fail these people wrote her glowing recommendations before they died. Sometimes they even left her money. Her son remembered being shown, when he was twelve or thirteen, a sheaf of these letters, for his mother was very proud of them. (Though beautiful, she was vain about few things.) The boy looked through the letters, seeing such phrases as "so efficient, and yet so gentle," and "I don't know what I'd do without Julia," and "Before Julia Martin was hired, I'd almost given up hope." He saw the word *hope* more than once and he couldn't help thinking that she lied to her patients, too. She told them what they wanted to hear, which inspired love, and continued hope. And money.

The older he got, the more her son became aware that he tended to be too hard on her; too judgmental. He hadn't gotten that from her, either, for she expressed often the idea that she didn't care what others did. Her only pronounced scorn was for meddlers, busybodies. Into this category she placed Aunt Agnes, their only relation, a kindhearted if slightly dim woman who often tried to "fix up" his mother with young men Agnes met at her church. She'd been doing this, his mother once let slip, since Julia was sixteen, and not one of those dates had ever amounted to anything. (Of course, she'd forgotten that Aunt Agnes had supposedly introduced her to "Ramey Senior," at a church social; and of course, he didn't remind her.) Aunt Agnes had raised Julia from the age of four, when the child's parents had died, their car veering into an embankment for no apparent reason, but as the years passed her sense of duty to Agnes diminished, even as her aunt's fluttering concern grew more intense. (On those occasions, increasingly rare during Ramey's teenage years, when they visited Agnes, she would sometimes fret privately that Julia needed to "meet someone," which puzzled Ramey since Julia was obviously doing well, and had never complained of loneliness in her life; he supposed that Agnes was tormented by some original, unfulfilled sense of duty toward her dead brother, so long as Julia remained unmarried. Perhaps she, too, considered Ramey a little bastard.)

They moved every couple of years, and her son noticed that each time they were further away from Agnes's house in Druid Hills, and eventually his mother began to speak of leaving Atlanta entirely, perhaps living in the country one day. Did Ramey have any interest in farming? his mother asked, shortly before her son's high school graduation. They hadn't even discussed what he would study in college, she said, with a rare laugh; had Ramey given any thought to that?

The moment had come. Ramey said, "You know that girl I've been seeing, Elise Mattison?"

"What? That new one, that curly-haired blonde . . . ?"

"Yes, but she's not new. We've been dating since the beginning of senior year."

His mother stared, her quick dark eyes fixed on him in a way they seldom did; usually her gaze was roving, restless. It was a Wednesday evening, past eleven o'clock. His mother had just gotten home and, still in her white uniform, had made herself some milk and graham crackers in the kitchen. Ramey had wandered out from his bedroom, a book in his hand: a paperback about how to pick a college or university, which had startled Julia into initiating this conversation.

"But what about her?" his mother asked. "What does she have to do with—"

"We've decided to get married and move to Athens. She wants to be a vet, so she's going to the University of Georgia."

"A vet?" his mother said blankly. "But are you—"

"I don't know what I'll study," he said. "I'll figure that out, eventually. The point is that I want to marry Elise."

3

His mother reached behind her, for a chair-back; until this moment Julia had seemed immune to emotional distress. Ramey watched as if from a great distance. He did not know what would happen next. He'd always assumed that his mother was invulnerable, even her beauty worn like a shield, smooth-surfaced, daunting. Her dark hair made a curved frame for her face, and was fastened neatly in back, just above her starched collar; beneath heavy brows she had eyes of a chill slate-blue, fine bones, a slightly prominent nose. Her body was compact, giving an impression of strength—the limbs slender, ropy, with a rope's fibrous toughness beneath the smooth-gleaming olive skin. He hadn't a doubt that if he left her and Elise in a closed room, his mother would emerge the victor as surely as she emerged a final time from each of her patient's rooms, with dry eyes and clean hands.

So she would survive even this, he thought. And so would he.

He said, "It's only sixty miles. You can come and visit us."

Expressing this preposterous notion, his voice had become a monotone. He watched as his mother—her face slightly paled but otherwise expressionless, betraying nothing—pulled out the chair as if completing a casual gesture. She sat. She tilted her head in his direction, her lips twitching upward in the effort to smile, but her eyes didn't quite meet his. Yet they were dry, like his.

Ramey folded his arms across his chest, listening.

She said, "But you're so young. These days, young people don't . . . "

"Some do," Ramey said.

She spoke more quickly. Already her mind had recovered and was thinking, working.

"This may sound strange, coming from your mother, but maybe you should go slowly, at first . . . you know, just live together for a while. I mean, you kids are just eighteen, and you don't know the first thing—"

She stopped herself, out of tact. So he presumed.

"It doesn't," he said. "Not at all."

"It doesn't . . . ?"

"Sound strange," he said. "Coming from my mother."

He regretted each word as it came out. He suffered the unwelcome memory of a recent night with Elise, when he'd tried with his jaw grinding to hold back, he'd only just entered her but the savage visceral warning had arrived too late and he came in a shameful desperate surge, his eyes clenched. Next time he'd be more careful, he vowed: he'd force his mind onto something else. And he'd done just that.

4

Now his mother's eyes had turned a darker, duskier blue; it took some effort not to look away. He noted with a thrill of envy that her facial bones had relaxed, shifting to a kind of compliant slackness, a surrender to the moment—the inevitable moment—while his own face had tensed so that his eyes and jaws ached, and he felt at the base of his skull the beginnings of a headache, a bad one. He'd been plagued with headaches since early adolescence. Occasionally his mother would hand him a tablet or capsule, prescription analgesics whose names he did not know. Julia herself never took so much as an aspirin.

Now she said, as though diagnosing a subtle ailment, "You're still angry, aren't you. After all this time."

Ramey said: "Look, I've got my own life to lead."

She smiled vaguely. "You do," she said. "You do."

They stared at each other, the mother with her thick dark eyebrows lifted slightly, the son whose crossed arms now felt locked into place.

Ramey heard, despite the pain throbbing now in his ears, so warm, sickish, hurtful, nonetheless he heard: "I'll tell you about your father, Ramey. I'll tell you the truth."

He stood with hot eyes, wanting to run out. He stayed.

II

After finishing high school, she moved out of Aunt Agnes's house, over the woman's whining protests. Julia loved her aunt, but . . . but she hungered for independence. For years her teachers, and the parents of her acquaintances at school, had remarked that she was mature for her age (her voice went lower, in what must have been modesty, relating this to her son), and this was the 1960s, after all, a time when young women routinely lived alone. And there was money she hadn't been told about, handed over during that same heady spring of her senior year, on her eighteenth birthday: money held in trust since her parents' death and managed scrupulously by Aunt Agnes, who hoped that her niece—a daughter, almost!—would live at home while she pursued an education, or a husband, or took her first full-time job. Instead Julia rented a tidy garage apartment owned by an elderly couple, both rather frail, the wife suffering from bone-marrow cancer, and in exchange for light housekeeping and companionship Julia paid only a nominal rent. The job suited her well, and the idea of a nursing career first entered her thinking. Julia visited her aunt on Sunday mornings, and sometimes attended church with her, but despite the woman's entreaties it was clear within a few months that Julia Martin enjoyed her new independence and would never dream of returning home.

She was somewhat extravagant, at first. She refurbished the garage apartment, hiring painters, indulging in custom-made drapes and even a few antiques. She developed a taste, too, for conservatively tailored but expensive clothes of the kind Agnes could never have afforded, on her schoolteacher's salary. By the time Julia began thinking seriously of nursing school, she had gone through most of the money and had obtained, in addition to her caretaking job, a clerical position in a small branch library near her apartment. By the spring of her twenty-second year, her prospects had suddenly darkened; or at least, she corrected herself, the change seemed sudden to her. She hadn't been given to thinking much about the future. Occasionally she went out with young men she met at the library, or at the church socials to which Agnes sometimes dragged her, or even with men she encountered in the neighborhood as she walked old Mr. Hennigan's ill-tempered chihuahua. (The dog had belonged to Mrs. Hennigan, but the woman had finally succumbed to her illness the year before; Mr. Hennigan, though he'd always despised the dog, kept it around for sentimental reasons.) Yet Julia seldom dated such men more than once or twice: she struck them as aloof, she supposed, or even forbidding, as if some presence not unlike that nervous, menacing chihuahua were always there between them, even when they were alone.

One man did persist, for a while: a newly divorced young attorney, very handsome (she supposed), with a smooth rambling voice and, he confessed, a "fascination" for Julia. They had five or six dates, and her life might have gone in another direction entirely if Mr. Hennigan hadn't suffered a massive stroke and died, causing a second influx of his children from various parts of the country. They'd been friendly to Julia after their mother's death, but this time they were decidedly cool: Mr. Hennigan had left Julia a small bequest—a "remembrance," the will termed it—of ten thousand dollars. As was their right, the children gave Julia sixty days' notice to vacate the apartment. The house was being sold, they told her. Thank you for the kindness you have shown to both our parents.

Julia asked for the chihuahua; and the children, though puzzled, surrendered it gladly. Yet the dog, confined in the small two-room apartment, drove her to distraction. A few days before she moved out, she took the dog quietly to the vet to be put to sleep.

She moved to a larger apartment, in midtown, in an old red-brick building off Piedmont Avenue. Again she spent much of her money refurbishing the place, though the process gave her less pleasure this time. (She spoke the word "pleasure" in an offhand, sighing voice that brought a twitching movement, perhaps of sympathy, to Ramey's lips.) She'd put off nursing school for another year, and had increased her hours at the library, which was now a thirty-minute drive from her apartment. She bought a newer car, but it began immediately to give her trouble. Somehow the lawyer had gotten her new phone number, though she'd paid to keep it out of the directory, and at last, during one of his pleading harangues, Julia calmly hung up the phone. His energy was oppressive, finally. She feared that he would show up at the library, but he stayed away. Now when the phone rang, it was always Aunt Agnes, and to Julia the future seemed a narrowing dark tunnel that pulled her forward against her will, eroding her youth and vitality slowly, by degrees, the way Mrs. Hennigan's cancer had reduced her to a sack of useless bones.

And she was only twenty-two! his mother laughed, darkly; and with her whole life ahead of her, as Agnes often remarked. Yet Julia hadn't been able to view her life that way.

At about this time, Agnes introduced her to yet another young man at church. His name was Ned—honestly she couldn't remember what his last name was. Tall, ruddy-skinned, with reddish-blond hair he wore in a crewcut, whether in defiance or blind ignorance of the current fashion Julia couldn't be sure. His very seriousness was anachronistic, and appealing: he'd studied business and real estate at the state university downtown, he'd gotten his broker's license and now worked in his uncle's office, he wore short-sleeved white shirts and the same narrow red tie to work every morning. His good-luck tie, he told Julia. He wore the tie to church, too, and on their half-dozen dates, and on the night in Julia's living room when, after coffee, he got to his knees and with no trace of irony expressed his undying love and his fervent desire to marry her. His smallish mild-blue eyes were narrowed, aching; in the lamplight his pink scalp showed through the crewcut, and as she stared down at him, amazed, Julia had the stray thought that he must have visited the barber that very morning, thinking ahead to their date and what he planned to say. . . . Yet her own response had surprised her far more than the proposal itself. She'd said, sputtering, "Well, yes— thank you."

He hadn't been put off by her awkwardness; perhaps her lapse in poise made her answer seem the more sincere. She didn't know. She recalled that he went off, happily, after giving her a quick shy breathless kiss on the cheek.

7

For he'd been conventional, she said, her voice dropped to a murmur, in matters of sex. Though he seldom spoke of his religious convictions, she knew this meant they were ingrained and unexamined—like his conservative politics, his desire for success, his belief in family life—and therefore unshakable. It was Julia herself, she told her son, her voice kept low, who'd had to initiate their intimacy, though she'd accomplished this subtly enough, no doubt permitting Ned to believe that the initiative was his own. She'd used age-old feminine tricks, or feminine *wiles* if Ramey preferred: it wasn't much of a challenge, really, since she felt that even ingrained religious principles and the codes of Southern chivalry and "respect for women" were thin barricades indeed against the storming ferocity of youthful male desire; and she'd proved herself right, of course. Yet she couldn't help (so her son felt, believing his mother relatively incapable of objective self-analysis) focusing on the deceit itself, a plan that seemed neat, swift, heartless, and in its own way, beautiful, in the manner of intricate glittering webs woven from the bodies of spiders and the minds of sociopaths, Ramey thought, savoring the words, *spiders and sociopaths, sociopaths and spiders,* but after this brief indulgence he willed his mind not to ramble, to speculate, to judge, and merely allowed his mother to tell her tale.

Ned and Julia had developed a routine more appropriate to a couple in the middle 1950s than the early 1970s. On Friday nights, Ned would be exhausted from his long work week and they'd simply talk on the phone, though sometimes for hours, Ned speaking with a droning but persistent enthusiasm of properties and contracts, recent and impending deals, the personal quirks of his clients and colleagues. (Julia imagined him lying in bed with the phone trapped between ear and shoulder, fresh from his bath, in his jockey shorts: pink-skinned and innocent, a kind of overgrown adolescent. Though Ned was far too modest ever to discuss what he might or might not be wearing.) Occasionally Ned would refer to their "future" together, make shy laughing references to kids and mortgages and the terrors of middle age, and before they hung up he said invariably, quite quickly, "Love you," and Julia answered softly, also quickly, "Love you, too."

That was Friday. On Saturdays they went shopping, saw movies in the evening, and afterwards went out for Italian or Mexican food; when they returned to Julia's apartment Ned would kiss her at the door like a high school kid, whispering "See you in a few hours," and then return swiftly on Sunday mornings and escort her to church. In the afternoons, still dressed up, they would visit Aunt Agnes or Ned's parents, who lived on an old farm west of Atlanta, and then they returned to Julia's, Ned watching ball games or reading the paper while she prepared their dinner. These Sunday night meals were the high point, as Ned often told Julia, of their weekends together. She made his favorite foods: manicotti, baked lasagne, meat loaf smothered in tomato sauce; squash, string beans, black-eyed peas; and peach pie or apple cobbler for dessert. Ned's impetuous proposal (or had it been carefully and nervously planned?) came on the second or third of these Sunday evenings, and soon after that Julia began dreaming ahead, watching the calendar, calibrating the secret rhythms of her blood in the effort to bring the future, *her* future, into being. She could not pinpoint the moment when she first knew her terrible longing for a child. Rather it seemed that the longing, once acknowledged and identified, had always been there, consuming her the way intense pain or joy can obliterate other states of consciousness, render future and past into mere dreamlike notions, lacking much substance, for at such times there is only the pressing urgency of *now*.

It was much the same, she supposed, with a man's erotic need: the blind madness of the present moment consumes or simply denies all obstacles and defenses. Thus she felt calm and confident and even, in a detached way, regretful, on that Sunday evening in mid-April when the doorbell rang promptly at seven P.M. On that day Julia had sent him away after church, saying she had housecleaning to do, and some last-minute shopping. In fact, she'd merely wanted the afternoon to herself—a languorous bubble bath, extra time for primping before a mirror. That week she'd bought a new dress of close-fitted black silk, the bodice low-cut but not provocative, the skirt pleated and quite short, in the style of the day—perhaps four inches above the knee. There were new nylons, shimmering and expensive; her shoes were little more than a few thin straps, also expensive, elaborately designed in gleaming black leather; her only jewelry was the slender gold chain and heart-shaped locket Ned had given Julia a few weeks ago, on her birthday. She had brushed her dark fresh-washed hair back from her face, revealing her dramatic widow's peak and smooth forehead and her tiny but exquisitely molded ears. Except for a coating of pale lipstick, she used no cosmetics; Ned had once referred to makeup as unnatural. Though she'd bought a new and costly musk perfume, at the last moment she'd decided against wearing it. Her body emitted its own scent, she reasoned. She would depend upon that.

After dinner, they sat in the living room. Rather than closer, Julia sat farther from Ned than usual—hugging, in fact, her side of the sofa. This caused him to edge closer, just as something dreamy and abstracted in Julia's manner—with a tinge of melancholy, perhaps—focused his attention and, fairly quickly, excited his desire. Was something the matter? he asked. No, nothing was. Did she want—? But he didn't know how to finish this question, so he took her hand; and when her gaze would not meet his, he touched her cheek. Romantically, she told Ramey (with a sigh of what must have been wistful remembrance); using the backs of his fingers, drawing them slowly downward from cheekbone to jaw. That's when she felt the wholly unexpected miracle of tears. She hadn't planned for them; hadn't supposed herself capable. Yet they pooled in her eyes quickly, but not quite to the point of falling—just clinging, glistening, and then she heard "Poor baby" and felt his body heat coming near. Her eyes closed the moment his lips touched hers, so that the tears spilled and lubricated the quick heated series of kisses that brought his body closer, ever closer. He was squirming, she told Ramey quickly, her headshake suggesting fastidious distaste. His response, she supposed, had something to do with the wetness of their faces, their hot cheeks slick with tears, Ned's opened mouth sliding downward to her throat at which point she heard his telltale guttural murmur, repetitive, unconscious, letting her know that everything had begun and, in a sense, ended, and that the responsibility was no longer hers. Now, with impunity, she could urge things along, adjust a leg or elbow to make the process easier, help with a recalcitrant snap or button, respond to every move closer with an accepting sigh or murmur, until finally they lay on the sofa in a massive ungainly heap, heartbeats and breaths calming, skin drying and cooling, Ned's mind (she presumed) beginning slowly to function again; to cast backward, or forward; to ache with regret, or defiance; to replace the consciousness of all-but-sex with the embittered mind that is removed from sex but cannot escape its ongoing central power, attached umbilically and hovering, circling, all around it. Thus a wide range of implication, she told Ramey, was held in Ned's simply whispered, "I'm sorry," and as for her whispered reply, "I'm not," she left that to Ned's or Ramey's or God's interpretation. The men in my life, she laughed, as though mocking the pathetic grandness of it all.

Then she paused, adding that their leave-taking was brief. His posture remorseful at first, hers shy and demure: had not such scenes been replayed millions of times, in living rooms all across America? Though she hadn't pondered this at the time. Rather she'd been startled again, even more cruelly than when those renegade tears had sprung to her eyes. Seeing Ned out, handing him his jacket and the red tie (which had slipped off, and down between the sofa cushions), she felt suddenly the pleasure of his strong male body atop and inside of hers; felt her own responding passion follow like a succession of building waves, threatening to engulf her consciousness itself as she stood there bidding him goodbye. How strange that her pleasure should be so delayed, she thought in wonder; almost, she supposed, as though she'd been doing something else at the time. The final wave descended into her body with a quiet, dark-toned, heartbreaking murmur: it was the moment she first heard the baby's voice inside her, as if uttering a promise or plea, and of course Ned mistook her look of faintness and wonderment for some meretricious aftershock of shame or fear or worry.

"It's all right," he said, his self-possession regained. He bent to place a clammy kiss on her cheek. "We'll talk this over tomorrow. After all, Julia, we're in love, aren't we?" The question seemed merely rhetorical. "So it's not the end of the world, but the beginning of one."

She blinked her eyes, at this unexpected surge into metaphor; she saw that his face was ruddy, glowing, *manly*. The sex had enlivened him, and she supposed he'd just learned something about himself, taken a step into masculine worldliness. It was all there in his new confidence and smugness, and now within the cool resonating shell of her body she knew again the keen anticipation she'd felt for weeks at the prospect of closing the door behind him, and forever.

"Yes," she'd told him, faintly. "I know."

"Call you in the morning, hon," he said, going out, and as he went down the hall Julia focused deliberately on the white scalp visible beneath his haircut, especially across the jutting back bones of his skull.

"All right!" she called after him, wanting at the last minute to sound forgiving, even friendly, hoping that later he might decide to remember that.

The next morning, her phone service was disconnected promptly at nine, just as she had ordered; the boxes and bags already packed and waiting were transported downstairs by the movers in less than an hour. Her new apartment, smaller and less expensive, was on the edge of downtown, not far from the university where she would soon begin her nursing studies. For a long while, even Aunt Agnes (who had a weakness for Ned) did not have her new phone number, which was published under the simple listing "J. Martin" (there were twelve others like it), but secretly Julia held to the idea that Ned's pride would forestall any extraordinary attempts to seek her out. According to Aunt Agnes, he continued regular church attendance, always nodding politely in Agnes's direction, until about two years later, when he suddenly disappeared. A friend of Agnes's thought that he'd moved to Arizona—or was it California?—where the real estate market was more promising, but the woman couldn't say for sure. It was only a rumor that she'd heard, she insisted; a story told at two or even three removes.

Somehow, the mystery of Ned's eventual destination suited Julia's temperament, as did the specificity of that last memory, her standing there at her doorway, watching him walk toward the elevator, his scalp illuminated in the meager hallway lights. Time served only to embellish the memory, until she could follow his gleaming scalp and jutting skull bones into the elevator and behind the closed doors, where she could not help imagining him denuded of flesh and hair altogether, standing there solid but doomed in his very bones. This image, she said quietly, would haunt her all her life: Ramey's father's skull and erect skeleton, wearing a thin red tie and trapped in that elevator, descending.

III

Ramey's first semester at college outlasted his marriage. Silently one November afternoon he drove Elise to Atlanta, where she boarded a train to Birmingham, to the home of an indulgent aunt. For now, she was giving up her studies—the stress of the past three months had undone her—and she felt too ashamed to stay in Atlanta, with her parents. At the station, he kissed her good-bye and, to his horror, Elise apologized to *him*. He saw that she considered herself emotional and weak and dependent. In Birmingham, she planned to enter therapy for a while. Ramey was too exhausted to argue or explain.

Watching the train churning out of the station, he thought suddenly of his grandparents who had died years before Ramey's birth. Almost as an afterthought to her story, Julia had remarked that *she'd* been angry, for a long while, but had given it up. Her father had been a drinker, evidently, and it seemed likely that he'd been drunk on the day their car had wrecked so mysteriously; or that his drinking had precluded his tending to some needed repair to the car's engine; or that it had, in some other way, brought him and Julia's mother to this final pass in their lives. Years later, with a nurse's efficiency, she'd sought out records of the accident and learned that the impact was so terrific that her parents had literally to be picked out of the wreckage, bone by bone.

Yes, she'd been angry for a while, but had given it up.

In mid-December she phoned Ramey, for the first time since his move to Athens. He'd supposed that she had been angry when he and Elise decided on an elopement; they had sent Julia a postcard several weeks later. Or perhaps she wouldn't have called in any case. Exchanging some initial banter with his mother, Ramey wondered if she'd heard, somehow, that Elise had left and would soon file for a divorce. If she had, he couldn't imagine how their conversation might run.

But no, she'd merely called to ask about Christmas. It was just two weeks away, she said, laughing—could Ramey believe that?

He heard the loneliness in her voice and closed his eyes.

He said quickly, "We're going to Elise's—her folks are big on that kind of thing, family get-togethers and such. I can't get out of it."

A long silence across the wires. Then her voice came almost meekly.

"Oh well . . . then soon after New Year's," she said. Then, in a quick surge: "I want to get to know you and—I mean, to know Elise—and though it may sound strange, coming from your mother, I always want us to be friends, from now on. We can be friends, Ramey, can't we . . . ?"

He couldn't answer; he felt as if a bone had lodged in his throat. Already he'd met another girl—her name was Janelle—in his American history class. She was forthright, long-limbed, athletic—nothing like Elise and nothing like his mother, and he was thinking that perhaps he would tell Janelle, or some other girl who succeeded her, the story of everything that had happened to this point in his life. Perhaps then he could answer his mother, he thought. Perhaps someday he would figure out the story, but it was one he'd tell when he was ready to tell, and stop when he was ready to stop.

The Boarder

PEOPLE enter your life in the oddest ways!—something I've often observed to Ralston, without his exactly agreeing. Ralston is my husband: fifty-five, soft-spoken, and solid as a brick building, but he isn't much for philosophical remarks or stepping back to consider the long view. He just plows right along, one day after another, and you've got to admire that. He likes most people, but doesn't have the easily piqued *curiosity* about them like I do, and so it's doubtful that he'd ever have met Professor Coates—in the odd way I met him, or any way at all—if I hadn't had what Ralston calls, dry-mouthed, one of my "bright ideas." In my opinion he'd also have missed a most profound and illuminating experience, though there's little chance of Ralston admitting to that.

My idea, to be plain, was that we take in Professor Coates as a boarder. He and I had met in the cleaners one day, the one I've patronized for twenty years or so, where I'd just gotten in line behind a small-framed youngish man in a tweed jacket. He stood quietly holding up a dress shirt on a hanger, the sleeves lifted up to show underarms that had been . . . well, pulverized, it looked like. In a snap I saw that they'd used much too strong a chemical for the underarm stains and that the young man should get a new shirt, but the clerk— a tiny, red-haired girl I'd never cared for—stood there shaking her head. And then, out of the young man's mouth, came the most amazing words: "Oh, very well. I hope you don't mind my having asked." The girl blinked, half-smiled in a smug way, and it was then I had one of my "impulses," as Ralston calls them. I just *had* to see that young man's face, so I stepped around and got on tiptoes (I'm a rather petite woman) to peer over the shoulder of the ruined shirt.

"I couldn't help overhearing," I began—and not to brag or go on about it, I had the manager out front within five minutes and a new twenty-dollar bill in Professor Coates's hand. The red-haired girl had left for her lunch break, in something of a huff.

Anyhow, that's how we met, and out on the sidewalk we got to talking. He interested me right away because he seemed so helpless

14

and had such excellent manners. He spoke in this odd, kind of formal way, not off-putting or affected but like he hadn't yet got the knack of talking like ordinary people. For instance: "You were extremely kind to intercede for me like that." And a minute later: "Why, a cup of coffee at your house would be delightful. How hospitable of you." Now I found this way of talk most intriguing, especially since the man looked normal in every other respect. Professor Coates was about thirty-five, with dark hair neatly cut, and eyeglasses with thick rims tinted the same deep brown as his eyes, and slender clean hands—the nails *exquisitely* clean and well tended—and a generally shy and kind-hearted aura to him, the sort that's very appealing to a woman. And he looked at you so directly, with such friendliness and gratitude, that you couldn't help but love him right away ("love" is exactly the right word, but don't jump to conclusions: I'm old enough to be the professor's mom and besides, despite all the little digs I'm nuts about Ralston). It's just that I found Professor Coates . . . well, so interesting, and also vulnerable somehow, undefended. An attractive trait in that rough-and-tumble world out there, so I was tickled pink when he accepted my invitation for coffee—after all, I told him, I lived just around the corner, and no, it wasn't any trouble at all.

So we went. And sat there talking. And having coffee, and later some lemonade, followed by a plateful of macaroons. And we talked some more. The experience, I tell you, was beyond anything I could have expected. Granted, I did most of the talking at first. I told him about Ralston and his work down at the tire store, and about our daughter Sarah who had just flown off to college the month before, and about our sixteen-year-old spaniel, Lucky, who'd died in her sleep just a week before that. I said how upset Sarah had gotten, insisting that Lucky had somehow sensed that she was going to abandon her, how it was all her fault and now she wasn't going, after all!—those few days had been terrible, probably the worst we'd ever lived through as a family. Ralston had spent a couple of hours up in Sarah's bedroom, talking in a gentle, persuasive voice, and when he came out he looked gray as ashes and said that Sarah had decided to leave a week *early* for college, she'd get there the day the dorms opened and try to busy herself with— But then I stopped myself; I'd felt a little catch in my throat. "Enough of that!" I said to Professor Coates, laughing it off. "I guess you're not interested in an old lady's troubles."

This wasn't completely honest, I suppose, since all the time I talked Professor Coates hadn't moved his damp brown eyes from mine. He sat very erect, every now and then taking a small sip of the coffee, looking concerned and thoughtful; his listening so closely made me a bit self-conscious.

"On the contrary," Professor Coates said, in his polite way. "Your story is very affecting. You must have a great deal of strength."

"Strength?" I said. I didn't understand.

"Inner strength," Professor Coates said.

No one had ever told me such a thing, and I felt that I'd earned the professor's respect without even trying. Certainly I'd earned his trust, since right away—and this is what I'd never have expected—he began talking about his own past life. Somehow I'd pegged him as a timid, withdrawn type, but actually he spoke in a frank unhurried voice, the rhythms pleasant and convincing. As he talked, I imagined this as the same voice he used to teach his classes at the University. For that's what he talked about first—his one-year appointment in the History department, his heavy work-load of preparing lectures and corresponding with other professors and writing a book (a long, complicated book, he said with a sigh) about Napoleon's last days. He'd moved to Atlanta in August, he said, but after two months he still didn't know much of anyone here, and he often thought that there wasn't much point—he had so much work to do, and he'd be moving somewhere else when the school year ended. The more Professor Coates talked, the more wistful he sounded. When I got up for the lemonade and cookies I said, "Go on, go on," and by the time I sat down again he'd already started talking about his parents.

Something awful had happened, he said. He broke one of the macaroons neatly in half, but then put both halves back down on the plate. The previous year, he said, he hadn't done any teaching. His mother had become very ill and he'd returned to Boston last September, to help take care of her. His father was retired but depressed—"severely depressed," Professor Coates said—and couldn't do much. Cancer, it was; a hopeless case. As the doctors had warned him, things went from bad to worse, and before Christmas she was gone. But that was only the beginning, in a way, because then he had to tend to his father, which was really much more taxing than his mother's care had been. In a slow, mournful voice Professor Coates told me that his father had died suddenly—that is, by his own hand. He didn't specify how, and of course I didn't ask. Big tears stood in my eyes; I took a swallow of lemonade to wash down the lump in my throat.

"That's—that's awful," I finally managed.

Professor Coates opened his long immaculate hands, palms up. "Thank you for listening," he said, his voice remarkably calm. "Over where I'm staying, it's pretty isolated. I really haven't made very many friends."

"Where *are* you staying?" I asked.

"Oh, just in the faculty quarters," Professor Coates said, shrugging. "Actually, it's quite a nice—"

"Why don't you move in here?"—the question and the idea came at the same moment, but I didn't regret my words. Ralston often says that I speak before I think, but what was there to think about, really? It was the perfect solution.

"You could stay in Sarah's bedroom," I said, talking faster now that Professor Coates was shaking his head. "I've often thought to myself, we should take in a boarder, we really should"—this was a white lie, I guess, but maybe I'd *felt* it, without really *thinking* it—"and since Mr. Parks and I sleep downstairs you'd have plenty of privacy, and your own bath. You could have dinner with us, too. I'm not a bad cook, and I—"

"Mrs. Parks, you're far too kind," and I could tell by his face that he was both alarmed and pleased by the invitation. The alarm I understood—it seemed too sudden, it was ridiculous when you thought that we'd only met a couple of hours ago. I've always had faith, however, in my woman's intuition—I have this knack for seeing to the heart of a situation, even Ralston will grant me that. Sometimes you have to proceed slowly, though; you have to bring people around.

"Well, at least come for dinner tonight," I said. "You can meet my husband, and we'll talk about it."

He paused, looking pleased despite himself. "I'd be delighted to come for dinner," he said, "but as for the other—" He stopped, reaching down for one of the macaroon halves.

We could discuss the matter, of course, but I knew that the thing was as good as done. I felt happy—completely, absurdly happy. So there was nothing left to do but reach across and take the other half of Professor Coates's macaroon. We sat there for a while, smiling, chewing happily. There was nothing more to say.

Granted, the idea of a boarder caused a tiff between Ralston and me. I'd told Professor Coates to come for dinner around seven, thinking I'd have a couple of hours to break the news to Ralston, calm him down, win him over; but naturally he picked that very evening to stop by his brother Ferris's house for a beer, so that when he got home at six-thirty I had to explain everything in a rush. We were in the dining room, where I kept straightening and restraightening the three plates, the silverware. I didn't much want to look at Ralston.

17

"Honey?" I said at last, adjusting a candle in the silverplate candelabrum we'd gotten for our twenty-fifth anniversary, from Ferris and his wife Julie. "Shouldn't you get cleaned up? I told Professor Coates seven o'clock, and it's already—"

"No," Ralston said, from behind me.

I turned around. He looked clean enough in his work khakis, his silver-white hair combed back neatly from his crown. Yet his eyes had darkened; he looked tired and angry at once.

"Then at least change your clothes, OK?" I said, keeping my voice light. "See what I'm wearing?" And I lifted my arms, turning smartly like one of those models on TV, showing off my sky-blue linen with the gathered sleeves and hoping to get a smile out of Ralston.

"I don't mean that," he said, the twin creases between his eyes getting deeper. "I mean *no* to the whole idea. No, no, no."

He pulled out his chair at the head of the table, snapping the cloth napkin onto his lap. "Let's eat."

"Ralston, I've invited the man for dinner. He's a very nice man, and I want *you* to be nice, too."

Ralston put down the fork he'd been holding above his empty plate, mockingly. The corners of his mouth drooped.

"For heaven's sake, Lily. Did you really ask the man to *live* with us? Without discussing it with me?"

He was weakening. I hurried over and sat in my usual chair, leaning close to Ralston and speaking in a near-whisper. "It's only for a few months, sweetie, only till the end of the school year. Then Sarah will be coming home, but in the meantime won't it be nice to have someone in the house? It's been so quiet around here."

"*You* live here," Ralston said, but I saw the little glint in his eye that meant I'd won. "So it's never quiet."

I reached out and pinched his forearm. "Scalawag," I said.

"But a perfect stranger, Lily," Ralston said. By now, even his shoulders had drooped. "A man we don't even know—"

"He's a lonesome fellow, I think," I said quickly, bringing out the ammunition I'd stored in my head all during the afternoon, "and it's the Christian thing to do, isn't it? I'm sure that Father Dalton would approve. And it'll bring a little money in, of course, and maybe he can even help around the house—you know, small repairs and such, and on top of that—"

Ralston had lifted his palm, so I stopped.

"It'll depend," he said.

"Depend? Depend on what?"

He threw me a look that said, *Dumb question, Lily!* Experience had taught me not to react to this look, so then Ralston said: "On *him*."

The doorbell rang.

"Fine," I said, getting up, smoothing my dress. "You'll see that I'm right, then. You'll be forced to *admit* that I'm right."

And, of course, he did exactly that, for Professor Coates was a completely charming dinner guest. He brought flowers for me, a bottle of Chardonnay for Ralston; he remarked on my dress several times and didn't seem to notice Ralston's khakis. And if I say so myself, the meal was delicious. Swiss steak, new potatoes, Caesar salad; and my famous raspberry cheesecake for dessert. During the meal Professor Coates asked us a good many questions, but nothing personal or inappropriate; he asked about Ralston's work down at the store, he asked about our church after I'd mentioned something about Sunday Mass, saying that he'd been raised as a Catholic, too, though unfortunately he had "lapsed" in recent years, and most of all he asked about Sarah, assuming that she was the favorite topic of conversation for both Ralston and me, which of course she was. This was the point, in fact, when the professor finally won my husband over. Ralston had been a bit reserved and stiffish up to now, but he leaned forward and asked Professor Coates eagerly about the college Sarah had chosen—was it really as well regarded as Sarah thought, would it give her the best possible chance for getting into law school, presuming she did well? Did most of Professor Coates's students, especially his freshman students, seem *happy* in their new lives, did they get over their homesickness quickly, did they make new friends?— and for that matter, what was college like, exactly? Professor Coates reassured him on all points, telling him about the social activities, the counselors, the sheer excitement of college life for most students. We shouldn't be alarmed at not hearing from Sarah very often—that was a good sign, in fact; it meant that she was just too busy to be homesick.

Ralston sat back from the table, satisfied. "How about some brandy for Professor Coates, Lily?" he asked, to my great surprise. "We still have that bottle, don't we?"

He meant the bottle from our little anniversary party, eight months before.

"Yes, of course," and as I poured brandy in the kitchen I heard Ralston saying to Professor Coates that if he'd like to board with us for the rest of the school year, that would be fine with him. For reply, I could hear only the professor's polite murmuring, but I felt sure that he would accept. During the dinner, it occurred to me that we had found out very little about him, and of course I didn't allude to the sad story about his parents. Having unburdened himself, perhaps he now felt embarrassed; and I wondered if his barrage of politely worded questions were a way, partly, to avoid revealing more about himself. A very shy man, this Professor Coates! And how pleasant it was, to be able to help him! Feeling a bit sly, I lifted one of the brandy glasses and made a toast to myself, for having accomplished so much in one day. The liquor burned in my throat and stomach, like the sweet glow of charity itself. Then I refilled the glass, and went back to join my husband and our new boarder.

For a long while, the arrangement worked perfectly. Professor Coates kept to himself most of the time, but he took his meals with us, and occasionally joined us for an evening of TV in the den. What a polite, well-groomed man he always was!—never a hair out of place, always wearing one of his tweed jackets and his carefully polished shoes. (Ralston and Professor Coates had made a Sunday morning ritual of polishing their shoes together, the professor his Bass Weejuns and Ralston the chunky black wing-tips he wears to church, the two looking for all the world like father and son as they worked and chatted.) Nor did he seem to mind our simple ways, commenting often on how "cozy" our house was, repeating every week or so how "eternally grateful" he felt to have lived here for a brief while, just like a member of the family. I noticed how often he mentioned his departure the following May, as though reminding himself that his "family member" status was temporary, or reminding us that he didn't intend to overstay his welcome. I'd feel a bit melancholy then, but with Sarah coming home for the summer I couldn't suggest that he stay any longer and decided to just enjoy him while I could.

So, everything chugged along perfectly during the fall. Only one thing bothered me, and that was how I kept feeling I didn't really *know* the professor very well, despite all the time we spent together. When I brought this up to Ralston, he said I was being silly: Professor Coates was a grown man, he needed his privacy; and there was an age difference, too. For that matter, Ralston said, in an irksome, commonsensical voice, what does he know about *us*, exactly? We're just an aging couple who watches TV on Saturday night and goes to Mass on Sunday morning. How many of *your* deep, dark secrets have you confided to the professor, Lily? I told Ralston that I wasn't talking about "deep, dark secrets," only about getting to know the man. What had his childhood been like, what made him happy or angry, what did he think about right before he went to sleep, what were his dreams about the future?—that kind of thing. You expect too much, Ralston said flatly, and then he added: Also, remember that he's not a Southerner. He's from New England, right? From Boston or somewhere? That's a different kettle of fish, you know.

There was no point in arguing with Ralston, but the truth was that the longer Professor Coates lived with us, the more curious I got. I guess I should blush to admit this, but a few times, while doing the cleaning, I lingered in his room a bit longer than necessary, knowing that the professor wouldn't return until late afternoon. (Not that much cleaning was needed: he kept his closets neat as a pin, the jackets and slacks organized by color, dark things on the left, shading to tans and beiges on the right. That tickled me, somehow. His drawers were orderly, too, the socks arranged in matching pairs, the jockey shorts folded and neatly stacked.) Externally the room was pretty barren: while Sarah had covered the walls with posters, lined her dresser with keepsakes and framed pictures, and kept a menagerie of stuffed animals on her bed, the professor hadn't added any personal touches. He'd bought an ordinary bedspread of white chenille, and though I offered to do it, he made the bed himself every morning. He left the walls bare, and on the dresser there were only a few magazines, a small box of stationery, and a little brass tray holding spare change and some matchbooks. I knew that the professor didn't smoke, so I did examine the matchbooks. They were all from a place called "The Den," with a midtown address, and none of the matches had been torn. One had something written inside: the initials "D.J." with a phone number. Probably a colleague of his from the University, I thought; maybe "The Den" was a lunch place. Among the matchbooks I also found a small strip of paper with a neatly printed sentence: "History is no more than a lie agreed upon," followed by the initials "N.B." Another colleague, I guessed, though the message didn't make much sense to me. Anyhow, I didn't go further than that. In the back of his bottom drawer, under some knit shirts, there *was* a small packet of letters, but I wasn't that much of a snoop. I closed the drawer with a sigh, and never opened it again.

When Sarah came home at Thanksgiving and Christmas, the professor took off for Boston, so it happened that our daughter never met the man who'd begun inhabiting her room. The arrangement was "okay by me," she said, but she refused to stay in the room, sleeping instead on the lumpy sofa in the den. That hurt my feelings a bit, but Ralston said that Sarah was going through "a phase" and it was probably best to let her alone. Otherwise she seemed happy, though. She made all A's and B's her first semester, she had a boyfriend ("sort of," she qualified), her clothes had gotten deliberately sloppy and more colorful; and she'd started frizzing her hair, tying it together in a kind of ponytail perched on the very top of her head. For once, though, I did agree with Ralston: I wasn't worried about Sarah any longer, and when she left the day after New Year's the melancholy lasted only an hour or two. And besides, I was looking forward to the professor's return, later that week.

He came back on a Saturday evening, but almost immediately went out again. I must admit, this bothered me. I'd fixed him a nice dinner and put it in the refrigerator, wrapped in foil, but Professor Coates just said, "I ate on the plane, thank you. Quite a delicious meal." It was almost ten o'clock, but he rushed upstairs and took a quick shower, then changed into jeans and a sports shirt. During the fall he'd often gone out on weekend nights, by himself—for a movie, he said, or just for a walk around the neighborhood. Though I'd tried once or twice, I'd never managed to keep myself awake until he got home, so I knew he stayed out late. Now we were having a cold snap, though, and when I heard him move lightly down the stairs I came out from the den. "My, it's such a cold night!" I said, laughing. "Why don't you come on back, have some hot chocolate with Ralston and me? You can tell us about your trip." Professor Coates smiled politely, opening the hall closet and taking out a short leather jacket I hadn't seen before. A Christmas present, maybe, though I hesitated to ask. He looked tired; even the smile seemed a bit forced. (Now Lily, Ralston had said over the holidays, when I'd expressed curiosity about what the professor was doing that very moment, you've really got to let the man alone. He's an ideal boarder, but he isn't a—a personal *friend*. Now, I didn't agree with this at all, but I said nothing. Didn't Ralston understand that the professor was lonely? That he needed someone to bring him out, get him to talk a little about himself?) He zipped up the jacket and said, "Thanks, but I'm meeting a friend of mine. I called—um, I called her from the airport, and—" He broke off, looking embarrassed. "Oh, well," I said, flustered myself, "then don't mind me! We'll talk tomorrow—have a good time!" And he was gone.

Now I'd better confess something: I felt jealous. But, to my credit, almost immediately after that I felt happy for Professor Coates. I remembered the matchbook and amused myself with a guessing game for the rest of that evening—that is, guessing what the "D" stood for. Diane? Darlene? Dorothy? It was a pointless game, of course—there were dozens of possibilities—and I didn't even mention to Ralston what the professor had said. I knew he would be irritated if I were even thinking about the professor's private life.

So, I had to keep my own counsel where the professor was concerned. There was a lot to think about, I must say, for if anything the professor became more secretive that winter. He started missing dinner and arriving home later and later from the University, his briefcase bulging. He'd mentioned that he had a heavy teaching load this semester, and he was trying to finish his book by May, and there was so much new material on Napoleon, it seemed a new book was published every other day. . . . We'd stand talking at the foot of the stairs, the professor in his beige overcoat, his hands and nose reddened from the cold (though he owned a car, he walked the half-mile to campus no matter how cold the weather, no matter how I chided him), his body dragged down on one side by the weight of the briefcase. But he wouldn't put down the briefcase; wouldn't let me take his coat and damp shoes and lead him into the kitchen for a nourishing dinner, or some hot chocolate, or hot tea and lemon to keep him from catching a cold. It was seven-thirty, it was eight o'clock, I *knew* he hadn't eaten a thing but still he'd back up the stairs, thanking me anyway, apologizing, touching his glasses between the eyes in an odd gesture he had (for the glasses hadn't slipped out of place) and saying sorry, he had so much work to do, papers to grade, and some reading, he was really very sorry. . . . And then I'd be left standing there, my neck aching as I peered upward into the dark.

Lose something, Lily? Ralston said smartly one night, passing by.

As the winter dragged on, the professor's company got scarcer, and when he did show up for a meal—breakfast, usually—he looked awful. Except for his red-rimmed nostrils he'd gotten white as the tablecloth, that kind of dead-white people get when they don't sleep right or exercise or take any vitamins. His eyes were dull and glazed, and he'd murmur that he hadn't slept well, he knew he'd be fine if he could manage to get some rest. By now, even Ralston was getting a bit concerned, and he jotted down Dr. Hutter's name and phone number—that's our internist—in case Professor Coates wanted a checkup, or maybe something to help him sleep. The professor mumbled his thanks, folding the slip of paper inside his wallet. "I really *do* regret," he said carefully, his eyes not meeting Ralston's, "having been such poor company of late."

"My goodness, don't apologize!" I broke out, before Ralston could answer.

"You see," he began, "I've been troubled by—well, something of a personal matter that I—"

"Professor Coates," I said, reaching out my hand and patting his,

23

"don't feel like you owe us any explanations—none whatever. Your private life is your private life, and we understand that."

I glanced at Ralston, thinking he'd be pleased, but instead he shot me a threatening look—a *scowl*, it was—that made my heart jump. Ralston isn't a big man, but he has a fleshy face, thick neck, dark quick-moving eyes, and when he gets mad that combination can be fearsome. The skin hardens, the neck thickens, and the eyes have the effect of freezing you in place. You can't move, and you can hardly speak.

"What—what I meant—" I stammered.

"Why don't you let Professor Coates finish?" Ralston said, in a polite voice that was curiously like the professor's but that Ralston used only when he was furious.

"I—I'm sorry, I—"

"Please, don't trouble yourself," the professor said, and I'd no idea what he meant. I looked back and forth between him and Ralston, but they were both looking down at their plates, embarrassed. Then the professor rose quickly, saying he'd better be off. I didn't say anything, even though I noticed that he'd forgotten to take the multiple vitamin I'd put beside his plate; he hadn't eaten his scrambled eggs, either. No sooner was the professor out the door than Ralston left, too, so I got up and started cleaning the breakfast dishes, feeling sadder and more bewildered than I'd ever felt in my life.

I stayed melancholy for a long while, feeling that I was in a kind of fog and that I didn't know what I was doing. I noticed the professor's exits and entrances—he left earlier and earlier in the morning, sometimes stayed gone until nine P.M. or later, and on weekends stayed out late at night and then slept until long after Ralston and I got back from ten o'clock Mass—but I no longer went out to greet him in the hallway, or tried to coax him into the kitchen for food or conversation. February passed, and March; we began making plans for Sarah's visit during Easter vacation, though we hadn't asked the professor about his own plans. I started worrying about what would happen if they both planned to be here—who would sleep where, would the situation be strained, etc. And something else troubled me: all during the fall, Professor Coates had called home frequently—at least, I assumed he was calling home, I knew he had a couple of brothers still in Boston—and I remember feeling gratified that he kept in such close touch with his family. At the end of each month, the professor would ask about the long distance charges—sometimes they were more than a hundred dollars—and would promptly write me a check. After the Christmas holidays, though, the calls abruptly stopped, and I wondered if his overwork or stress or whatever was bothering him had made him decide not to call home for a while, so that his family wouldn't worry. That would be just like him, I thought. So considerate of others, he always was. That's one thing about Professor Coates that never changed. No matter how much he kept to himself or how badly he seemed to be feeling, he always took the time to compliment a new hairdo of mine, or a dress he thought was becoming; and every once in a while, he'd repeat his thanks for having him as a boarder. These days, I didn't know how to respond, since his boarding with us had seemed to coincide with such a difficult period in his life, but nonetheless I appreciated his comments and wanted to say to Ralston—though I didn't dare—that I wouldn't have missed knowing Professor Coates for the world.

Despite what happened, I still feel that way. Now that the shock has worn off; now that enough time has passed that Ralston and I have talked the matter over, not only between ourselves but with Father Dalton down at church. It was Father Dalton, after all, who pointed out that we'd given Professor Coates a "room in the inn," so to speak, and tried to ease his way during a time of great suffering. Nonetheless it wasn't ours to judge, Father said, in response to some complaint Ralston had made (in a low, surprisingly meek voice) about Professor Coates's having been dishonest, in a way; having lied "by omission," as Ralston put it. But no, it wasn't ours to judge. I couldn't have agreed more, and was happy that Father Dalton was so understanding and open-minded. Maybe it rubbed off on Ralston, for this time I didn't get the usual smart remarks—the "I told you so," the "See what you get" kind of talk. No snide references to my "impulsiveness," my "harebrained schemes." We've reached a kind of truce, it would seem, where our different views of the world and other people are concerned. Finally, after all this time, we're even.

The shock was the main thing, I think, for in the past it was always yours truly who ended up surprised, or disappointed, or hurt by people I tried to befriend. Ralston, on the other hand, tended to be smug, as though taking in stride the quirks of other people and the world at large; nothing surprised *him*, he'd have you believe. The incident with Professor Coates did surprise him, though—surprised the hell out of him, if you'll excuse my language. It goes to show, I guess, that something good can come out of even the most tragic circumstances, and to this day I believe that the whole experience *was* illuminating, *was* profound—though Ralston certainly would not agree.

It was just another Sunday morning, in early April. I'd had breakfast ready at eight-thirty, like always, and of course Professor Coates hadn't come downstairs; it had been weeks since he had risen before noon on a weekend day. Last night, though, I'd stayed up extra late—I was watching one of those old forties melodramas on TV that I love so much, this one with Loretta Young—and it had crossed my mind that maybe Professor Coates *would* come home before the movie ended at one A.M., and maybe we would have a little chat. But no. I turned off the set, and even dawdled in the kitchen over some hot milk and graham crackers, but still no professor. I went on back to the bedroom, and by the time my head hit the pillow I was asleep.

At breakfast, Ralston and I were chatting about this and that, nothing special, and I was just about to go and change my dress for church, when we heard a sudden noise from upstairs. A crash, it sounded like, followed quickly by two or three more. Ralston had pricked his ears, his coffee cup suspended in midair. "What on earth—" he began, but then we heard other sounds—a series of muffled, heavy grunts, like you hear from boxers when they're fighting. Professor Coates's room was catty-corner on the other end of the house from where we sat, so the sounds were blurry, but nonetheless that was my first thought: fighting. Two men, fighting. But then I thought of soft-spoken Professor Coates and knew I must be imagining this. Though Ralston would often say, later, "Why did I just *sit* there," I knew he had the same reaction. It sounded like one thing, but had to be something else.

At such times, of course, thoughts race through your mind: maybe he's moving the furniture around? maybe he's exercising? maybe he bought himself a TV and is watching something noisy and violent? But then came a loud thud that made the walls tremble even down-stairs, and Ralston and I exchanged a wide-eyed glance. A door slammed, and we heard the loud, thumping footsteps coming down—making a racket, I knew, that Professor Coates had never made in his life. Then, at the doorway of the breakfast room, he appeared: a tall, mustached man wearing boots and blue jeans, and a very soiled light-blue sweatshirt. He had dark bushy eyebrows, big red-knuckled hands. I noticed the hands because he thrust one arm forward, as if pointing or accusing, his finger shaking in our direction.

"Look, I need some money," he said. "Do you people have any money?"

Ralston said at once, "Just what's in my wallet."

The young man wriggled his fingers. "C'mon, hurry up." I saw how nervous he was, his eyes reddened, his body moving constantly in little jumps and spasms. His longish dark hair looked electrified, standing out in all directions. When Ralston held out the wad of bills, the young man snatched them the way Lucky used to snap her dog treats out of our fingers. He turned and ran out of the house.

Feeling limp, scarcely breathing, I followed Ralston to the front door, which the young man had left standing open, and we stood watching as he raced Professor Coates's little car—some kind of hatchback, I think—backward out of the driveway, then down the street with a loud squeal of the tires.

"My Lord . . . ," Ralston whispered.

At the same moment we turned, gazing up to the top of the stairs.

"Professor Coates . . . ?" I said, but it came out as a croak and I knew he couldn't have heard.

Then Ralston squeezed my wrist, trying to pull himself together. "Wait here," he said.

He climbed the stairs three at a time, and of course I wasn't far behind. At the bedroom doorway he said again, "My Lord . . . ," and gestured me back with his hand. For a moment, I obeyed. I heard my husband's low murmuring inside the room, as though he were comforting Professor Coates, or gently questioning him. Then I heard him talking in a louder, more businesslike voice: the one he uses on the phone.

I crept forward, just barely peeking my nose and eyes inside the doorway. This sounds cowardly, I know, but I was truly frightened; I believe that my teeth were actually chattering. And then I saw him. Lying on the bed, one arm splayed outward. His glasses had been knocked off: later they'd be found on the floor, underneath his desk. His face was pale, and there was a long streak of blood along one side of his mouth, like saliva. His eyes were open but dead-looking; glazed over. No, I thought, please God, please Mother Mary, no no *no*. . . . When Ralston finished ordering the ambulance, he dialed again and asked for the police. All the time I stared at Professor Coates's face: so pale, so dead-white, except for the thread of blood out the side of his mouth. His T-shirt and the mussed white chenille bedspread were also streaked with blood, stray blots and wriggles of blood, random designs. I felt myself becoming sick.

I turned and hobbled down the hall, into the upstairs bathroom.

When the ambulance arrived, they loaded him quickly. The driver told Ralston not to worry, that he was in shock but would be fine; there seemed to be no serious internal injuries. A broken wrist, maybe a couple of broken ribs, but nothing to cause undue concern. . . . When the police arrived, they were amazingly callous; or so *I* thought.

27

Later Ralston remarked, philosophically, that we led a sheltered life, that maybe we were to blame for being so shocked, so defenseless. . . . I didn't understand what my husband meant. The policeman who did the talking—a short, jowly man in his forties—said this wasn't unusual, not in Atlanta; this happened all the time. He seemed rather pleased, somehow. I didn't know what he meant by "this," exactly, but a part of me was too angry to speak, part of me still too frightened. I kept glancing around the room at the bloodstained bed, the broken desk leg, the papers scattered everywhere; I was already picturing myself cleaning up the room, slowly and methodically. I clung to that.

For the next day or two, Ralston and I talked very little about what had happened. Occasionally we'd give each other the same wide-eyed look we'd exchanged at the breakfast table that morning, as though we were reliving the incident together; and yet we were apart, too, because we couldn't talk about it. We didn't have the words, it seemed to me. On Monday morning Ralston did go down to the hospital, but was told that Professor Coates couldn't have visitors except immediate family members; later that day, one of his brothers would be flying down from Boston. That night, I happened to answer the phone when it rang, and it was the brother, Jason; he said he would like to come over at once, if convenient, and clean out the professor's things. He called the professor "Jim," which sounded funny to my ears. After we hung up, I stood by the telephone table a long while, understanding that we would never see Professor Coates again. After a few minutes Ralston came up behind me. "Don't worry, Lily," was all he said.

Jason Coates turned out to be a slightly older, darker-complected version of the professor; and he looked fleshier, stronger. It took him and Ralston less than half an hour to load the professor's things into the man's rented car, and then we were all standing at the front door together, awkwardly saying goodbye. Mournful and slump-shouldered, Jason stood there a long while, as though there were something more he wanted to say. And then, looking chagrined, he brought out that the professor *had* been well enough to see visitors, but he felt too embarrassed, too ashamed. He never dreamed of our having to encounter that—that acquaintance of his, Jason said, dropping his voice even more. As for the money and the damage, he would send a check from Boston as soon as he was able; and above all, Jason said, the professor wanted us to know how grateful he was for our being so kind to him, during these past eight months.

"He says he's never known such fine people," Jason said, with a quick smile. "And as for myself, I'd like to thank you, too. For being so good to my brother."

"But," I began, "I still don't understand—"

"Hush, Lily," Ralston said. "We were glad to have him," he told Jason Coates. "And you tell him not to worry. We know it wasn't his fault."

Suddenly Jason looked anxious. "You know," he said, "he has had some personal problems. There was a—a person, someone he was involved with up in Boston, and it ended very abruptly last year. Jim has a knack, it would seem, for choosing people who aren't good for him, who don't have his best interests at heart. It amazes me, really, that he found you people." Jason smiled, ruefully.

"I found *him*," I said. "But I still don't—"

"Tell him we wish him well," Ralston said. "And God bless." I could hear in his voice—though Jason probably couldn't—that he wanted to end this conversation. As he held my wrist I could feel the tension in his fingers.

"I'll tell him, and don't worry about him, *please*," Jason said, and he was gone before I could even get his address or phone number. So I never found out how long it took Professor Coates to recover, or whether he went on to another teaching post the next fall, or whether he finished his book on Napoleon. Whenever I brought any of this up, Ralston would say shortly that it didn't matter if we knew these things or not.

Anyhow, despite Ralston the incident never quite went away. For several weeks there was a change in the atmosphere, somehow; when Ralston and I talked over dinner, or during the TV commercials in the den, we sounded awkward and a bit false, like people rehearsing their lines in a play. I suspect he was thinking, as I was, that everything would change when Sarah got home in mid-May, but actually the opposite happened: for Sarah, once as talkative and carefree as her mother, had become a different person in the last nine months. She moved all her things back into the professor's room—that is, *her* room—but not only had she gotten sloppy and a bit "wild" in her dress, as we knew from her visits home, but was quieter, moodier, spending long hours alone in her room, reading and listening to music, and writing letters that she rushed out of the house every morning to mail. (During her first week home, practically her only words were the daily request for stamps, her eyes not quite meeting mine. I'd stall for a moment, staring at this girl who had once been, people said, the spitting image of me, petite and auburn-haired and, if I may say so, very pretty. Delicate, pointed features; very fair skin. But she'd ruined all this with heavy eye makeup and the frizzed hair and the bright loose-fitting clothes, and I hardly knew her. Soon enough, I began to think that Sarah—our new boarder—was as much of a stranger as Professor Coates had been.)

Finally, one Saturday morning after Sarah had taken off for the post office, I began crying over my scrambled eggs. I don't cry often, as you might guess, but when I do it's quite a sight. I can't hold back, you see. Great racking sobs, like hiccoughs. Tears running like a faucet. When Ralston said, "All right then, let's go see Father Dalton," I could only nod and let him lead me out to the car.

Mostly I've reported what Father Dalton said, but I did leave one part out, and that was about the letters. This part even surprised Ralston, I believe. You see, the day after Jason Coates's visit I was cleaning the professor's room yet another time when I saw that someone had thrown some papers into the wastebasket, and of course I recognized the letters I'd glimpsed in the back of the professor's drawer. Evidently Jason had thrown them away, and naturally I wondered about this. It seemed a callous thing to do, but maybe he knew more than I did? Were the letters somehow linked to whatever was troubling Professor Coates? Sitting in the little reception room at the rectory, I remembered that I'd recently glimpsed some letters of Sarah's, too, in the very same drawer; and of course I hadn't touched them, either, much as my fingers itched. Anyhow, I told Father Dalton about retrieving the letters from the wastebasket, and noticing they had a Boston return address, but no name above the address. The handwriting was small, neat, precise; "Dr. Jim Coates" was how they were addressed. After telling him about the letters—there were five of them, all folded inside the same pale-blue envelopes—I asked Father Dalton if it would be all right (if it wouldn't be "sinful," I suppose I meant) if I opened them.

Ralston jumped in his chair. "Lily, what on earth—"

But Father Dalton had raised his hand, shushing Ralston; *he* didn't seem surprised.

"Why would you want to do that, Mrs. Parks?"

"Because—because then it might make sense," I told him. "It's not idle curiosity, I'm not a snoop," I said quickly, "it's just that it's so hard, not being able to know people. Not feeling that you really *know* another person, even when he lives right under your own roof."

"Father, she's been very upset—" Ralston began.

"Even my own daughter, now that she's home. And even—"

"Lily!" Ralston said, his neck thickening. "You're not making sense."

Ah, my stern husband, my protector!—actually, I knew him very well.

Then, for a long while, Father Dalton spoke. Again he mentioned Christ, and how he taught forgiveness without explanations, without conditions. He suggested that just as Christ's life was a mystery, so was each of ours, and no matter how we might try, there's no getting to the genuine heart of another person. Not even when they live in our own house, he added gently. But knowing one another wasn't finally important, he insisted; it might even be considered a wasted effort. All of life, finally, was a mystery, Father Dalton said, but a mystery made bearable by Christ's unstinting love.

It was a very nice speech, I guess, but Father Dalton never did get around to answering my question. Months have passed, and I still have the letters, tucked into the back of my own dresser drawer. I haven't opened them, I think, because I'm afraid they *won't* tell me much, or at least not enough, and that certainly they won't ease the hollow feeling that has gradually settled in my heart, and that stays whether Ralston is nearby or not, whether I'm having a good day or a bad one. Though I try to stay cheerful, I'm no longer the person who'll just start talking to someone on the street, as I did to Professor Coates; and even with friends of ours, even at church, I'm aware that I'm not quite as friendly, don't laugh as much. She's getting older, people must say, if they notice at all. I'm fairly sure that Ralston hasn't noticed.

So, we go about our lives. Ralston is next in line for manager down at the tire store, then retirement and a good pension in six more years. Sarah's back at college, and I guess I understood too late that she was a separate person from myself, and that we've never really known each other. Maybe we'll become friends one day, close and confiding friends . . . ? As for Professor Coates's letters, I'm sure that I'll never read them and also sure that I'll never throw them away. Whenever I remember them, though, I become thoughtful for a moment—it's like praying, almost—and my heart lies hollow and silent as that empty room upstairs.

Private Jokes

I F ONE started, it was hopeless for the other. Russell would glance across a crowded restaurant table, a blond eyebrow raised; Chloe might catch his eye during a business meeting, the hint of a smile on her wide lips. No matter what set them off—some innocent remark, usually, by a perplexed outsider—the others had to sit waiting, no longer surprised or offended after all these months, while Russell and Chloe finished laughing, Chloe bent over in a silent paroxysm, one arm held across her middle, Russell's shapely blond head thrown back and his turquoise eyes wet with tears. After thirty seconds, or a minute, they'd pull themselves together and invariably Russell said, "Sorry, really sorry—a private joke," and he'd throw his amused clear glance at everyone but Chloe.

For her part, Chloe would wipe the corners of her eyes and say, insincerely, "Yes, we're very sorry. Please forgive us."

That night in bed, they would surrender to a storm of laughter. "Did you see Meecham's expression?" Russell cried, clutching a pillow to his face. "And Okira going on and on, completely unflappable—"

Chloe held her stomach, trying to catch her breath. That morning a Japanese visitor to Chloe's architectural firm had started talking out of the blue about an instance of sexual harassment in his own company, saying how rare such cases were in Tokyo as compared with the United States. It so happened that Meecham, Chloe's vice president, had approached her only the week before to ask whether Chloe needed any "help" with Russell—whether Russell hadn't become "bothersome" to her, in certain unnamed ways. Meecham had long cherished a hopeless infatuation for Chloe, and it had taken all her effort to keep from laughing in his face. That morning, as Okira droned on without any awareness of what was happening, both she and Russell had succumbed at last.

"I don't know if he wanted to stand up and denounce me, right there on the spot," Russell said, lifting a corner of the pillow so Chloe could hear, "or whether he just wanted to confess his own crimes."

"The latter, I'm sure," Chloe said, lifting up on one elbow, feeling suddenly exhausted. She remembered the parade of emotions passing across Meecham's dull face—fear, anger, jealousy, shame. "There was that day in the copy room, after all, when he literally *cornered* me. And made his little schoolboy's speech."

"Chloe dear," Russell intoned, with Meecham's hollow precision, "we've been working together for eleven years now, side by side—"

"And that other time, in Manhattan—" But again her tanned limbs and breasts shook with laughter; she couldn't go on.

"He seized your hand, in the back of a taxi! Protested his undying admiration—!"

Chloe thought: I'm choking, I've got to stop. She got out, "On our way to a business meeting, yet. Five minutes later we were walking inside a board room, Meecham's face had totally caved in—"

"Oh, poor Meecham—"

Again they dissolved into giggles.

There always came a moment, usually the following day, when Chloe would say, severely: "We've got to stop. We really *must*."

"I know," Russell said, contritely. "I'm sorry."

"It's not your fault," Chloe said. "Not entirely, I mean. But we've got to separate them, our work life and the—the other."

"I agree," Russell said. "Absolutely."

She looked over, irritated. "We're not at the office *now*," she said. "Stop sounding like my secretary."

"I didn't mean to sound like a secretary," he said, pouting. "And by the way, I believe the title is administrative assistant? Actually, I meant to sound like a yes man. I'm a yes man by nature, you know."

She pushed back her heavy dark hair with both hands, smiling. "Are you?" she said, coming toward him.

It was Saturday morning, or Sunday afternoon.

"Oh yes," Russell said.

"And you'll say yes to anything? Anything at all?"

"Oh yes. *Yes*," Russell said.

Early that summer, as Russell made preparations to move in, Chloe began to complain—half-seriously—that their relationship interfered with her work.

"I don't accept that," Russell said, lightly. "You've been traveling more than ever."

"Maybe, but my mind's always *here*," Chloe said, tilting her wide palm toward the glittering, white-and-silver living room spread before them. They sat snuggled in a corner sofa, drinking brandy. "I've started daydreaming," she said, "which I never used to do. I'll sit imagining you in the spare room, bent over your drawings. Or padding barefoot out of the bathroom to get the phone, a towel clutched to your waist."

Russell laughed. "When it does ring, it's always you."

"Are you complaining?" she said, pulling back.

"No, I'm saying the time spent apart doesn't matter. Because we're still together."

"By talking on the phone?" she said, irritated.

"No, by using our imagination," he said comfortably. He took a long swallow of brandy.

Chloe frowned at him, not only because his daydreaming about *her* seemed unlikely. She felt obscurely that Russell, possessing the very traits for which Chloe herself was famous—his blond, clear-cut looks only emphasized his coolness, his self-containment—had somehow usurped her best self. Next to him she often felt grubby, needy. She was hardly accustomed to that.

"You're so sure about everything," she challenged him.

The turquoise eyes sparkled, ingenuous; but this might have been a ruse, a private joke of Russell's own. "Of course," he said. "Aren't you?"

When they met at a cocktail party, in early April, it had been Russell who appeared grubby, but in such an appealing, "Bohemian" way that most of the women's eyes—and some of the men's—lingered on him, assessing. New to the city, he'd been an obscure friend of the host's, the younger brother of some slight acquaintance. In a roomful of tailor-made suits and thousand-dollar dresses, he'd worn wrinkled khakis and a snug-fitting knitted shirt, speckled here and there with paint. Though the sleek head was impressive, his blond hair cropped close and tapering invisibly toward a tanned, elegant throat, he had several days' growth of beard (of a darker, golden blond) and a bright, carnivorous look about the eyes. He seemed to be drinking rapidly, the eyes straying about the room. More than once, they had snagged on Chloe.

"You must be a painter," she'd said smirking, when he finally came over. It was the first of many cruel remarks.

"And why not?" he asked.

Chloe glimpsed the flash of cleverness in his eyes, belying the bland, turned-down smile and the vague shrug of his shoulders.

"In this crowd, artists are a rarity," she said. Already she felt uneasy.

"You don't consider yourself an artist?" he said, and Chloe had felt the first tug of their complicity, which however had little to do with art.

She'd said, in a steely voice, "Hardly."

She felt annoyed, as always, that her reputation preceded her. Not that she wasn't proud of her work, but the pride (like the work itself) was somehow irrelevant. That is, irrelevant in certain situations, if not downright damaging. She'd been aware since childhood of her intimidating effect on the male of the species (women tended to pity her) and by now her success in business had sharpened that effect almost unbearably. At forty-two, Chloe had a dark, highly stylized beauty edged subtly with bitterness. As in her high-rise apartment uptown, her colors were white, cream, silver; she wore heavy silver bracelets, an occasional piece of jade. Her wide mouth and eyes, her heavy dark hair and brows, her way of walking and gesturing that implied a collected, considered power—Chloe's apparent invulnerability had more than once been construed as menace, though it was merely a triumph of style. (Once, as she joined a roomful of colleagues in a Chicago hotel, she overheard a bitchy male voice inquiring where "that Amazon" had gone. Chloe had walked directly toward him, smiling—he looked stricken, utterly miserable—and had stayed deliberately close to him all evening.) People claimed that no appropriate mate for Chloe—no one good enough—existed, but the truth was that Chloe, after a few close calls in her twenties and early thirties, had simply decided to avoid marriage. She was too busy with work, she traveled too much, she told herself that she was vain and selfish. She could never suffer the compromises, the oblique surrenders of power, that a marriage would entail. In recent years, following upon the string of close calls, there had been a series of youngish, handsome, quite interchangeable men who entered her life through a revolving door, it seemed, sharing her apartment, suffering both her contempt and her generosity, and at the appropriate time leaving by the same door, without bitterness. They understood how Chloe lived, and in any case exited her life materially or socially advanced. There had been a flight attendant who wanted to become a model, a professional football player whose career had ended at twenty-five, and even—shameful to admit—a headwaiter. Occasionally she received letters from them, notes of gratitude. Thank-yous.

But they'd all been dark, mustached young men—Chloe's type. None had been an "artist."

"I've been doing some oils," Russell told her casually, that first evening. "I'm trying to get one of the midtown galleries to take me in. No luck so far, I'm afraid."

Somehow she'd felt he was lying—he seemed too lucid, too pleased with himself and his surroundings to be an artist—but she would later feel amazed to discover that he'd been scrupulously truthful from the first moment.

"Shouldn't you be in New York?" she asked skeptically.

He shrugged again; she felt the appeal of the wry, downturned smile, and determined to resist.

"I guess I'm not that ambitious," he said, smiling.

"Have you met Cal Reinert?" she said quickly. "He's an old friend, runs a small but quite well-known gallery on Highland Avenue. He's always looking for new talent."

"Really?" said Russell, careful to show little interest.

"Yes," she went on, "but most of his younger artists—well, they're *quite* ambitious."

Against her better judgment, she let her eyes catch onto his, and a moment later they were laughing. It had been the first of their private jokes.

All over town, people owed Chloe. She'd been instrumental in obtaining the work of a well-known New York artist (she'd met him in the Village, at a small brunch) for Cal Reinert, and by the end of May the plans for Russell's one-man show were underway. Already he'd been written up in the Features section of the Atlanta paper, and had been interviewed for the local arts and entertainment radio station operated by the University. Except to Chloe, however, Russell had yet to make a sale, for he placed absurdly high prices on his work. At first she'd been amused by this, finding it ingenuous and charming; then she'd become annoyed, and finally enraged. A local art patron had visited the gallery and offered Cal Reinert eighty percent of Russell's asking price for a small watercolor, half a dozen lilacs in a vase. But Russell had refused to lower the price. "What's the point?" he asked Chloe, hands on his hips. "That's what it's worth to me, OK? Otherwise I'd rather keep it." Chloe tried to keep her head. "You'll get a bad reputation," she told him. "Temperament people will put up with, but not stupid arrogance." Pretending to disregard this Russell said, "Just wait till the show, and we'll see if I'm overpriced. I plan to charm the pants off everyone." Chloe heard herself ask "Is that a threat?" and a moment later Russell said, frowning rhetorically, "My dear, I'm not *that* subtle" and there had been a beat, two beats, and Chloe had no choice but to laugh.

Lately, however, she felt that she'd been laughing rather less often. Her first impulse of uneasiness with Russell had only intensified with time, despite the bantering, witty tone they maintained both at work and in private, and despite the careless abandon of their passion. Perhaps it had been a mistake to offer Russell the assistant's position, but he'd begun to insist on "earning his keep" and in any case he painted only at night, usually after Chloe fell asleep. For someone who spoke so frequently about his "career," in fact, he painted rather seldom. "I meant it, I'm not ambitious," Russell said one night, after her casual query about his work. "Quit badgering me, will you?" She'd lain quietly for a moment, staring at the ceiling. Only Russell would ever talk to her that way. "I was only asking," she said, her whisper soft, apologetic. "I didn't mean—" And she'd broken off, perplexed, suddenly attentive to herself rather than to him. "Goodness," Russell said, turning droll as he approached the bed. "We're looking *lovely* this evening."

Lingering often in front of mirrors, she understood that she hadn't looked this well in years. Somehow her bold, rather angular face had softened, relaxed into some other Chloe, less perfunctory, less alert. Droll or not, Russell had been the first person in her life to use the word "lovely" about Chloe. Looking into the mirror, she saw her thick dark hair looking burdensome, as always; her heavy brows nearly met above the severe, gold-flecked eyes; tiny lines like diagonal cuts bracketed the wide mouth. Nonetheless she looked softer. Milder. As if compensating for this she found herself deliberately frowning at her subordinates, or at some innocent acquaintance. One night, after Russell had closed the spare room door behind him, Chloe's maiden aunt had phoned from Birmingham, inquiring in her tentative way if she might come to Atlanta, next weekend perhaps? It had been so long since their last visit.

And Chloe had said at once, "It's not convenient. There's a friend of mine, he's having a gallery showing this Saturday. I've got to help."

"I understand, dear. Perhaps the week after?"

"Perhaps," Chloe said.

It was her first conscious rudeness to Miriam, Chloe's only living relative. Ever since the death of Chloe's mother, six years ago, Miriam called two or three times a year, timid but persistent, never failing to use the word "family" in her first few sentences. Powdered and smiling, "sweet" in a way that grated on Chloe's nerves, Miriam would leave her white-painted front porch and her petunia beds for a few days of sitting perplexed in Chloe's glittering apartment, alone all day but uncomplaining, paging through glossy magazines until Chloe arrived home. The two went shopping, they went to museums, they went to dinner; they had nothing at all to say to one another, but by now Chloe had become resigned to the visits. At least Miriam never nagged or complained, never asked questions about Chloe's private life. One time, Miriam had emerged from the spare bedroom with a pair of brief-cut red nylon shorts—they had belonged to the ex-football player—and had asked, blinking, "Chloe honey, are these yours?" At such times she was even grateful for Miriam.

The next morning she said flippantly to Russell, "I hope you're happy. My poor auntie Miriam wanted to come visit, and I said no."

An absurd smile had spread across her face.

"Auntie Miriam? Who's that?" Russell said, wrinkling his nose.

And Chloe became aware, vaguely, of turmoil at the office. The secretary who might reasonably have expected to get Russell's job had quit, without warning; Chloe hadn't bothered to replace her and now the other secretaries, she'd gathered, were grumbling about overwork. When Chloe's architects were in town they treated Russell coldly, but with deference. Chloe began to notice that except for Meecham they never referred to him in conversation, even indirectly. These were men in their forties and fifties, and she supposed they considered Russell an embarrassment. Her eyes darkened at the suspicion that they laughed at her, remarked that her vanity (or worse, her emotion) had blunted her good sense. Distressed, she found herself confiding in Russell.

"Who cares what they think?" he said lightly, bending down with one eye closed. It was late on Friday, the night before the opening; Chloe had gone with Russell for "one last look" at the collection before tomorrow's showing. Russell felt that Cal had hung the pictures, especially the recent large oils, much too close together.

"Isn't that one crooked, just a hair?" he asked. He held out one thumb, squinting.

"I don't know, Russell. Why aren't you listening to me?"

"I'm listening," he said. "I just don't like what I'm hearing."

"What?" She felt her cheeks going pale.

Russell lowered his arm and looked at her. "Those people don't count," he said coldly. "Haven't we agreed on that?"

"I wasn't aware that we'd agreed to anything."

"You should never compromise," Russell said, in his edict-giving tone. "Not with me, not with anyone. It doesn't become you."

She thought of Miriam. "I don't compromise," she said. "But I don't care to be laughed at."

"We don't live that way, you and I. Not *us*," he said, and for a horrified moment she saw his lower lip starting to tremble.

"Russell, don't be angry," she said, touching his arm. "I shouldn't have said anything, not now. Not when you're so preoccupied." She added, wanting to make light of all this, "After all, you're an artist. I keep forgetting that."

Touching him, she'd felt the adrenaline surging through them both. Their intimacy, she thought, had become more than she could bear.

He'd curled his lower lip under his teeth, forming an odd smile. "I'm not an artist, only a perfectionist."

He watched her coolly, with that level, glittering gaze he'd used on the paintings.

"What, am I perfect?" Chloe said lightly, starting to laugh. But she felt her face hardening; the blood rocked in her veins.

"I hope so," Russell said.

Shaken, Chloe went home alone. For several days, furtively, she'd been indulging in daydreams, eerie formless patches of time during which she sat remembering, drifting. Yesterday afternoon Meecham had entered her office without knocking and there she sat, half-reclined in her chair, recalling some odd incident in her childhood: running up the porch steps after school, her long hair swinging. Her hand had frozen on the front door, for she could hear her parents arguing inside. She couldn't remember the particular disagreement, only the abandoned viciousness with which her parents spoke, her father's voice squeaking with rage, her mother's equally harsh, unremitting. She'd stood listening a long time, exhilarated by her own jumble of sensations, her queer bitter joy. Never had her parents argued in front of Chloe; theirs was a Southern household, genteel, protective of children. More than once Chloe's father had remarked uneasily that Chloe was so "bright," so "attentive"—she seemed to notice everything. Even at ten or eleven she had known that to enter the room while they argued would represent a grave indiscretion. She'd gone down the block, her pulse racing, her parents' voices a grating music in her head, and by the time she returned (scraping her shoes, this time, on the porch steps as she mounted) her mother had disappeared into the kitchen and her father had looked at Chloe from the newspaper on his lap, his smile widening around his pipe. . . . So that when Meecham entered Chloe's office her own mouth had widened, remembering. Meecham had stood rooted in shock at the dreamy smile on her lips, but after a moment he stammered that he needed some time away from the office, could he beg off the trip to San Francisco he'd scheduled for next week, there were pressing concerns that required his attention, matters of some urgency— Of course, Chloe had said, wanting to laugh. Don't worry, she said, I'll make the trip myself.

She'd meant to say to Russell, last night, "My God, we're giving Meecham a nervous breakdown"—but then she'd forgotten.

Daydreams. Forgetfulness. It wasn't like her, this restless drifting state of mind, this inability to focus or make decisions or really, in any meaningful sense, to think. Yet she didn't mind. The business could run under its own power for a while, she mused, her profession-al mask was formidable enough to get her through. Perhaps she needed a vacation from thinking. A witticism she might repeat to Russell: Since meeting you, I've taken a vacation from all serious thought.

She made herself a drink, wondering whether Russell would come home after finishing at the gallery or would punish her by staying elsewhere for the night, as he'd done once or twice before. It didn't matter, she supposed. She didn't want to argue. Russell had become so solemn lately, no longer in a joking mood. Chloe had quickly seen that his gallery showing was more than simple vanity, even though his work (so Chloe believed) was surprisingly tame and conventional. She didn't understand Russell's absorption in his painting. At times, she mused, in the heartless objectivity solitude always brought her, his artiness seemed overwrought, a shade too practiced. Sometimes he came to bed in a campy mood, scoffing at his own work ("my child has been most incorrigible this evening"), unconcerned, careless. At other times she heard his fist smashing the table, canvases hitting the walls, and he might come storming from the room with his eyes clouded over, unfocused. She thought, I will never get to the heart of him. Yet she experienced delicious fear that here she sat, trying.

He came home after two in the morning, sat on the side of the bed for five or ten minutes, then finally crawled under the covers with his clothes on, even his shoes. At first Chloe pretended to be asleep, then thought better of it. She feared he might hear the pounding of her heart.

"You're all right?" she said.

"Yes," he answered. "Go back to sleep."

"Don't worry about the show, Russell. Your work is good."

He paused a long time. "You're the only person in creation," he said slowly, "who thinks so."

He climbed out of bed, undressed, and crawled back beneath the covers.

"Russell?"

"I think I have it," he said, snapping his fingers. "I'll leave the arrangement just as it is, but have them all facing the wall."

"That's not funny," Chloe said. There had been such rancor, such desperation in his voice.

"It's funny," Russell said.

The reception was so crowded that Chloe glimpsed Russell only a few times during the evening. Deliberately unemphatic in a pale yellow dress, wearing no jewelry, Chloe found herself eavesdropping as she milled around, trying to glean what people really thought of the paintings. She heard the usual inane praise and laughable comparisons—weren't those small watercolors, the exquisite outdoor scenes, reminiscent of Dufy? didn't these recent, blaring oils show the influence, though an entirely *assimilated* influence, of Jackson Pollock? But also she heard one or two sharp, muttered asides: that the champagne, at least, was remarkably good; that the ridiculous prices on Russell's "vapid" pictures at least might prevent some poor soul's actually getting stuck with one. Exhilarated and ashamed, Chloe found herself savoring these remarks as though they were any more objective or well-considered than the mindless praise, and out of guilt she began looking for Russell, at first casually, then with an emotion approaching desperation. Yet he was always surrounded, and Chloe kept being snared by her own admirers. Once she stepped back from a squared pillar and suddenly there he was, talking to a man in his fifties, balding, fatuous, very rich; Chloe recognized him as a friend of Cal Reinert's, a retired international banker who fancied himself a collector, she couldn't recall the name. At the sight of Russell she caught her breath. Tonight he'd worn a beige silk jacket, an open-collared shirt, the gold chain Chloe had given him for his birthday last month. The turquoise plaid shirt matched his eyes, now trained on the other man with such mingled intensity and mischief. Chloe breathed shallowly, thinking that Russell seemed at once intimate and foreign, sleeker than ever, tanned and blond and elegant, yet unaware of her. They might never have met, in fact. He might lift those sparkling eyes at any moment and stare right through her.

Half an hour later, the crowd beginning to thin, she came upon Russell from behind; he stood talking in a quiet, confiding attitude to Cal Reinert, so that Chloe felt like an intruder. She hesitated. "Oh yes, he's very well-connected," she heard Cal Reinert say, "and not only in Atlanta. Scoggins knows people in New York and San Francisco, even in Paris—" Then Russell interrupted him, speaking

41

in a soft, urgent voice; Chloe couldn't hear. She stepped forward. "Russell?"

"Chloe!" Cal Reinert said, his voice booming. "I've hunted for you all evening, where have you . . ." but then a passing woman spoke to Cal, bent to whisper something in his ear.

"Well, what do you think?" Russell asked Chloe, but there was no lift of his eyebrow, no little smirk.

"I've been walking around, spying on everyone," Chloe said, smiling. "It seems you're a hit."

She felt uneasy beneath his long, steady gaze.

"But what do *you* think?" he said. His mouth seemed to tighten.

Her tongue felt heavy, uncooperative; it refused to form the lie they both waited to hear.

Finally she managed, "I think it's a cause for celebration, don't you? Before I left home, I put some champagne in the refrigerator."

"I think we've had enough," he said, smiling coolly. "Any other ideas?"

Shrugging, Chloe took a last swallow from the glass she'd been carrying all evening. The warm champagne tasted stale, sickly-sweet.

"Meecham backed out of the San Francisco trip, so now I've got to go. Want to come along?"

"Won't that keep everyone whispering?"

"Maybe. It doesn't really matter."

"Won't I be in the way?"

"Probably," she said, her mouth widening.

But Russell looked thoughtful. "I suppose I could visit some galleries," he said, "while you're doing whatever it is. Transforming the skyline."

They looked at each other. "Yes, I suppose you could," Chloe said.

It had often been said of Chloe that she was nobody's fool; that she wasn't born yesterday; that invariably she got the last laugh. Her father had first used these clichés, but they'd been repeated so often, down such a lengthy chain of quite various men, that Chloe had little choice but to believe her own legend. The most intelligent man she'd ever dated, a strong-willed and opinionated restaurant owner with whom she'd shared both an easy camaraderie and a profound mutual distrust for about six months, had told Chloe that she saw everything so fully and clearly that it rendered her heartless, and thus her success as an architect: she longed to remake the world along her own bold, bitter lines, and this required a style so aggressive and self-sufficing that naturally everyone (but especially men) adored her work. Russell's catty remark about her transforming the skyline had reminded Chloe of her earlier lover's comment—made, coincidentally, during his and Chloe's last evening together—which in turn recalled her father's discomfort, especially during Chloe's teenage years, whenever she turned her solemn dark eyes upon him. She was so perceptive, she noticed so much! he was fond of saying. No wonder she did well in school, in science and art and English, in everything (he laughed) except home economics; but then Chloe was no ordinary girl. Her father suspected her, Chloe felt, of covert behavior. Remarking in her presence, gaily, that she was "nobody's fool," her father would laugh uproariously, but Chloe would merely smile, and in her impeccable upstairs bedroom that night, or the next night, would carefully lift the phone, her finger releasing the button so gradually that her father and his mistress didn't miss a beat, continued to plan their next assignation, to make unkind jokes about Chloe's mother (resting in her own dimmed bedroom at that moment, in thrall to one of her raging migraines), and it was true that Chloe felt nothing, might have been heartless, as she perceived the flawed and even laughable design of this family, this sorry piece of architecture, this joke. Later, she would gladly escape her father's discomfiture and guilt (for he suspected that she knew; that really his infinitely clever daughter couldn't *not* know) by leaving Birmingham to spend six luxurious years at an Ivy League university and then a celebrated design school, spending money her father could ill afford, returning to the city the very summer he died in the arms of his mistress, overweight and pathetic and laughable. Within six months Chloe's mother's headaches had disappeared, and the two of them began to agree that the situation *had* been laughable, and they'd laughed quite a bit. Chloe's mother had met a courtly, homosexual widower whose companionship she shared until the day of her death, while Chloe herself had moved to Atlanta, had launched her notable career. Soon enough the past faded, dissolved away; it seldom entered her thoughts. When her mother died, Chloe returned home for the funeral, but she spent only one night in Birmingham. And that was all.

She seldom spoke of her family to the men she dated; or, in fact, to anyone. It all seemed so distant, so irrelevant. One of Chloe's suitors had remarked admiringly that she seemed not to have "grown up" like other people but to have been created just as she was, every detail perfectly rendered, implacable. Chloe had been pleased by the compliment. Most everyone she knew, and especially the men, had so obviously "grown up," nor was the process complete in most cases. Lacking the maternal instinct, Chloe had little interest in mothering a thirty-year-old, yet until Russell came along she'd felt herself drawn into such arrangements. However childishly expressed, Russell's autonomy was, she felt, real; he had something of her own sleek and irrefutable wholeness, as she had doubtless recognized during their first meeting, when she'd felt such an irresistible mingling of amusement and terror; and he had drawn from her, absurdly or not, the first genuine emotion of her adult life. Driving slowly toward home on the night of Russell's showing—he would catch a cab later, he told her, it was important that he talk to everyone, not offend any of his "contacts"—she thought seriously of her father for the first time in years, remembering how ludicrous he had seemed, how pathetic. As a teenager she had felt herself secretly allied with his mistress, whom she envisioned as blond, fey, thin as a whippet and unnaturally selfish, rather than with her father in his romantic foolhardiness, or with her mother who lay quite literally in the bed she had made, awash in pain. Instinctively Chloe had scorned these victims, these comic buffoons. She'd looked upon them, she thought now, as she'd recently looked upon poor Meecham, as personalities existing only in two dimensions for people like herself and Russell. Stick figures, Chloe thought bitterly. Jokes.

The next evening, Russell told Chloe he'd decided against the trip to San Francisco. The gallery showing had energized him, he said; he wanted to hole up for a few days in his work room, seeing absolutely no one. There was no reason for him to be at the office, was there, while she was out of town? . . . They sat on their corner sofa in the living room; the cleaning service had visited that morning, and Chloe stared at the zig-zagging tracks the vacuum cleaner had made along the carpet. She felt slightly dizzy.

"Is that all right?" Russell asked. "Do you mind?"

"Mind? I don't mind," Chloe said vaguely. She kept her eyes averted.

"Chloe, are you feeling well?" Russell asked. He sounded uneasy, apprehensive. A tremor of pity passed through Chloe.

"I'm just tired," she said rising. "I'll go to bed, do you mind? My plane leaves at seven in the morning."

"I'll take you to the airport. If you like."

"All right," Chloe said.

During the next hour, she heard him puttering around downstairs as she packed her bags. His little sounds were so domestic, proprietary. Waves of pity swept through her. She'd rehearsed the speech in her head all day, had planned to deliver it this evening—but her nerve had failed her. For all her experience, firing people hadn't gotten any easier. Her first theme had been that Russell was meant for art, not business; but of course he'd see through that. Next had come the "interference" idea, arguing that the office and her own work had begun to slip beyond Chloe's control, and naturally she couldn't jeopardize . . . but she quailed, imagining the contemptuous look *that* would earn her. Finally she'd settled on a closure that matched—very satisfyingly, from an aesthetic standpoint—their beginning, something wry and jocular, even jokey. We mustn't upset poor Meecham any longer, we mustn't slow the development of contemporary art, something like that, why shouldn't they end with a laugh, why shouldn't Russell leave as the others had, admiring and free of bitterness, even mildly grateful? Yet in the end she'd lost her nerve. She felt dazed, addle-headed. Not herself at all.

Tomorrow, then. On the way to the airport.

Around ten o'clock she closed the bedroom door and picked up the phone to call Miriam. It might be best, next weekend, to have company in the apartment, and of all people Miriam might help create a balance, signal a return to normal life. But instead of a dial tone Chloe heard laughter—wheezing male laughter, entwined with Russell's distinctive soft chortling. The wheeze Chloe recognized instantly as that of the collector, Cal Reinert's well-connected friend. Her face flaming, Chloe wondered only for a moment what object of ridicule, what splendid joke, could have inspired their laughter, so full and abandoned that neither man had heard her lift the receiver. When the moment passed, and Chloe heard Russell draw his breath for speech, she understood that his words were superfluous. She put the phone down.

For a few minutes Chloe paced with her arms folded, feeling like a prisoner in her own bedroom. Only when she paused before her bureau mirror, staring, did she give way to the ache in her abdomen, her lungs, her throat. Glimpsing beneath her dark helmet of hair the eyes of a wounded girl, and a mouth drawn into a knot of pain and worry, Chloe laughed aloud.

Fever

D URING the year I was ill with rheumatic fever and was kept home from school, my mother and I would spend our afternoons watching forties melodramas on TV. This was the early sixties, the pre-assassination sixties, and at that time the overheated passions of those movies didn't yet seem impossibly distant; far from inspiring cynical laugher, the aching eyes and hearts of Loretta Young, Susan Hayward, and Jennifer Jones brought to any observer, male or female, adult or child, a quietly personal thrill of recognition and longing.

That year, my mother had all but relinquished housework; she spent mornings toying with new hairstyles or phoning the dress shops downtown, hoping something new had come in; whenever someone called her, she spoke in a fey, girlish voice, as though I were not in the next room. Her manner held a new urgency, I thought, a sense of plunging, original effort, as in some desperate audition for the role she'd been born to play.

I believed she had fallen in love.

She had not fallen in love. Her afternoons weren't spent with a lover but on our living room sofa, holding my feet as we watched our movies, though often I gazed at her instead of the TV, awed by a pink silk scarf at her neck that I'd never seen, or some bewildering new arrangement of her hair. I believed she had fallen in love and at night I stared at my bedroom ceiling, another screen, watching as she drove off with the stammering mailman, or the pseudo-cheerful manager down at the Piggly-Wiggly, or the flat-topped football coach at school. These were the only men in town, that I knew of, who were young enough, and reasonably handsome, and unmarried. They weren't John Gavin or Tyrone Power, but I supposed that they would do.

I did not suppose, on the other hand, that anything had come between my mother and father. Though nearly twenty years older than his wife (a situation much more usual then), my father clearly loved her, though it seemed a fond, remote love, lacking much evidence of passion. My parents exchanged cheery-voiced hello's in the mornings and dutiful pecks when they said good night. My father was past fifty by then, his arthritis already begun, and his bedtime was usually much earlier than my mother's. By the time I was ten, he would sometimes retire before I did, leaving her and me—especially on weekends—to watch old movies late at night. That's when our addiction started, I believe. It had some vague connection to forbidden things, to emotions indulged but not acknowledged, to the release we felt—though we did not acknowledge this, either—at the sight of my father's salt-and-pepper head retreating down the hall. Half an hour later my mother and I would be making popcorn, or pouring hot cocoa, or heaping squares of fudge onto the single plate to be wedged between us on the sofa, our eyes bright as we exchanged happy but forgettable kitchen conversation, a prelude to the much deeper and abiding pleasure of the movie that lay ahead.

During the year I stayed home from school, we watched movies nearly every afternoon on the Million-Dollar Movie Showcase. Since I would have preferred to be at school, I felt something of the invalid's self-righteous indulgence, and although my mother occasionally sighed that this was a "work day," and she really ought to be doing other things, I knew that her guilt attending these lazy afternoons was itself a source of pleasure. So we were long accustomed to our routine when, late in the spring, the Showcase featured a melodrama called *Leave Her to Heaven*, with Gene Tierney and Cornel Wilde, which had a puzzling but profound effect upon my mother.

In this movie, Gene Tierney the beautiful woman marries Cornel Wilde the handsome novelist, and it seems all will be well, except that Gene Tierney is sick with jealousy at the thought of Cornel Wilde giving love of any kind to someone else. She is even jealous of her own younger sister, Jeanne Crain, a sweet girl who would never consider committing adultery with Cornel Wilde, but to whom Cornel Wilde, rather unwisely, dedicates one of his novels. Gene Tierney is not the type who needs much in the way of evidence, and the book dedication sets her dark pained eyes aglow.

Meanwhile, Gene Tierney has also become jealous of Cornel Wilde's crippled kid brother, because Cornel Wilde loves him, too, and she feels that even such exemplary fraternal love somehow cuts into the love Cornel Wilde should feel for *her*.

Finally they go to a lakeside resort, so that Cornel Wilde can write, but he insists on bringing his crippled brother along. In the movie's climactic scene, Gene Tierney takes the boy (who is about eleven, my own age as I watched this movie with my mother) out into the lake while her husband is busy writing. As part of his physical therapy,

47

the boy has been learning to swim, so now Gene Tierney suggests that he see how far he can swim out from the boat. When he gets into trouble and starts yelling for help, Gene Tierney just sits there, behind her dark glasses. Gene Tierney just lets the boy drown, because then there will be one less person with whom to share the love of Cornel Wilde. The camera closes in, of course, on Gene Tierney's stony expression as she watches the boy drown, and the dark glasses make the scene especially effective. On the day my mother and I watched *Leave Her to Heaven* on the Million-Dollar Movie Showcase, the host said that the movie's director had claimed that Gene Tierney should get an Academy Award for that scene alone; but, as it turned out, she lost to Joan Crawford. She was "completely overlooked," according to the host, who seemed extremely unhappy about it.

"Imagine that," my mother said, rubbing the soles of my feet in her absent-minded way. "She didn't win the award. . . ."

I tried to make a joke. "I guess they left her to heaven," I said, but my mother didn't seem to hear.

It was May and already hot outside and my mother wore a white sundress with spaghetti straps and lime-green piping. Her honey-blond hair was swept back on both sides, fastened with stylish gold-toned barrettes. I tried to imagine her sailing off into the sunset with Cornel Wilde, even though I knew she would prefer John Gavin. Until we saw *Leave Her to Heaven*, the movie that had impressed her the most was *Back Street*, starring John Gavin and Susan Hayward. In that one, John Gavin is married to a rich but mean-spirited woman, and Susan Hayward is a fashion designer who has everything in life but John Gavin, the man she loves. At the end, he lies in a hospital, dying from wounds suffered in a car accident which was caused by his wife who was not only rich and mean-spirited, but also suicidally unhappy. By then, it's a relief to everyone that she's dead. Her being dead allows for a final scene in which Susan Hayward comes to John Gavin's hospital room and reaffirms her undying love through a blur of tears, just before he breathes a final time.

We watched that movie twice during the year I was home with rheumatic fever, and I remember that once my mother wept softly to herself over the ending, but then rubbed at the tears quickly with her fists, not wanting me to see.

That was the first time I wondered if she were in love.

By mid-May, when we watched *Leave Her to Heaven*, we had dozens of those movies under our belt, so I was surprised when she snapped off the TV and said that she shouldn't have allowed me to watch that particular one. What Gene Tierney did was simply too awful, too unspeakable, and scenes like that generated the wrong kind of excitement in your heart. (For Gene Tierney had become even more desperate; when killing off her crippled brother-in-law failed to earn her the undivided attention of Cornel Wilde, she finally proceeded to kill herself, but made the suicide look like a murder. She planted some "evidence" which suggested that the sweet-natured Jeanne Crain had been her sister's killer.) My mother glanced at me, worried. Because of my rheumatic fever, my young heart was supposedly in danger, so that sports were forbidden, as were running, or riding a bicycle, or energetic play of any kind. The previous summer, while I sat in my Jockey shorts on an examining table, our family doctor had shown me a heavy medical reference book that had pictures of diseased hearts in it. This was what could happen, he said, to people who had rheumatic fever and failed to take care of themselves. Entranced, I stared at photographs of deformed hearts, so swollen and scarred, so burdened by calcified dead-white tissue that they scarcely resembled hearts at all. Coiled in upon themselves, seeming to writhe upon the page, they suggested great tormented seashells, I thought, that might have been salvaged from some other planet. There was nothing human to them.

The photographs had their effect, and from that moment on my complaints about staying home from school, about staying indoors, took on a rhetorical blandness. After watching *Leave Her to Heaven*, and hearing my mother say that exciting movies should also be forbidden, I didn't even flinch. I had grown resigned to my enforced boredom. I had no particular reason to protest, so I merely waited for my mother to explain. She had kept watching me, standing near the silent TV with her arms folded.

Instead of meeting her look, I stared at the lingering silver dot in the center of the TV screen: stared until it shrank down to nothing.

Did I know, she asked finally, that Gene Tierney had been a truly evil woman? My mother wasn't sure if the movie had made this point as clearly as it should have. She wasn't sure that she hadn't detected a bit of sympathy for Gene Tierney somewhere in the movie, though she couldn't put her finger on it.

I said that I didn't know.

Didn't know what? she asked. If Gene Tierney was evil or if the movie failed to make clear that she was evil?

I said I didn't know that, either.

49

I got my fun where I could, that year. I had begun developing the kind of wit, and a viewpoint on the world, that would later be termed "caustic," and my mother already had had reason to claim, wrinkling her nose, that I had better watch my mouth.

Sometimes my mother unconsciously preened before me. Now, still standing beside the TV, she made a single turn in her white sundress, letting the skirt flare a bit; I noticed then that she was wearing a new kind of lipstick that resembled pink frosting. Eleven years old, wearing my summer uniform of T-shirt and cut-offs, and possessed of a fragile heart, I half-sat and half-lay on the sofa, the only male audience she would ever have. (Her behavior around my father, of course, was far more conventional; by 5:30 that afternoon, the sundress and lipstick would be gone, and she would resemble a youthful version of Donna Reed.) As she finished her twirl, which was her way of expressing the drama and emotion left over from the movie, she said: "Well, you'd better *know.*" But then she came forward and tweaked my nose, in a gesture dating back to my earliest boyhood ("Look, I've got your nose!" she would cry, poking her thumb out from between two fingers. "What shall I do with Lennie's nose, I wonder?"), and then she sat in a chair, across the room. She merely sat, watching me, and I sat watching back.

This wasn't so unusual. Often we didn't know what to do with the stilled amber time between the end of the Million-Dollar Movie Showcase at 4:00 and my father's arrival home. We'd sit there in the living room, the blinds still half-drawn (to prevent glare on the TV screen), a few stray dust motes visible in the air, and we would look or not look at each other, feeling neither happy nor unhappy, knowing that unlike good Loretta Young or evil Gene Tierney or misty-eyed Susan Hayward we could do nothing with the terrible fever of the roused love inside us, which was objectless, ravenous, and self-consuming, and which left only an astonished silence in its wake, like that following the noise of a television set that has been switched off abruptly.

Finally I said, "Did she"—and I meant Gene Tierney—"think that her husband's love was like a pie, and that if his little brother died then that was one more piece for herself?"

I was thinking of a few years ago, at school, when they had used drawings of pies to teach about fractions.

"Yes, something like that," my mother murmured, lifting her arms in a sudden but languorous stretch. Her arms were no less white, I was thinking, than those of Jennifer Jones in *Madame Bovary.*

I wasn't thinking, not then: She's only thirty-two years old.

"If she was wrong," I said, "then how *does* it work?"

I spoke in the childish sing-song I often used with my mother that year, a voice implying that I didn't care what the answer was; or that somehow it was the rhythmic give-and-take of our dialogue, not the words or their meaning, that mattered. Though my mother often looked as dreamy and abstracted as if she were, in fact, in love, her voice implied that she understood this, too; she knew that we were merely pleasuring ourselves, for a brief time; that next September I'd return to school, of course, and her current phase ("just a phase I'm going through!" she had sighed once, when I'd asked about the new clothes and hairstyles) was only that, a phase, and meant nothing, just as our idle late afternoons meant nothing, and even as those forties melodramas meant nothing, really, in the context of actual people and the world.

I wonder (though I didn't then) if she was thinking of me, back in school next year, rambunctious, unself-conscious, involved in my classes and sports, perhaps finding my first girlfriend?—while she waited here.

She came back to herself, frowning; but it was a joke-frown like Carole Lombard's or Greer Garson's, implying that here was a crazy question from a crazy kid.

"How does *what* work?" she asked.

Unexpectedly, I blushed, too embarrassed to say the word *love*. But the room was dimly lit, and I didn't think she saw the blush.

I was trying to ask did she love my father, that kindly but distracted silver-haired man who looked old enough to be *her* father.

I was trying to ask did she love him more, or me more.

I was trying to ask whether, if I were strong and robust and, at this very moment, playing football after school, instead of lying in a forced months-long immobility to benefit my useless heart, she would then love me more, or less, or the same?

I wanted to ask, Will it ever stop rocking through our veins, will anything stop it, will it ever cool down, fade away, leave us in peace, ever?

But I didn't have the words, of course.

My mother said, "No, I shouldn't have let you watch that one," but I could tell she no longer meant it. She was thinking of something else. She stared dreamily past my shoulder, as if through the wall, or into the future.

Then she said, "Gene Tierney didn't know about love, that's for sure." Her voice had strengthened, and even in the faint light I saw the flush in her cheeks and the sudden sheen of her eyes, making me wonder if she didn't feel a little pity for Gene Tierney, too, in spite of everything.

She repeated, still gazing past my shoulder, "She never even *knew* what it was."

Nickels and Dimes

I HAVEN'T been here ten minutes when she gives me that look. You'd think she'd know better, working here in Grady's ER, but she can't be more than twenty-two, skin fresh as a baby's, so maybe she's just out of school. Still clinging to her Florence Nightingale fantasies. My calling her Florence, trying to make a joke never mind that I'm hurting like hell—stabbing pains in left thigh and side, left arm surely broken—is what earned me that look in the first place.

Roughly translated, the look means something like this: How did you get in this fix, anyway? You don't seem to be drunk, you don't strike me as a moron or a psycho. I'm detecting a glimmer of intelligence now and then, and you look young and strong, and reasonably healthy. So what are you doing here? Would you kindly explain yourself?

Maybe I'm reading too much into just a look, but I've gotten enough of them, these past few weeks. Like I said, it's a rough translation.

"How fast was the car going?" she says now, gingerly touching my ribs.

"About twenty, twenty-five. He tried to veer off, but too late."

We're both looking down at my side. There's a visible gash, but to my surprise it's not bleeding. This may sound strange, but I'm disappointed. And that's not all. When we first came in here, Florence draped my shirt over the portable wall-on-wheels that divides us from the next cubicle, but if the smell hit her nostrils, she didn't show it. It's two months since the shirt saw a rinse cycle, almost a month since my last full-fledged shower. When she asks me to raise my left arm, I hesitate a second but not because of the pain.

"I don't think it's broken," she says, frowning. "Just a sprain, maybe. We'll get one of the docs in here . . ." She turns and peers beyond the partition. When she first led me in here, there was a big black Mama sitting next door with a carving knife stuck in her head. Not her cheek or her neck—her head, just above one ear. It looked like some sort of weird Afro headgear, and I didn't see any blood. Even Florence was startled, but the Mama just smiled and said hello.

53

"It's a good thing you didn't pull that out," Florence had told her. "You'd have been in trouble, then."

"I knows better," the Mama said. "I done been here befo."

Now I can hear Florence asking her, "Honey, has a doctor seen you yet?"

I don't hear the answer because I'm staring at Florence's rear end, so beautifully outlined by the starched white uniform as she leans around the partition. There's a swelling in my pants, so I guess I'm still alive.

Now Florence glances over and I think she catches me looking. She doesn't show it, though, so maybe she's savvier than she lets on. Which makes me like her even more. All the time I'm thinking this, I forget about the pain and about getting knocked into West Peachtree and hit by a three-ton red Buick.

"Honey," she says (and I'm thinking, how nice if I hadn't heard her call the black Mama that), "just wait for a minute, would you? I'm going to see what the hold-up is."

She hesitates, giving me that look again—it's brief but unmistakable. I'm not imagining it.

"Honey, I'm not going anywhere," I tell her, and I even manage a little wink.

The cops delivered me here, though I asked for an ambulance. "Those're mighty expensive, son," the older cop said. He was fat and friendly, though he never looked right at me. (I've had considerable trouble, lately, in getting the visual attention of other folks; I'm wondering if there's some new comic book idea here—*The Invisible Guy*.) "C'mon," the cop said, "I'll drop you off." Then he said, "Good luck, son," as we pulled up to the glass doors of the ER; his skinny younger partner hadn't said a word. I waited a second, all of a sudden feeling scared and wanting the big one to walk me inside. But I told myself that my daddy was dead and you do not get a replacement. I said, "Thanks, sir," and hobbled clear of the car.

When I get scared, I get jokey, so when I found the reception desk I emptied both my pockets' worth of change onto the counter. The young black chick working the desk was on the phone, but she watched from the sides of her eyes. There were four nickels and seven dimes, along with some pocket lint. There weren't any pennies and I was glad. Even the silver coins looked small and grimy under the bright fluorescent lights. "Ma'am?" I said, though she was still on the phone. "When you've got a minute, I'm interested in buying me some first-class medical care." And I laughed, which felt like a white-hot

poker stabbing my side. I doubled over with the pain. "Sir," the
receptionist said sharply, one palm over the mouthpiece. "Would you
please sit over there and wait your turn?" I glanced toward one wall,
where a row of the sorriest-looking critters you could imagine sat on
bright-orange plastic chairs. I straightened, and I guess the strain
showed on my face; the receptionist's eyes softened a little. "I'll bring
you some forms to fill out," she said. "In a few minutes." I nodded.
"Sorry, I was just—" But even though it had been a joke, like I said,
there wasn't any point in explaining. With the edge of one hand, I
scraped my change back off the counter. I sat against the wall like I
was told.

Seeing my little pile of coins reminded me of something Daddy
used to say. When Rafe and I wanted to go to the movies, or to play
pinball down at the A & W, he'd dig in his pockets and roll his eyes
and complain how we were "nickel-and-diming" him to death. He'd
be smiling, though; I knew he was proud that he had the change to
give us. Unlike his "good-for-nothing" kid brothers who'd dropped
out of school and wandered off, never to be seen again, Daddy held a
good job in the tire plant until one morning when the plant machin-
ery mistook his arm for a hunk of unformed rubber. By then, Mama
had been dead six months and he'd been drinking quite a bit. Had he
gotten drunk on the job, gotten careless? He never told, and after
sitting up in the house for a while, getting his disability, he never said
much of anything. Just stared at the TV. If you said something to him,
he muttered answers nobody could interpret. So Rafe and I just decided to let him alone. One time we were at Daddy's house, a Sunday,
all three sitting in front of a ball game, and Daddy muttered something about a beer. When I came back from the kitchen I said, "Okay,
here it is, but Daddy, you're nickel-and-diming me to death, you
really are." I rolled my eyes just the way he used to do. Rafe laughed
out loud, but Daddy's eyes stayed glued to the TV. It was that day
when Rafe and I decided: just let him be.

My brother and I worked at the tire plant, too, but a few months
after Daddy's funeral I got laid off. Rafe found out he was sick during
that same week. I was over at Rafe and Marsha's, and I said, "Brother,
we sound like a goddamned soap opera." Rafe laughed, but Marsha
had been crying, and she gave me a look straight from hell and ran
out of the room. Shoot, I knew what leukemia was, but I felt sure that
Rafe could beat anything. Ever since we were kids, he'd been the calm
and steady one, harder-working and better-liked, even though I did
better in school and much better with girls. (Rafe looked just like
Daddy, and I often wondered: did Daddy think I took after his van-

ished kid brothers, good-looking rascals who never did anything for the family? If he thought that, he never said it.) So I just let the word "leukemia" wash right past me; even after I'd gone flat broke and moved in with Rafe and Marsha, I tried not to think about it. But I saw he was getting sicker and sicker; I knew Marsha wasn't just being a hysterical woman, though I thought it to myself, what with all her worrying night and day (and out loud, really loud) about the plant maybe laying off Rafe, too, just to keep from paying his medical bills. I'd point out that they couldn't do that; it was surely illegal. Of course, I didn't know what I was talking about, and for opening my mouth I'd get further looks from the realm of Beelzebub.

Pretty soon, I figured, Marsha would be asking Rafe to kick me out. "Has he looked at the want ads lately?" I overheard her asking, out in the kitchen one morning. "Is he even trying?" "Hell yeah, he's trying," Rafe said, though I didn't hear much conviction in his voice. "You know how things are in this city nowadays, if you ain't finished college. Atlanta's just turned into a little New York, if you're asking me." This didn't sound like Rafe, and I wondered if it was something he'd heard from Daddy. "Besides," Rafe said, "he's still all riled about Cindy, you know? I know he don't say nothing, but—" That's when I closed the door to their little spare room and plopped back down on the bed. In fact, I *had* been reading the morning want ads, and Marsha knew it—while she was cooking Rafe's eggs I'd asked if I could borrow the paper—but now I stared at the newsprint and the little red circles I'd made and it all started to blur. I pushed the paper aside, kicking my legs until the sheet dropped to the floor. I decided that I'd have it out with Marsha. Rafe was her husband, sure, but he was my brother, and I intended to pay back every dime they'd spent on feeding me. We never had this airing-out, though, because Rafe took a turn for the worse that very day, and never came back from the hospital.

So, to answer Florence's sweetly puzzled and sympathetic look, that's how I joined the ranks of the great unwashed. She could read the form, if she liked, that I filled out for the ER receptionist. Age twenty-six, three years of college, four point five years of steady work experience, though granted I spent every check as soon as I got it. Marital status, single, though I came awfully close. Too close, maybe. For almost everything else, I put "none" (Employment, "none," Insurance Coverage, "none," Next of Kin or Other Person Who Will Be Responsible for Your Bill, "absolutely none—sorry!") but maybe there's enough information that Florence could figure it out, if she tried; and who knows, maybe she will.

I was certainly glad, I'll tell you, when she came out between two cubicles and said, "Eustace, James," looking around her with a pleasant expression as though meeting Eustace, James, would be the high point of her life so far. I'd started to get depressed, sitting out there with my colleagues in the plastic chairs. There was a woman with a puffy dark-bruised face; she kept cradling her arm, and moaning. There was a tiny black man with bright yellow eyes and, it seemed like, no eyelids—not that I looked too closely. There were a couple of teenaged guys who mumbled to each other nonstop, high on something, but I couldn't see that either one was hurt. One of them coughed a lot, though. And soon after I filled out the forms, in came the black Mama with the knife in her head, looking calm as you please. They took her right inside, probably figuring she wouldn't do much for morale out in the waiting room. By the time Florence showed up, they'd brought in two women from a pretty bad car accident. One was unconscious, but the other was screaming to beat the band. They lay on gurneys in the hallway, and a black orderly had set up IVs, but after that they were pretty much ignored. The loud one kept calling for her mother, and for someone named Fred. The thin gurney mattress had soaked through, and her blood had started to drip onto the floor.

So I said to Florence, as she led me to the cubicle, "Now wait a minute, this is Disneyland, right? I must've taken the wrong bus stop, huh?"

She smiled and said, "Very funny." And it was.

Now, though, she's been gone a long while; the doctors here must be in short supply. My arm is throbbing, and my left side feels hot and raw, but what's strange is that I focus on my stomach. When I get in bad situations, it always acts up. Those last few times with Cindy . . . that day I understood I was really on the street . . . that fine morning a few weeks ago when some black guys rolled me in an empty parking lot over on Eighth, took my sleeping roll, watch, corduroy jacket, and my little stash of grimy pathetic wadded-up dollar bills. My stomach goes into heavy turmoil at such times, and good luck sneaking into some store or restaurant to find a bathroom. . . . But the good news, as they say, is that the doctor—his name is Ogilvy—turns out to be nice. His smile is really sweet, he calls me "Sonny," and he clicks his tongue while doing the examination. The bad news is that he looks to be about a hundred and twelve years old, and I can feel his hands shaking as they move along my side. They're cool and papery, like a granddaddy's hands. But I guess I'm not in a position to be choosy.

"Did they get the driver?" he asks, writing some shaky notes on a little pad.

"No, but they'd probably like to give him a medal," and then I could kick myself for saying that. For it's then that he gives me the look, too. Who *are* you, Sonny. And Florence is hovering over by the partition, her usual sweet and puzzled self. These are the villains of my story, I'm thinking. I can't have Nurse Ratched and Dr. Mengele, oh no. Can't get any kind of break at all.

So now Dr. Ogilvy tries some grandfatherly humor. "You're too smart a boy," he says, "to be playing out in the street."

I have to smile at that one; it's then I understand that I haven't been smiling.

"You got me," I tell him. "So what's the news. Is it broken?"

"No, just a bad sprain," he says, "but I'd like to keep you overnight, Mr. Eustace." All of a sudden, he sounds serious; I liked "Sonny" much better. "I'd like to do some X-rays," he says, "and see how that side is doing in the morning."

"Overnight?" I ask. "Well, I could stay in Florence's room," and I glance toward the partition.

Dr. Ogilvy looks in her direction, squinting. He doesn't get it. He probably hasn't gotten it in quite some time, I'm thinking, but I guess I shouldn't joke with the old guy.

"Look," I tell him. "I can't pay."

He ignores this. He tears the top sheet off his pad and hands it to Florence. "See what you can arrange," he says, and then he gives me that sweet smile again. Now I see that it's his professional smile and that he probably knows what he's doing, after all. "See you in the morning, Sonny," he says, his clodhopper wing-tips shuffling along the tiles as he goes out.

"You're lucky," Florence murmurs, helping me with my shirt. "Doc Ogilvy's retiring next year, but he's still one of the best. He'll take good care of you."

I start to say something smart, but all at once there's a catch in my throat. I manage to say, "That's good news. I haven't had much of that, lately."

She steps back, watching me. "I'll be right back," she says, and she looks blurry, like some kind of white-dressed apparition.

She says, "I'm going to get you something for the pain."

When I wake up, it's pitch black except for some sort of droning, or buzzing. I blink my eyes, and gradually understand there's a TV up near the ceiling. My mouth feels dry, cottony. I start working my tongue, trying to keep my eyes open and understand where I am. I guess I'm really here, an official guest of Grady Memorial Hospital. Hot damn, as Decker would say. He's this black dude out on the street who told me he'd gotten thrown in jail this past winter to get himself out of the cold. Said Fulton County detention was safer than most of the so-called shelters, and not quite as smelly. I'd met Decker first thing when I walked out of the Y, where I'd gone after Rafe's funeral and stayed until my cash ran out. When I called Marsha to ask for a small loan, she said in a grief-thick voice that the movers would be arriving any minute and to call her new number in a few days. So I waited, then used one of my remaining quarters and dialed the number and learned it would be cool tonight, showers likely, low in the mid-fifties.

That morning, Decker had caught my stymied look. Even though it was mid-April, he wore a navy pea-coat and a knitted cap pulled down past his eyebrows. He could've been thirty, or fifty—I soon learned that guys on the street all look the same age. He was a light-skinned dude, with sharp features and one gold tooth. Looked at me sideways, that first time, and asked for a light; before long he'd gotten a buck out of me and given me a short introduction to life out here. That's what Decker always called it—"out here." He laughed when I said I was looking for a job. He said I was lucky I'd missed the winter, and told me to keep to the busy streets at night and avoid Piedmont Park. We never hung together, really, but as the days passed he seemed to be everywhere, lounging against a parked car or rummaging through a trash bin at the next corner. I'll admit that I was usually glad to see him.

His scowling, slit-eyed face keeps coming to mind as I watch the static-filled TV screen. I've been wondering who's on the other side of the partition, and I can hear myself asking, in Decker's snide voice, "What's a room here cost, anyway? A hundred a day, two hundred? And who the hell is paying?" But I've done better than Decker ever could with his petty jail time (vagrancy charges, usually), and the big chip he carries on his shoulder. . . . It's then I catch myself. I'm thinking like one of them. And I catch myself again. One of *them?* I don't seem to fit anywhere, exactly, as if I'm waiting for someone to tell me which side I'm on, just who or what I am.

Like a three-ton red Buick, maybe. Splat, kid, here's what you are. Dead meat.

But not quite yet. I'm lying afloat in the never-never land of a hospital late at night. Vaguely I remember them bringing me up here, and helping me out of my clothes. Some black guy—for a second I thought it was Decker—gave me a sponge bath. He laughed whenever I said anything, showing huge white teeth. What was I saying? The shot they gave me had sent me high as a kite. I remember eating a little something, I remember stumbling into the bathroom, but mostly I drifted in and out of sleep as though my brain were filled with heavy fog. The pain was gone, sure enough. My worries too, for a while, all except that vague nattering about who or what I was, the way half-remembered dreams will tug at your mind in the middle of the day, like a pull at your sleeve, to tell you something you don't want to know.

Somewhere around dawn a nurse comes in and these vague thoughts scatter like confetti. I've begun to hurt, and hurt bad. Arm and side throbbing, a burning in my left thigh as if jabbed by a red-hot needle.

The nurse isn't Florence and my insides deflate like a kid's balloon. I guess she went home, or else is still down in ER and has forgotten me by now. What's that song?—oh poor, poor pitiful me. That's the one.

This new nurse—an older gal with iron-gray hair—bends to my ear. "I'm here to change the bandages. How are you?"

"Okay, I guess, but all of it hurts."

She asks if I want more medication. She says it's allowed.

"Yes, thanks, if it's all right."

"I'll let it take effect," she says, "before I start pulling on those bandages."

"I appreciate that, ma'am," I say sincerely. I'm lying here thinking to myself how wrong Decker was. When we'd shuffled through midtown together he'd whisper sideways in my ear about the prosperous folks passing by us, how they didn't give a shit about us and didn't even see us any more. Businessmen with their silk ties flapping in the wind, dressed-up women carrying briefcases and using their free hands to keep their hair in place—all of them in a rush, staring down at the sidewalk. I didn't see that they were particularly heartless, just hurrying, but it didn't do to contradict Decker. He'd raise his screechy voice and repeat himself until he'd worn you down. He had evil things to say about the police, lawyers, doctors, just everybody. Now I'm looking forward to telling him about Florence and Doc Ogilvy, though I know he'll think of some way to put them down. I guess it's the main difference between Decker and me: he's given himself over to being on the outside, whereas with me it's just a run of hard luck. I'm thinking that when I'm back on my feet and have a job, I'll drive through midtown and look for Decker and offer to help him somehow, if only to make him eat all his ugly words.

By eight o'clock the pills have kicked in, my bandages are changed, and I've had some oatmeal and juice. The guy behind the partition—I still haven't seen him—has turned on the "Today" show, where this black movie star is talking about his latest action-adventure. Behind his glossy smiling face I can see Decker's sly dirty one, mocking everything the movie star says. I'm in the midst of this daydream when Doc Ogilvy touches my shoulder.

"How we doing, Sonny?"

"You're a sight for sore eyes," I tell him, and he's grinning while he pokes at my arm and ribcage.

"Say doc, is there some way I could take a shower?"

He thinks a minute. "Make sure you face the water with your right side," he says, "and then just sponge on the left, around the bandages. You'll need to be careful for a while, you know."

"Gotcha," I tell him, and for some reason I start talking again about the money. "Listen, is there some way I can help out around here? I hate being a charity case."

"Down on your luck, are you?" he asks. "Got a place to live?"

"Not right now, but . . ."

"You're young, good-looking, and smart," he says, like he's talking to himself. "It doesn't make sense, does it?"

"No sir," I say, starting to feel embarrassed. "But it's just a temporary thing. I've had some college, you know. I'll be working before long. I mean to pay back what I'm spending here."

"Never mind that," he says. Finished with the exam, he pats the sheet around my chest and adjusts his spectacles and fixes his little blue-gray eyes on mine. I can see that he's a smart and shrewd old guy. His eyes aren't smiling but he says, in a kind voice, "Why don't you stop by personnel on your way out this afternoon, ask for Michelle. You could get something permanent, I'm pretty sure. I'll put in a word for you."

My heart is pounding so fast I can feel the first glimmers of pain come back to my ribcage. "Thanks, doc," I tell him. "I appreciate that. You know, there's this guy I met out on the street, and he thinks—"

I break off when I feel the crisp bill against my palm. I open my hand to see that it's a fifty.

"This should help till your first check," Doc Ogilvy says. "Pay it back whenever you can. And don't worry about the hospital bill, the government will pick that up. I'm sure you've paid some taxes before, haven't you?"

"Yes sir," I tell him, but I don't say anything else because I'm feeling so grateful. I figure he sees it in my eyes.

61

A little before noon the older nurse comes back with a small kit of bandages and ointments, and instructions for the next few days. From what she's saying, I can tell she doesn't know I'll be out on the street, and I'm glad of that. Maybe I'll use the fifty to check back into the Y, and then ask personnel for an advance on my first week's pay. I'm thinking fast and only half-listening to the nurse, but when she says, "Would you like another Percodan before we check you out?" I tell her yes, and I also tell her that Doc Ogilvy has okayed a shower. She watches me swallow the pain pill, and then she says, "Okay, I'll come back in half an hour, and then we'll get you out of here." I say, "Sounds good," wondering how she'd react if I told her I'd like to stay another week.

By the time I get in the shower, the pill is taking effect. I can move my arm better now, and those hot jabs in my leg are dying down. For some reason I'm excited and happy, keyed-up, and have to keep reminding myself not to get the bandages wet. Before stepping into the tub I glimpse myself naked in the bathroom mirror and of course that gets me thinking of Cindy, how we used to shower together and afterward watch in the mirror as we dried each other off, so slowly, sometimes laughing, other times serious and quiet, of all things I'd have to remember that now. But I can't help feeling hopeful, I feel like this past day or two is a turning point, maybe I needed that Buick to knock some sense into Eustace, James. (Didn't one of my high school teachers say, laughing, "You're smart, Jimmy, but you haven't got a bit of common sense"? No, nor common cents, either, but let's recall that she's the same teacher who made a pass at me, in her office, when I was still a sophomore, so maybe common sense isn't so common, after all?) But, in effect, Cindy said the same thing. I took her for granted, she claimed. We weren't going anywhere, she claimed, just drifting, whereas she wanted to build something with a man and not just float from week to week, paycheck to paycheck. She didn't want the same life her mother and aunts had lived—the life *my* mother and aunts had lived, for that matter—there was more to life than sex and laughter and cuddling in bed on Sunday afternoons, God knew I'd been valuable for that, she said laughing, about to cry, about to turn and walk out for the last time, but no, she said, she just couldn't invest any more time in this. She didn't want—and now she spat out the words, making them as ugly as possible maybe (who knows) so I'd be able to say, Good riddance—she said, in a low queer whisper, I don't want to be the wife of a factory worker, James. I want more than that.

So she did walk out, closing the door gently behind her. No slamming doors for her. No raised voices. Just cutting her losses, you might say.

Okay, I'm thinking, so it was like that Buick crunching a few bones, knocking the breath out of me, only Cindy had knocked the will out of me. For a while, anyway. Who's to say her new white-collar boyfriend hasn't walked out on her by now, who's to say he isn't a loser in bed and she's wishing like hell she knew where to reach me? She'll know soon enough, I'm thinking. Two, maybe three months at the Y, then enough saved for first and last months' rent on a nice apartment, and the phone deposit, and the utilities deposit, and so on, and then one quiet summer night I'll give her a call, I'll set candles around the tub, have the champagne chilled, who's to say all this isn't within my reach, here in the land of opportunity known as the U.S. of A.?

Okay, I'm letting the pain pill and this lovely hot water make me goofy, I'm smiling up into the shower nozzle and letting the water stream down my face like happy tears, I'm thinking of being in that tub with Cindy and yes I'm getting myself tremendously horny in the process (how long since I've felt horny, by the way?—for a while, I just let the street unman me) but the remedy's quick enough, two or three hard pulls, that's how long it's been, oh Cindy Cindy here I come, and I moan thickly into the streaming water like a wounded animal and stand there a few seconds with eyes closed, catching my breath, and I twist the faucets to *Off* and stand there dripping, panting, never mind that the bandages are ruined and maybe I'm bleeding a little, never mind that I've lost my family and girlfriend and have fifty bucks and change to my name, everything has turned around and I feel so clean and warm, that deep glow in my belly branching out in all directions, I'm healing, I'm getting well, I'm going to be all right.

I remember one of Decker's favorite phrases and murmur aloud, smiling, "Thank you, Jesus!"

But not in Decker's bitter chortling voice.

Well, the nurse gives me a *tsk-tsk* while she redoes the bandages, but we joke back and forth, talking about anything, everything, I'm so happy that it seems to be contagious. "Good luck, Mr. Eustace," she says in the lobby, once the paperwork is done. "You follow those instructions, now!" I tell her that I'll surely do that, and I have the weird idea that I ought to tip her or something, but that's ridiculous, I push the thought away. All at once I'm out on the street in the bland May sunshine, feeling wonderfully clean and naked under my clothes. Even the clothes are clean, courtesy of hospital laundry while I was in bed. When I see the bus approaching from the next block, I dig in my pockets for the change and count it up—ninety cents, exactly the right amount. I take this as a sign and I'm glad, I didn't want to break the fifty yet.

I get off at the Arts Center, and it's not ten minutes before I see Decker, over on the other side of Peachtree. He's leaning up against one of the white stone walls at Colony Square, hunched and bitter-looking, his knitted cap pulled down across his eyes. The noontime lunch crowd crisscrosses the walkways in front of him, well-dressed, chattering, but Decker stands there motionless, his arms folded. He's dark-clothed and grimy here in the warm sunlit air, his very posture a rebuke to the shoppers and office workers streaming by. Not that they see him, of course. But I see him, and I'm so intent on getting over there, lurching across Peachtree against the light, that I earn a few horn blasts from the heavy traffic and almost get myself knocked flat again.

"Hey Decker, how's it going?" I call when I get close enough. I'm determined to be friendly.

"Man, you got any money?" he says, but he still doesn't move, as if he's conserving energy. I'm not sure he even remembers me.

"Sure," I tell him. "Just got out of the hospital, though. Folks there were nice as hell."

It's then my stomach lurches: I forgot to stop by the personnel office and ask for Michelle, whose name alone made me want to meet her. So damned high on the pain pill that I forgot all about it.

"That right?" Decker says, with a nasty grin. "Folks just so nice, was they?"

"Listen, Decker, you've got it all wrong," I tell him. "Come on, I'll buy you some lunch. You want a burger?"

"Man, that Buick like to made *you* into a burger—that's how nice folks is." He laughs, but so deep in his chest you can hardly hear it.

"That was an accident. Nobody meant to—"

"What the fuck you talkin about, man?" Now he does move, shifting his weight from foot to foot. Uneasy. Furious. "Man, you done forgot that you got pushed into that street? Ain't you recalled that I was there and seen the whole thing?"

I stand there for a moment, stymied. Yeah, I could remember that the street was crowded, and somehow I'd gotten knocked off the sidewalk . . . maybe, now that I think of it, I can even remember a hand in my side, a hard and deliberate shove . . . but no, it had just been an accident, I wasn't going to be tainted by Decker's evil thinking.

"You're full of shit," I tell him.

"Better than shit for brains," he says, "walkin round talkin 'bout how *nice* folks is. Man, you gettin hit in the street was a big show for these folks, somethin to see on the way home from work. Shit, to them, that's all you're good for—something to shove in the street, and watch it get splattered all to hell."

"They treated me good at the hospital," I tell him. For some reason I'm breathing hard. "They gave me money."

"Sure they gave you money," he says. He looks away, coolly.

So I dig into my pocket and pull out the fifty. I know it's still the pain pill and I'm acting like a fool but all of a sudden I don't care, I wave the fifty in front of his veiled black eyes and then I grab his scabby dry hand and close it around the money.

"There you go, shithead, and don't say nobody ever did anything for you," and with that I turn around and start walking. It's half a block before I understand I'm walking in the wrong direction—I don't have a dime, literally, so I'd better be heading toward Grady. Turning, I can't resist glancing back toward Decker, needing to see the look on his face. But he's long gone, and I'm standing here like a fool. All around me are strangers, and my side's hurting again, so I duck my head and keep walking, starting to limp a little, thinking that some time must pass before something good can happen.

A & P Revisited

I N WALK these three girls carrying nothing but UZIs. Two of them are pretty butch, rough-looking: black leather jackets with studs, holey jeans, Gestapo boots. One has a mohawk and the other's hair is punk-dyed orange and lime green. Just inside the seeing-eye door, these two hold the guns like mallets, their expressions mean and off-hand, as if to say, "What, *you're* not carrying UZIs? Is this a wimp convention, or what?"

But we don't look at them long, because of the third one. My God, the third one. She's clearly the leader, and holds her gun Patty Hearst style; it's slung over one shoulder and looks really hot, you know? She's in leather, too, but it's a sleek burgundy color, sort of a jumpsuit, and her blond hair is permed out like one of those soap opera bitches. But her face is just an angel's—lips and eyes that would do Miss America proud, a tiny red heart painted near the top of one cheek. I sink back toward the cash register, and behind me, I can hear Dennis going, "Oh Mary Mother of God, I'm weak in the knees, I'm trembling!"

Dennis is married and Catholic, but he doesn't mean trembling from fear.

So they've made their big entrance, and now they come forward, step by step, toward the two working registers flanking the glassed-in manager's booth. Jergens is up there, of course, but he's busy at his computer terminal, going over receipts. Jergens is fiftyish, graying, and lives for Sunday and Wednesday night services at some holy roller church out beyond the suburbs, where he's a deacon. He doesn't see much, and understands less. We call him jerk-off for short.

Dennis whispers, as the girls position themselves near the end of our check-outs, "Give me what I deserve, sweet cakes, oh beat me, beat me!"

I sort of wish he'd shut up, as these girls don't look like they've got something pleasant in mind. Even the leader, standing there with her lieutenants on either side, has twisted her luscious bow-shaped lips into a smirk that's decidedly nasty, her left eyebrow arched as though she's looking at vermin, or might be posing for a statue called "Girl Triumphant." I peer down and see that she's wearing the Gestapo boots, too. I hear Dennis whispering, "Grind me under those heels, baby! Oh grind me down to nothing!"

So it looks like I'm in charge. I clear my throat and say, "Can—can I help you?" Never mind the little squeak in my throat, which always comes out when I get nervous. My dad says *he* had that squeak till he was twenty or so, and didn't start shaving till he was seventeen. I'm sixteen, and I've been shaving for more than a year.

The girls all exchange glances now, as if deciding whether to bother with an answer or not. I look back over my shoulder at the fossil standing across the counter, waiting for me to check out her cottage cheese and cat food. Dennis has a fossil at his register, too, but the odd thing is that these old white-hairs don't seem to notice that something is going on. It's the same with the other fossils, cranks, and dweebs still roaming the aisles behind us, their carts squeaking as they blunder through the store like rats in a maze. Both Dennis and I have said that once we get quit of these shit jobs, we swear, we'll never go food shopping in our lives, having seen it from the inside. We know too much.

So I'm clearing my throat again, about to repeat my question, when I see that the girls have settled something among themselves (though without saying a word), and the one on the left, the really butch one with the mohawk and a big jaw, steps forward and says, "We are lesbian rage. We are the lesbian nation."

Hearing that, I cut my eyes back to Girl Trumphant, my heart a sore lump in my chest. From Dennis' silence, behind me, I can tell he's feeling what I'm feeling. But all at once she smiles, gesturing Mohawk into the background where she belongs.

So those lips straight from heaven are smiling, and I think her eyes have softened a bit. Then G.T. finally speaks, with a sort of lazy confidence that sets my blood whooshing again. "Don't mind Jody," she says. "She don't mean it, she just reads too much. She's just showing off."

She has a lisp—instead of "reads," she says "weads"—and her mispronunciations are just the cutest thing. I can hear Dennis behind me, moaning.

Then the petite one on G.T.'s right, with the Technicolor hair, pipes up. "Yeah, we wouldn't have come to the meat market otherwise, would we?" she says. "I mean, like why would we even bother?"

By now I'm feeling pretty friendly and confident, so I put one hand out, palm up, as though willing to begin a reasonable conversation,

67

when suddenly G.T. says, "Wipe that grin off your face, buster. We're not here for a walk in the park."

Now the fossil at Dennis' register makes some sort of noise—a high-pitched, whining sound—and then the first girl, Mohawk or Jody or whatever you want to call her, points her UZI at the fossil and says, "Down on the floor, grandma. Face down, come on now."

And damn if *my* fossil doesn't get to the floor, too, splaying her arms and legs as if she's been practicing for this moment all her long and miserable life. Then glancing back to the aisles I see that every customer in the store decides to lie down, none of them saying a word, just spread-eagling out on the cold tiles alongside their carts. The only person in the store who doesn't understand what's happening is Jergens, still sitting up in his glass booth with his keyboard clacking away.

G.T., her lovely hard eyes on me, nods her head in Jergens's direction. "What's this mush-head doing?" she says. "Is he a retard, or what?"

Again I clear my throat, calling back over my shoulder. "Uh, Mr. Jergens? Would you like to come out here, please?"

But nothing, just more from the keyboard. Clackety-clack.

So Mohawk decides to lift her UZI into the air and send a few ear-splitting rounds into the ceiling, as if my polite question needed some violent punctuation.

Jergens finally looks up, frowning.

"Ho," Dennis says, arm crooked at his waist as he leans against his register. "A conscious life form, after all."

"Hush up," I whisper to Dennis, remembering every lesson in responsible behavior my father had ever taught me. "Can't you see this is *serious?* Can't you see we're in *trouble?*"

Inclining his head toward G.T., Dennis flutters his eyelids and says, "But brother, what a way to go."

Looking back to the glass booth, I see that Jergens has stood up behind his desk, and is peering down on the scene in front of him. Several times he adjusts his bifocals and deepens his frown another notch or two.

"Murphy, Anderson," he says, addressing us but staring at the girls, "what's going on here?"

Dennis says softly, "Can't you see, jerk-off? This is the lesbian nation." But of course Jergens can't hear.

"Young ladies, what are you—" Jergens begins, and I can feel the blood leaving my head as the old guy opens the glass door and struggles over toward the registers. He says more words, but we can't quite make them out. As for the girls, they're looking at him the way you might stare at a gnat on your arm for a few seconds before taking the trouble to mash it between your fingers.

"Young ladies, young ladies!" Jergens cries as he comes up to them, shaking his finger. "Don't you know this is the A & P? You can't bring those guns in here." He pauses, looking them up and down. "And your attire in general, I must say, is most inappropriate and, well—unfeminine."

Now Mohawk glances at G.T., as though requesting permission to blow off Jergens's head. I want to explain to them that this is just Jergens's Sunday school manner, that he doesn't know any better and isn't really worth killing, but I can see from the glint in G.T.'s eyes that she doesn't want advice from the likes of me.

G.T. says, enraged, "So you don't like our clothes, huh? So you think we're not dressed appwop—apwipp—" She can't pronounce the word. It's so damn cute I start shifting my weight from one leg to the other, unable to keep still.

"No, they're certainly *not* appropriate," Jergens says huffily, though I can see he's had time to get nervous. He's a bit more friendly when he says, staring at the gun barrel G.T. has slowly lifted in his direction, "So, did you girls need some help? Did you want to buy something?"

"Yeah," says the one with Technicolor hair, snidely. "Yeah, we're here to pick up some meat."

"I see," Jergens says, nodding. "Some nice rib-eyes, maybe? Or some lean chuck, ground fresh today? If you'll follow me back to the—"

"Keep it closed, fart-face," G.T. says, but again she lets her little bow lips curve upward in a smile.

"Holy moly, cook my tacos," Dennis sighs.

"We've already found what we want," G.T. says, staring at me. I notice that Mohawk is looking at Dennis, with a hard little grin, and Technicolor is looking back and forth between us, actually licking her lips.

"What we want," G.T. says, her smile broadening, "are a couple of nice little grocery boys."

Except she says "gwocewy" instead of "grocery." It's so cute I'm ready to die.

"What's that?" Jergens says, frowning. "I don't understand—"

"Oh, so you don't understand, do you?" G.T. says, and she demonstrates why she's the leader. After moving a few dainty steps to get herself in position, she lifts her UZI, closes one eye, and sprays the glass booth with an eight-second burst. The din of shattering glass is so overwhelming that by the time she's done I'm panting with excitement. There's just a few visible slivers, like stalactites, where the glass booth used to be.

G.T. walks back to her place between the others, calm as you please.

"Now do you understand?" G.T. says, mock-sweetly.

At that, Jergen hits the tiles. He lies spread-eagled like all the other fossils throughout the store.

"Well now," G.T. says, blowing invisible smoke from the barrel of her gun. "I guess that leaves just us, wouldn't you say?"

"Us?" Dennis says, almost frantic with excitement. "What do you mean, us?"

"You want to come along, don't you?" G.T. says, raising that killer eyebrow again. "You boys aren't going to resist arrest, are you?"

Except G.T. says, of course, "wesist awwest."

Solemnly, Dennis raises his hands and walks toward the girls. From her back pocket Technicolor whips out a pair of handcuffs and joins Dennis's wrist to hers.

"Now wait a minute," I say, as G.T. comes forward, followed by Mohawk.

"Wait?" G.T. says, as though she's never heard the word before. "What's he saying? Wait?"

"For heaven's sake," Dennis says, rolling his eyes. "Wave the white flag!"

I stand silently as G.T. cuffs my wrist to hers, and I'm taking small steps as they lead us out of the store. Dennis and I are still wearing our white aprons, and the little black bow ties the store made us purchase for $8.95. I'm thinking how ridiculous we must look next to these hot girls, but once we get outside—the girls parked their Toyota van in the handicapped spot, of course—I'm amazed that no one pays us any attention. There are dozens of other stores and hundreds of people ambling down the sidewalks, crisscrossing the parking lot, but their eyes are all trained forward and a bit glazed, as if they're extras from some movie called "Shopping Center of the Damned."

In any case, the girls have plenty of time to arrange us inside the van. G.T. is the driver, of course, and I'm next to her, and Mohawk is sitting guard by the passenger window. I can feel her rock-hard biceps pressed against mine. Dennis and Technicolor are in the back seat, all scrunched together on one side. Craning my neck, I can see purple lipstick prints on Dennis' jaw.

"Well, I hope you're happy!" I hiss at him.

"I am, I am!" he hisses back.

As G.T. starts the van, Mohawk glances to the back seat and then at me. "Say goodbye to your corrupt bourgeois existence," she says. "Bid farewell to the capitalist power structure and the disenfranchisement of women, people of color, and the poor."

"Oh Jody, for heaven's sake," G.T. says as she shoves the van into gear.

"Bye!" Dennis cries, pressing his face to the back seat window, waving. "Bye bye!"

Slowly the van pulls away, and we're swinging out along the front windows of the store. Squinting, I can barely make out the darkened forms of Jergens and the other fossils as they slowly begin raising themselves from the floor and brushing off. Jergens is limping toward the register—*my* register—and yes, I can see his hand reaching down into the cart, starting to check the fossil through. Then I think of my father, his saying the other night at dinner that the world isn't like it used to be; when *he* was a kid, he said, whining, on the verge of tears, people were nice to one another and you could walk the streets without fear and sleep soundly at night. Then I think of my mother, telling him to shut up. That's all I remember.

I ponder my words carefully as G.T. pulls out of the parking lot, onto the service road, and finally onto the expressway. She takes the inside lane and hits the gas pedal, hard. There's little traffic here on this balmy afternoon, there's nothing to hold her back. We're still cuffed together and as she steers the wheel, my left hand is jerked sharply to the side. I can feel the cold metal begin cutting into my flesh.

"Well," I say philosophically, thinking of the store and Jergens and my parents whom I would never see again, "I have a feeling that the world is going to be a tough place, from now on. I have this eerie sensation that—"

"Hey, cut the epiphany crap," G.T. says, though she actually says "cwap." "Otherwise, we'll be glad to take you right back to that shit-ass store."

"No, no!" Dennis squeals, and he and Technicolor break into a fit of giggling.

Mohawk has begun handing out lit cigarettes, and I see how hard G.T. sucks on hers, and so I start smoking, too. I decide that G.T. is right, and a great joy is released in me. It's like the clouds of smoke filling the interior of the van, making my eyes water and my heart

71

race like crazy. Light-headed from the cigarette, I'm thinking giddily that the world is fresh out of epiphanies, just like the store is usually out of our 99¢ specials.

The girls seem to sense the change in me, the last hold-out, and so Mohawk says aloud, "*Yeah,*" and G.T. lets out a whoop, her sweet little chin jutted out over the wheel. By now we're doing eighty, edging toward ninety. Grinning, I hunker down in my seat and get ready to ride.

Commitment

S HE'D never been good at waiting. When she got to the hotel, she paced the room lengthwise, door to windows. The windows overlooked a parking lot, and with each pass she scanned the rows of cars for her husband's BMW, muttering to herself, not hearing the TV that blared from the room's far corner. It had always been her habit to keep the TV on, for company, and when her husband arrived home from his office, or from one of his mysterious evenings "out," he'd rush around the house—the den, the kitchen, finally their upstairs bedroom where Carlotta waited—and snap off each set angrily. Their couples therapist, Dr. Jahnke, had asked Carlotta if she enjoyed angering her husband. He had asked Frank if he understood Carlotta's need for companionship at night—her yearning for security, fidelity, commitment. After three sessions Frank and Carlotta had decided to terminate therapy.

She glanced at her watch: three forty-five. Frank had said four o'clock but it was like Carlotta to be early, it was one of the curses of her life—like playing the TV all day and night, like smoking four packs of cigarettes a day, like this infernal pacing. By contrast, Frank was a slender, self-contained man whose impervious calm often threw Carlotta into raging fantasies of violence or self-mutilation. She had insomnia, and of course Frank slept as though their bed were a coffin. Often she could not eat (that is, she could not eat healthful meals: but she gorged on sweets, late at night, alone), and of course Frank's appetite was excellent. She did everything quickly, haphazardly, while Frank was slow, methodical, and thorough. He even ate slowly, chewing each mouthful exactly twenty-six times. She knew this: she'd sit in restaurants counting each drop of his jaw, watching dourly over her plate of uneaten food, smoking fiercely. What else had she to do with her time, since thanks to him the very sight of food made her stomach writhe in its own acids? Yes, he chewed each mouthful twenty-six times, never one more or less. When they left the restaurant Carlotta's food would be stippled with cigarette butts, the lipstick-smeared filters looking as if they'd been gnawed.

73

Now she glanced out the window, reached into her caftan pocket for another cigarette, lit the cigarette as she headed back toward the door. Then she saw the smoke curling from an ashtray on top of the dresser and thought, *Damn, not again,* then went to the ashtray and put the second cigarette there, too. The pair of lit cigarettes made her long for an intimate chat with a girlfriend over coffee, a tête-à-tête. She no longer had many girlfriends. According to Frank, she'd driven all their friends away with her erratic behavior. According to the therapist, her acute anxiety resulted from unconscious rage with which she must come to terms or perish. But she hadn't lost all her friends: she supposed there was still Emily. They'd met several years ago, in the aerobics parlor Carlotta favored when she went on binges of exercise and dieting. Since then, they'd joked often about opposites attracting, for Emily was one of those women determined to have it all—though divorced and still in her twenties, she had two kids and a high-paying job with an interior design firm, and she managed to date several men at any given time. Emily never touched cigarettes, liquor, sweets; she had short-cropped reddish hair that gave her the look of a pixie, and a spider-thin body that made Carlotta's eyes cloud with envy. For her part, Emily claimed to envy Carlotta the luxury of spending time alone, of being married and settled whether the relationship had troubles or not. For Carlotta had confided in Emily, over their Saturday brunches and post-aerobics cups of tea, about her problems with Frank: his tendency to detach, emotionally; her own inability to relax and handle each conflict as it arose. (She didn't discuss with Emily what distressed her most—her addictions, her periods of emotional instability; she could barely acknowledge these to herself, much less to another person.) Emily claimed that a troubled relationship was better than none at all, and not long ago had said something that stunned Carlotta: Emily claimed that she'd trade all the trappings of her life—her job, her looks, her romances—for a single ongoing attachment to another person.

It was Carlotta's recollection of her friend's peculiar, emphatic statement that caused the trouble between her and Emily, for one night she'd invited Emily and her current boyfriend to dinner. Though Carlotta couldn't pinpoint the moment her mistrust began, she'd felt by the end of the evening that Emily had paid more attention to Frank than to her own date. All evening Frank had seemed abashed and boyishly pleased when Emily spoke to him, and once or twice Carlotta had seen her touch Frank's forearm with her tiny white hand. For the next few days Carlotta had tried to forget about that evening, and with both Frank and Emily she'd maintained a brittle pretense of friendliness. But privately she was suspicious and enraged. When Frank worked late, she would dial Emily's number— hating herself, but knowing it must be done—and Emily's machine would answer. On the nights when Frank stayed home Carlotta would also call, but on those nights Emily always answered. Finally Carlotta had enough and began screaming into the receiver, ashes shaking from the cigarette in her free hand: "I might expect this of Frank, but not of *you*—not you, Emily!" She'd intended her voice to sound furious but it came out as a small child's cry of betrayal. Emily had reacted angrily, accusing Carlotta of "paranoia" and of having too little to do with her time. Carlotta had hung up on her, then stormed upstairs to have the same argument with Frank, who was already in bed and asleep. "Why are the two of you doing this to me, why!" Carlotta screamed, but Frank merely raised on one elbow—she had flicked on the overhead light—and gave her the dulled and unsurprised look of a domestic-war veteran. He said, "Lottie, I've asked you not to smoke in the bedroom, haven't I?"

She'd slammed the door and gone downstairs and slouched in one corner of the sofa, eating ice cream from an oversized mixing bowl. She'd turned on the TV—an old black-and-white movie from the forties, handsome men in tuxedos smiling cleverly at slender girls— but kept the sound off. Occasionally she wept but without bitterness or even much noticeable pain; perhaps the drugs and cholesterol in her blood had choked off the pain. She could not understand her life. From the beginning of her marriage she'd all but worshiped her husband, had denied herself for him, had felt committed utterly to him!— and this was her reward. The world belonged to skinny selfish girls like Emily, who befriended fat hopeless women to make themselves feel even more powerful and self-assured. So Carlotta's mordant but self-lacerating thoughts had run. In the two weeks since her accusations she hadn't spoken to Emily and had exchanged only monosyllables with Frank. Each day, she knew, she ate and drank and smoked a bit more, but she'd begun to believe that she no longer cared what happened.

Now she stood staring at the two lit cigarettes trying to decide which to put out. Her ingrained Catholic-school discipline suggested that she should finish first what she started first, and thus she should retrieve the first cigarette—there was more than half of it left, the rest had turned to a fine cylinder of pale-gray ash—and put out the second one, though carefully so as not to waste it. Yet she'd read somewhere that the part of the cigarette nearest the filter held the most tar, so perhaps she should let the first cigarette burn out while she continued smoking the second. But now the second (as she stood there watching, biting her lower lip) had itself burned almost a third of the way down, and her stomach had begun churning for she couldn't decide, she didn't know what to do. Her inability to make small decisions, the therapist had said, was typical of acute anxiety, as was her tendency to make important decisions impulsively and rashly. At the moment she lifted both cigarettes, one in each hand, as if examining them closely might help her toward a decision, there were three quick raps at the door. Frank always knocked three times—never two, never four. Carlotta stubbed out both cigarettes frantically and reached in her caftan pocket for another.

When she opened the door, she saw his eyes graze downward quickly— she'd complained to the therapist that he was always assessing her, judging her—and then he tried to smile, his eyes squinting as though he were trying to see through a fog.

"You like it?" she said, swirling the caftan as she turned in a circle. This was her Vanna White parody, and it usually made him smile.

"You look tired," she said. She wanted to step forward and hug him, but something kept her back—his look of weariness, or resignation. And her own disappointment, for he'd sounded so energetic that morning on the phone. Cheerful, buoyant, even a tad romantic, she had thought. His suggestion that they meet downtown this afternoon, and *in a hotel room*, had all but floored her; she'd been having a bad morning, feeling rootless and dissatisfied, chain-smoking by ten A.M. and already contemplating her first glass of wine. She'd begun to feel that maybe she'd been unreasonable, accusing Emily and Frank like that. She tried to see the matter from their point of view, and to imagine how bizarre her behavior would seem if they were innocent. Her husband's unexpected call had seemed a reward for this enlightened thinking. Normally, Frank called only to say how late he would be, and how sorry he was.

Of course, she'd agreed to come, and since he seemed to be rushed— Frank owned a small accounting firm, and early April was his busiest time—she hadn't asked for explanations. One of his favorite sayings was "Never complain, never explain"—he claimed that some famous tycoon had said this, Henry Ford or Andrew Carnegie. During her suspicious period she'd thought bitterly that he didn't complain about Carlotta and would refuse to explain about Emily. But now that was over. Her husband wanted to see her; his wanting to meet in a hotel (the Ritz-Carlton, no less) gave her a right to develop certain expectations. So she'd simply said, "Four o'clock is fine, Frank. And

I'm—I'm glad." Her husband had paused. Her husband often paused. But then he said, "I'm—I'm glad, too."

Facing one another in their sumptuous third-floor room of the Ritz-Carlton, neither Frank nor Carlotta looked glad. She thought he might be disappointed in her outfit, but the swirling pink-and-white caftan disguised her weight and drew attention to her still-pretty face, with its smooth poreless skin and girlish blue eyes; and her honey-blond hair, worn "up," made her look taller, a bit less dumpy— perhaps even sexy, she thought, with those wispy tendrils curling down around her ears and the back of her neck. It hadn't been that long, after all, since she'd inspired her husband's passion almost nightly, and he'd commented often on her soft skin, her fragrant hair. She'd spent most of the afternoon choosing her outfit, doing her hair and makeup. Yet his look of weariness and chagrin made her over-bright smile turn wobbly, uncertain. After doing the model's turn in her dress, she felt herself sinking into the room's thick carpet, her head slightly dizzy as though she were losing her balance: that same feeling she had after smoking too many cigarettes in quick succession. So she backed away from Frank, who stood in his usual solid, immovable posture near the still-opened door. Little danger of *his* losing balance, she thought—this smallish slight-chested man who nonetheless had strong, wiry arms, a good body from working out two hours daily in the gym, and lovely exasperating wintry-blue eyes that Carlotta found unreadable. She could not read them now, she thought, edging toward the bed—perhaps he was simply tired from working so hard? Perhaps he looked forward to this night as much as she did, and as hopefully?

She sat on the edge of the bed, feeling nervous. He'd stayed near the door, watching her. Now he smiled, but even his smile was weary.

"Aren't you going to light that?" he said.

She looked down, where the unlit cigarette dangled between her fingers.

"No, I'm trying to cut down," she lied. "It helps if I just hold one."

Her husband hated smoking, especially in women: it looked un-feminine, he said. And he didn't care for the smell. Dr. Jahnke had said that her smoking had a dual purpose, didn't it?—it was a self-destructive behavior, and it angered and repelled the husband she wanted so badly.

Her lungs fairly ached for a long draw on the cigarette, but instead she thrust her hand inside her caftan pocket and broke the cigarette in half, then crushed the remains between her fingers. Somehow that was pleasurable, too.

Frank came toward her, moved as though to sit beside her on the bed, then seemed to think better of it. Carlotta felt that if he touched her she would burst into tears. She hoped this would happen, but at the same time she dreaded it. She dreaded his reaction.

"Lottie?" he said, bending slightly as though urging her to meet his eyes. She was staring at the plush beige carpeting around her husband's wingtips. Holding her breath.

"Lottie, how are you doing today? Are you—"

"Today?" she said evenly. "Why is today different from any other day?"

Her heart felt sore, like an overused muscle, and she knew the pain showed in her face; nonetheless she looked at him. Her question had been sincere. She wanted to know.

Frank's cold blue gaze veered off. He gave that nervous tic-like smile she knew too well.

"Well, today's different—you're right. But it can be a positive difference."

She stared at him. "Do you know what I thought?" she said, listening for bitterness in her voice but hearing none. "I thought you'd intended some kind of romantic encounter—like a second honeymoon. A new beginning." The words sounded even more absurd as she said them aloud. "That's why I'm looking and smelling so nice this afternoon."

"You *do* smell nice," he said, but now it was Frank who stared at the floor; or he might have been looking at her white open-toed shoes. This morning she'd painted her toenails carefully, the same hot pink as the caftan. Helplessly she remembered their honeymoon in Bermuda and the night he'd sucked each of her toes gently, one by one. Her chest heaved and she felt she might scream if she couldn't have a cigarette. She wanted a drink, too—a stiff one. Her throat ached for that drink. Her eyes ached.

She said, "But that's not why we're here, is it."

Frank put his hands in his pockets. "I thought we should talk."

She rose and came at him, both arms raised, her small plump hands clenched into fists. How she longed to strike him, pummel him!— but her husband was strong and quick. Her caught her wrists just in time; he held them firmly. She hadn't managed even to graze him.

Tears spilled along her cheeks. "You bastard," she muttered. "You asked to meet in a hotel room, knowing I'd think—knowing I'd hope for— You brought me here to dump me, didn't you? You thought you could do your dirty work here, and then the maid could clean up afterwards. That's it, isn't it?"

In her chest came that vicious feathery itching which meant an attack of panic, hysteria, sheer mindlessness, of the kind she'd experienced only two or three times; so she took a deep breath, trying to forestall it. Frank had released her arms and now she rubbed at her face with the sides of her clenched fists. She wiped her hands on the caftan.

"Lottie, please calm down," Frank said. "Let's try to be reasonable about this." He sat on the bed himself, as though providing a good example. He patted the mattress next to him. "Come on."

She sat. She allowed him to put his arm around her shoulder. Her emotion seemed spent for the moment, and she felt that she could take anything. But she hoped he would hurry.

"First of all," he said, sounding almost amused, "I didn't bring you here to dump you, for heaven's sake."

She said dully, "All right, then, let's use one of Dr. Jahnke's euphemisms. You've discovered, let's see, that this relationship is dysfunctional, and that recent life-events have prompted you to decide on another course. Like, for instance, shacking up with a bimbo named Emily."

Frank was shaking his head. "Lottie, Lottie, not that again . . ." He squeezed her shoulder.

"You think this is just a joke, don't you," she said. "You've never shown me the favor of getting angry, or upset. Because it's never meant that much to you—any of it."

"Lottie, I—"

"Even when I had that last miscarriage—and Dr. Jahnke was right for once, I *was* happy about it, I didn't want to be pregnant—all you did was leave the house and play racquetball for a couple of hours. That night you slept as soundly as ever. I knew it was over, then."

Or perhaps she'd known long before? She and Frank had grown up together, attended the same Catholic academy, and beginning in fifth grade Carlotta had been the aggressor. It was the year her father died, and her sudden raw grief, that new and perplexing emptiness, had coincided with the sudden harsh clamor of sexual need. At first, she'd enjoyed teasing Frank—he was so shy, so serious—and sometime during their high school years, when rather suddenly Carlotta had become pretty (she'd tinted her hair a lighter blond, her figure had become shapely, womanly) he had started teasing back. Despite his ferocious sexual drive Frank was a good Catholic boy and they'd married soon after graduation. They used the rhythm method for a while, but around the time he'd become a C.P.A. Frank talked often of wanting to be a father, and indeed those two or three years had

79

been the raging heart of their sexual life together. Though Carlotta became pregnant at once, she miscarried in her fourth month. Their internist said that she had "nervous problems" and advised her to quit her drafting job. At first she resisted—she loved her job—but Frank sounded so plaintive when he spoke of wanting children. He came from a large family himself, and still visited his parents every Sunday after Mass (sometimes with Carlotta, but more often without; she felt that his family disliked her). His faith kept him sane, he told Carlotta, sternly. He'd always planned to have a family, at least four or five children: he'd thought she understood that. As it happened, she hadn't quite understood—had she not been paying attention?—but after several weeks of agonized indecision and a couple of unannounced dinner-time visits by the parish priest, Carlotta finally agreed. On the weekend after her last Friday at work they went for a three-day vacation to Key West and made love seven times. Instead of the birth control pills she'd been taking secretly since her miscarriage Carlotta swallowed the pale-yellow Valium tablets her internist had prescribed.

In fact, Carlotta didn't want children, and she felt that somehow her body knew this even when she did not. After her second miscarriage Frank glowered around the house for weeks, began working late at the office, developed friendships with other men—former classmates from the academy—who enjoyed racquetball and marathon running. Alone at home, Carlotta kept taking her medicine. The fits of shaking she had experienced before the miscarriage returned at times, and often she washed down the Valium with a glass of wine. Slothful as her husband was athletic, she let the maid Frank had hired do the housework, and she cooked only the simplest meals. She loved cheeseburgers, tacos, thick steaks, and baked potatoes loaded with sour cream and cheese. After dinner, when Frank went back to the office or to the gym, she watched TV and either sipped more wine or ate chocolate sundaes topped with strawberry jam and whipped cream. This dessert was a consoling reminder of the banana splits her father bought her at the Dairy Queen when she was little—Carlotta had adored her father—but the food tended also to diffuse the effects of her afternoon Valium, so she took another tablet at night to help her sleep. If Frank was in the mood for sex when he got home, the tablet helped her through; if he turned over in bed, ignoring her, it helped her through that. Just before her second miscarriage her shakes were so bad that her gynecologist—a man with a Jewish-sounding last name she'd picked at random out of the phone book—told her that being pregnant did not agree with her. Instead of Valium he gave her a new prescription for birth control pills and listed the names and numbers of three psychiatrists. Two were women, and she crossed off their names at once. The third name was Dr. Jahnke.

Carlotta saw Dr. Jahnke by herself for a while, and he reassured her that she was not crazy. He didn't believe in minor tranquilizers but he did prescribe an antidepressant and another drug to help with her anxiety. Once in B. Dalton's she looked up the second drug in a reference book and saw the designation "antipsychotic" and shut the book at once. That's what she got for sticking her nose in the doctor's business, but at once she thought of movies she'd seen about crazy people given shock therapy and crammed into straightjackets. Dr. Jahnke laughed when she told him about this, and said again that she wasn't crazy. He suggested that Frank should come to the sessions, too, since his talks with Carlotta had revealed that the issue of commitment was paramount in this marriage and that he needed to hear the husband's side. During the first session, Frank admitted calmly that he'd had three affairs within the past year. He felt tremendous guilt, he told the doctor—he didn't glance at Carlotta—but also tremendous loneliness and frustration because he feared that he would never be a father. Dr. Jahnke suggested that he address his frustrations directly to Carlotta, but when Frank began to speak Carlotta interrupted him and asked if he wanted a divorce. That way, he could marry someone like Emily, she said in a brittle but reasonable tone; someone who could provide him with children. Frank said at once, "Marriage is a commitment for life. You know I don't believe in divorce." Carlotta said that neither did he believe in illicit affairs, did he, and Frank said that he'd never claimed to be superhuman.

After she and Frank decided to terminate therapy with Dr. Jahnke, she visited her old internist and got another Valium prescription, then visited the Jewish gynecologist and got some more birth control pills. She made both these doctors' appointments for the same day and afterwards she felt jubilant and congratulated herself by drinking an entire bottle of champagne at home by herself. Then she cried for three hours. When Frank got home, she apologized for being so fat and so ugly. She was shaking violently. Frank said he had a racquetball game and hoped she would pull herself together before he got back.

That had been three weeks ago. Then she'd pulled herself together and invited her friend Emily for dinner, and look where that had gotten them. But she'd never wanted to believe that her marriage was over, and that was why Frank's phone call had instantly changed her despair to that frantic self-deluding sense of hope. This was the first time she'd dressed nicely and used makeup or perfume in months. Before donning the caftan she'd mounted her bathroom scale and had been relieved that the digital display read 149, for lately she'd been topping 150; but then she recalled that she'd denied herself all last week—no fried foods, no desserts, even a special low-calorie white wine—and this seemed a paltry reward. A reading of 149, instead of 150! She gazed into the floor-length mirror at her lumpish pale body until the image began to blur and then she donned the tent-like caftan quickly, swabbing her cheeks with the sleeves. The Valium she took was her last, and she vowed to refill the prescription on her way to the Ritz-Carlton; or, she thought, on the way back. She couldn't decide because she wanted to believe that her time with Frank at the hotel might mark a turning point in their marriage, meaning that she wouldn't need the pills, but then she was repelled by the idea of equating her husband's love with a tranquilizer. So she'd deposited the empty prescription container in her caftan pocket, intending to toss it into the trash can in the garage, on her way out. But she had forgotten, so on her way to the hotel she stopped at the drug store, after all. Sitting in her car, in the parking lot of a busy shopping center, she took two of the pills without water. Merely to swallow them made her feel better. Outside her car was an ordinary spring afternoon, and women not very different from Carlotta were drifting in and out of the stores and parking lot as though trapped in a dream. What secret did they possess, that she did not? Why did their husbands come home at night, when hers did not? Some of the women dragged along children by the hand, but Carlotta could scarcely focus on *them*; with a brutal twist of her hand she started the car. The Valium, she reasoned, would begin taking effect by the time she reached the hotel.

Frank had kept his arm around her but her own arms felt paralyzed, held close to her body. Yet her fingers kept working busily, toying with the crumbled cigarette pieces inside her pocket.

Frank said, "Feeling any better . . . ?"

She glanced at him, sideways. "Oh yes," she lied. "I was just thinking . . ."

She stopped because she hadn't been thinking at all. But Frank was waiting.

"I was thinking that—that this was a good idea. You know, getting away, having a chance to talk—"

"That's right," Frank said calmly. Somehow she wished he were less calm. Those times in Dr. Jahnke's office he'd been edgy, his face creased with tension. He'd admitted freely that he had difficulty in

82

talking about his emotions, or in dealing with his wife's. That's when he said the only conscious emotion he felt was his desire to be a father, and Dr. Jahnke asked if "conscious emotion" were not a telling phrase; then he'd asked if wanting to "be a father" were quite the same as wanting to have children. Frank hadn't answered either question, and at that moment it was Carlotta who had felt calm, and strangely gratified. But that had been their last session with Dr. Jahnke.

"You know," Frank said now, "I've been doing a lot of thinking lately. I've been aware of how much I've failed you—how I haven't paid enough attention to your needs. Dr. Jahnke agrees with that, and so does Father O'Neill."

"Father O'Neill?" Carlotta said blankly. "You've been talking to *him* about—"

"About you—I mean, about us. That's why I visited Dr. Jahnke, too. I wanted to make sure I understood the situation."

Carlotta stared at him. All this time she'd thought Frank had been immersing himself in work, in sports, in weekend visits to his parents—all in the attempt *not* to think of her. She didn't know whether to be pleased or frightened.

She said, "Frank, I don't know what they've told you, but—"

"They've been worried, Lottie," her husband said gravely. "They think I've been neglecting you."

There were no more cigarette pieces left in Carlotta's caftan pocket: only fine grains of tobacco which she sifted through her fingertips, over and over. "Well, that's because—"

"That's because I haven't understood your needs," Frank said. "Just as you haven't understood mine."

His arm felt heavy, oppressive along her shoulders, so she drew away from him, trying to smile. "Honey, it's not that I haven't understood—I know you want kids, and so do I. But the point is that we're not ready. For one thing—"

"You're right, Lottie," Frank said, nodding. She heard the patronizing tone in his voice—as if he were speaking to a child—but she tried to ignore it. At least he was trying to communicate, she thought. He sat there trim, erect, handsome, his plaid sports shirt and khaki pants neatly pressed, looking every inch the accountant on his day off: leaving this hotel, free and unfettered, he might easily attract the glance of some young girl. . . . Carlotta closed her eyes, then opened them. Hadn't Frank just said he felt committed for life? To her husband, words were like numbers, he took them seriously; each sentence was a vow. So she would trust him, she thought. She would cling to his words.

83

She began to cry, softly. The pills she'd taken had begun to relax her body, so that her shoulders slumped as if her very bones had softened. Her tears were gentle, painless, as though leaking harmlessly from the confused gauzy mass that her mind had become. Yes, she thought, she must listen to her husband. She had filled herself with other things, false things—food and drugs and smoke—but now she must let her husband enter her, through his words and the faithful love that lay behind them. Perhaps they would make love on this bed and she would become pregnant and conceive a child on this very day. Like her husband, she wanted a child. Like him, she believed in miracles.

She edged back toward him, curling one arm around his waist; she felt the hard muscles of his stomach tensing, wary of her. She pressed her soft fragrant cheek against his throat, murmured something inaudible, then understood that her hand had wandered downward, had begun fiddling with his belt buckle, clumsily. All at once she began to giggle, and that's when her husband pulled away.

"Lottie, we can't—" He stood, gazing down at her; then he looked down at himself and readjusted his belt. For that moment he looked boyish, studious, preoccupied—unaware of her. Fiddling with his pants. She remembered her anguished fantasies of him and Emily together, undressing one another slowly. Unaware of her. He'd laughed at her accusations, treating her like a child, but suddenly she knew that she'd been right. Again that terrible feathery rage expanded through her chest, a bodiless shriek that required a voice, *her* voice; but she would not lose control. She clamped her lips shut and went to the fancy French telephone beside the bed. She lifted the receiver and punched Emily's number.

"Lottie?" Frank said vaguely. "Who are you—"

Emily answered on the first ring. Her vague, tentative "Hello?" said everything, Carlotta thought in triumph. She blurted into the phone, in the few seconds before Frank strode forward and snatched the receiver from her hand: "Emily, it's Carlotta. Frank told me everything, everything! You miserable bitch, he told me what you did!"

Emily said, faintly, "What did he—" But that was the moment when Frank grabbed the phone.

"Lottie, sit down," he said sternly. "You're hysterical." Then he turned away, putting his lips to the mouthpiece. He said, "Lottie's not well, Emily. I'll call you later— What? No, not yet."

As he spoke, Carlotta wandered away. With her husband's back turned, she felt happy and free. She went to one side of the ornate cherrywood bureau, stared for a moment at the tasteful accessories arranged along its gleaming inlaid surface—a teal-and-white porcelain biscuit jar, an exquisite gold-leafed clock, a small Greek bust in veined marble of a young woman, noble-looking, slender, lovely— and with the side of her arm swept all these items off the bureau and onto the floor. The room's plush beige carpeting was so thick that this minor catastrophe hardly made a noise, but nonetheless Frank whirled around, shouting, "Lottie, my God!" She didn't bother to glance at him, but she heard something: he must have dropped the telephone. She'd already headed for the tiny silk-shaded lamp on a corner table, with its base of filigreed brass—she lifted the lamp by its shade and flung it against the wall. Then she picked up a large crystal ashtray, so heavy that it weighed down her body on one side, and aimed it at the mirror above the bureau. She missed. Instead the ashtray thudded against the wall, leaving a modest gouge mark, rather disappointing. . . . But then came another, similar sound, and Carlotta turned, her mouth opened vaguely, eyes rimmed in white, and Frank stopped before he reached her: someone had knocked at the door.

Some time later, Carlotta again sat on the edge of the bed, listening to her husband. He spoke in a slow, methodical voice; his wife listened closely. She took her hands from her pockets and folded them in her lap, like a docile schoolgirl. She watched his calm severe profile as he spoke.

They were no longer alone, but the others were quiet, too. They were listening to Frank.

". . . and I'm guilty of many things. I've been avoiding the issue, hoping that somehow the problem would just go away, that you'd get better on your own. . . . But after talking with Father O'Reilly, I knew I'd been evading my responsibility. He said something that I found touching, Lottie. He said, 'For the time being, perhaps *she* must be your child.' And that's when I knew—I'd have to take care of you, I'd have to do what's best. . . ."

Carlotta felt that despite his words he'd grown abstracted from her, strangely distant; as though his words were really spoken to himself, repeated in that dogged, slightly tedious rhythm, like a stubborn prayer. She was part of that prayer, the word "Lottie" spoken in her husband's low aggrieved voice, but somehow that was not her; somehow he was ignoring *her*, she thought. Yet her anger had gone, vanished. That feathery, wild sensation had passed away; her breath came calmly, evenly.

"I—I'm not a child," she said.

She kept watching Frank from the bed, her mind so gauzy from the

Valium that it felt separate from her body—her body shivering beneath the caftan, hands clasped in her lap—and the tears blurring her vision and wetting her face felt distant, too, as though the real Carlotta were trapped through some tragic error in this mass of flesh, this bloated trembling woman who kept repeating a phrase that Carlotta herself had not willed: "I'm not a child, I'm not a child. . . ."

No one heard. Facing her, this sudden crowd of men: she saw Frank, she saw Dr. Jahnke, she saw a couple of younger men who watched her vacantly. She yearned back to that moment when she'd swept those items off the bureau, flung the lamp and the ashtray: she'd never behaved more sanely in her life. She'd felt cleansed, whole, and a vague smile of fulfillment had played about her mouth. Now she wanted to explain to these men, patiently and calmly, but instead she heard her own broken, sobbing voice: "I'm not a child, I'm not . . ."

Dr. Jahnke was bending low, cupping his hand beneath one of her arms; the two young men he'd brought along approached her other side. They were urging her upward, gently, and Dr. Jahnke's familiar voice was saying, "We'll talk on the way, Carlotta. All the paper-work is done, everything is arranged, and in the long run I know you'll agree this is for the best. . . ."

Carlotta wanted to say, But where are we going? I'm not crazy, I've never felt saner in my life! But her voice said, "I can't have a baby, so does that mean *I'm* a baby?"

Dr. Jahnke smiled, gently, keeping one of his hands firmly beneath her forearm, her other arm grabbed by one of the faceless young men flanking her other side. She was being led from the room, slowly. In the distance, near the bureau with its oval-shaped mirror that she had failed to shatter, her husband stood looking small, tidy, forlorn. She gazed back at him, and floating near his shoulder, in the mirror, she saw the blotched tearful face of a woman she would never acknowledge.

She heard someone speaking, with a girlish bitterness the men could not hear: "I've been bad, haven't I? I've been very, very bad . . ."

At the last moment Carlotta glanced again over her shoulder. There her husband stood, tight-lipped, arms folded over his chest. And that bobbing ugly face, near his shoulder . . . ? It had vanished, she thought vaguely; it was nowhere to be seen.

Child of My Dreams

AT HALF PAST eleven the doorbell rang: Emma would remember the time, since she'd gone into the kitchen to wash her coffee cup right after *Wheel of Fortune* and had reached across the sink, with a little grunt, to close the window. She hated to run the air conditioner, but here it was only April and already in the nineties, the air sticky as tar. She resolved to make some lemonade before lunch, paused before the window unit in the dinette and twisted the switch to HI, then went to the living room and cracked open the front door.

"Yes? Can I help you . . . ?"

On the little white-painted stoop waited a young pregnant woman and an even younger man who had taken a step backward when Emma spoke. Now Emma opened the door wide. Her attention went instinctively to the woman, who wore her reddish hair tightly curled and was amply fleshed even apart from the pregnancy.

"You're Mrs. Sands, ain't you?" she asked, smiling blandly. "The real estate lady said you lived here?"

Emma blinked, putting a look of kindly bewilderment on her face while her mind raced into the past. They'd lived in this house for twenty years, and she remembered that even back then some young men or other had handled the sale. She recalled his dark head and Rayford's salt-and-pepper one, tilted in the same direction as they examined water stains on the bathroom ceiling.

"Excuse me?" Emma said, smiling dimly through the screen. "I'm afraid I don't—"

"See, we used to live here," the pregnant woman said. She came a step closer; only inches separated her and Emma on either side of the screen. Up close, Emma could see that the woman was about thirty or a bit older: a few lines rayed out from the plump folds of skin around her eyes. She had a round, fair face, lined with tiny droplets of sweat at the hairline. Yet she wasn't exactly homely, just as she wasn't exactly fat: she had a pleasant, rosy quality that attracted Emma at once.

"Here? In my house?" Emma said. "Is that right?"

"Yep," the woman said, her eyelids dropping a moment in what must have been shyness. "A long time ago, though. You've been here a while, I reckon."

"My goodness, yes," Emma said. "Since '68, in fact. I remember because it was the year that Rayford—that's my husband—got his big promotion."

"We're just in town for the day," the young woman said. Now she pressed her nose against the screen, squinting into the dimness past Emma's shoulder. "I wasn't but five when we moved away—out of state, I mean, and we just ain't made it back to Georgia before now. I sure would like to glance inside, if it wouldn't be too much trouble."

Emma had a moment of giddy panic—she and Rayford seldom had visitors, and when they did she hardly knew how to behave. Rayford had always said that she was too timid, too much of a shrinking violet, and now she felt a childish thrill—half pleasure, half delicious fear—as she opened the screen door and stepped back to let them pass. Really, she told herself, she had nothing better to do. Eleven-thirty to one o'clock was her slowest part of the day, since there was nothing on TV and since she often felt tired about now, but not sleepy enough for a nap.

"Now look, Templeton," the woman was saying to the small-framed man who followed her inside. "Now this is *nice*."

"If I'd have known you were coming, I'd have straightened up a bit," Emma said dishonestly, following the woman's gaze around the living room and knowing there wasn't a doily out of place. "But have a seat, won't you? Now when did you live here, exactly? Was it just before us?"

"Not *just* before," the pregnant woman said cryptically. "Just *before*."

Emma blinked. "We moved here in '68," she repeated.

The woman turned and held out a fleshy pale hand, which felt damp and overwarm to Emma's touch. And she couldn't help noticing the jiggling flab on the woman's exposed arm—the outfit she wore had no sleeves—or the big half-moons of sweat darkening the fabric halfway down the sides. Stiff reddish hairs curled out from the gaping arm-holes and Emma wondered, not for the first time, at the things young women did these days—or failed to do. But the outfit itself was pretty enough, a blue floral maternity top that ballooned out over a longish, rather crooked navy skirt.

"I'm Janine Whitehead," the woman said in her blunt way, "and this here's Templeton."

Emma shook the man's hand, too, telling herself that these were definitely country people and hoping that Templeton was the man's first name and that Whitehead was his last. She thought he looked very peculiar, standing next to this oversized woman: small-boned, slump-shouldered, he had a carefully trimmed mustache and pale quick-moving eyes. The eyes met Emma's for a second and then skittered off, like a child's. Yet he had big hands and thumbs—*huge* thumbs—that he kept hooked inside the front loops of his jeans. When Emma saw, alarmed, that his fly gaped partway open, she quickly glanced away.

"I'm pleased to meet you," Emma said, embarrassed. "I don't get much company these days."

"Is that a fact," the woman said, still looking around.

"My husband, he works out at the paper mill—he's a foreman, has been for years," Emma went on, wondering if she sounded ridiculous. These people didn't want to hear about Rayford, but as always when company arrived she had one central problem: what did you talk about?

"Is that a fact," Janine Whitehead repeated, and now her rather blurred, colorless gaze settled on Emma. She added slowly, "You sure got some pretty thangs in this house." Keeping her little dull eyes on Emma, she wiggled a plump hand toward the high, narrow hutch by the TV where Emma displayed her silver and china. "That's a purty silver service," she said. "We didn't have nothing like that when we were coming up—did we, Templeton."

The young man had stayed a foot or two back from the pregnant woman and now Emma thought he looked meek but also rather sly. He smiled lopsidedly, one end of his mouth moving and the other not, and when he spoke Emma caught a whiff of something strong, sickly-sweet; but surely he hadn't been drinking, this early in the day?

"Nope, I reckon not," he said in a bland sing-song, as though agreeing with Janine Whitehead were customary with him. Emma decided he must be a younger brother, not the husband: they'd both lived here long ago, she thought, and now they were back, on a little vacation or something, and wanting to see the house. That made sense, after all.

"Would you like some lemonade?" Emma said pleasantly, noticing how the woman's eyes kept straying around the room and even squinting out toward the dinette.

"That'd be nice," Janine Whitehead said, rubbing her bare arms as though she'd caught a sudden chill. "But won't Mr. Sands be wanting his lunch?"

"Oh no, he eats out at the mill," Emma said with a sigh. "I have my lunch by myself, nearly every day. In fact, if you'd like a bit of something—"

"We ain't hungry," Templeton said at once. "We done et."

The pregnant woman gave an abrupt, surprised laugh. She came forward and patted Emma's shoulder. "C'mon, I'll give you a hand," she said, but something about her—maybe it was her close, fleshy odor—made Emma stand aside.

"Oh, I couldn't let you bother, Mrs. Whitehead," Emma said quickly. "Why don't you have a seat on the sofa, you and your—that is, you and Mr.—"

"Call me Janine," the woman said, winking broadly. "And he's not Mr. anything—he's just Templeton."

Grinning, Templeton showed that one of his front teeth was missing.

"Besides," Janine said, "I want to see the kitchen. My mama used to make the best homemade biscuits in town, right out in this here kitchen. . . . Look, sit down and rest yourself," she called over her shoulder to Templeton—she spoke rather bossily, Emma thought— but by then the woman's heavy, clumping stride had taken her halfway to the kitchen, and Emma had no choice but to follow.

Much as she fought it, Emma had always felt afraid before strangers, and this Janine Whitehead's being from the country didn't help. They were so confident, these country people!—so blunt, so sure of themselves! When she and Janine got to the kitchen, Emma resolved not to feel intimidated.

"Really, don't trouble yourself," she said, reaching into the cabinet next to the refrigerator for the lemonade pitcher and squeezer. But she saw that giving a hand had only been a figure of speech with Janine, who had plopped herself down into one of the vinyl-covered chairs and now let her eyes swoop around the kitchen just as she'd done in the living room. She looked disappointed, Emma couldn't help but notice, and Emma felt a little crestfallen herself as she followed the woman's gaze.

"Is something wrong?" Emma asked.

Janine exhaled heavily. "Well, you ain't done much with it," she said in her forthright way. "You keep all the nice stuff in the other room, I reckon."

"Well . . . yes, except for my silver drawer," Emma said awkwardly, patting the drawer beside her and trying not to feel offended. Such people didn't know any better, she thought. Seeing that Janine's stomach protruded even more noticeably, now that she was seated, Emma decided to change the subject.

"I see you're expecting a little bundle," she said, dropping her eyes to Janine's mid-section.

"What?" Janine said, but she looked down, too, and then brought her arms forward as though giving herself a hug. "Yeah, that's right," she said offhandedly. "Number eight, I reckon."

"Number *eight!*" Emma gasped, all at once picturing a stair-step of little redheads, each one missing a front tooth . . . But no, she told herself, that small-framed young man out there wasn't a day over twenty-five and could *not* be the father. She couldn't bring up such a delicate topic, so she set her mouth and started grinding the lemons. It was too late, of course, but she wished she hadn't answered that doorbell after all.

"What about you?" Janine asked her. "How many you got?" She lifted one of her elbows and began rubbing it briskly with her palm; the tip of the elbow had been bright red, and now got redder.

"Oh, we don't have any," Emma said, hearing the sharp regret in her voice. This was her one "sensitive subject," as Rayford called it, and one they hadn't discussed in years; but even though she was past sixty the thought of babies—of babies, and children, and all she had missed in her life—still flooded Emma's mind at the oddest times. In her twenties Emma *had* borne a child—a very difficult breech birth, but the baby had not been alive—and the doctor said ruefully that she wouldn't have another. After a period of bitter grief she'd had a long spell of distrust and skepticism toward doctors, refusing to believe what they said, keeping the antique hope chest (a family heirloom, and a wedding gift from her mother) stuffed with the tiny blankets, nightgowns, booties, and other nursery things she'd assembled during those excited last months of her pregnancy. The doctors were wrong, she'd told her mother, and her mother's friends, and any other female who would listen. The doctors were definitely wrong, she told Rayford softly, late at night, curling her forefinger under the lobe of his ear. She had trusted her hopeful instincts for a while, and then she was thirty—and thirty-four—and thirty-eight—and though she refused to throw away the hope chest and its contents she did stop talking about pregnancy or babies or anything associated with motherhood at all. In those days you seldom discussed intimate details with anyone, even your own mother (how Emma resented and envied the young girls on her soap operas, who discussed such things in the same intense, cheery voices they used to talk about their jobs or their clothes!), and so she couldn't talk to anyone, least of all

91

Rayford who had mumbled a few sympathetic words about "women's troubles" on that first night, the night she came home from the hospital and cried her eyes out, but after that had shied away from Emma whenever she wore a long face and, if he felt his own grief, never complained. So she had no one, really, except herself, and for quite a while she kept that self busy with scrubbing the house, and redecorating every year or two. This was her one flaw, her one female weakness—she had redecorated constantly throughout her forties and even into her fifties, sometimes replacing every stick of furniture in the house and inspiring Rayford to complain that when he left for work in the morning, he never knew if he'd find the same living room when he got home. Which prompted Emma to ask, after stewing for several days, if she didn't keep the cleanest, prettiest house in town, after all?—and without the expense of a maid?

That was the closest they'd ever come to an argument, in all their long years of marriage. Now that they'd both mellowed somewhat, Rayford spending his spare time playing dominoes or cards with his friends from work, Emma watching her soap operas and game shows during the day and redecorating only as needed, and neither of them discussing or even thinking much about the past—now they had a pleasant routine, Emma often thought, they were still the best of friends and what more could a woman want from life? Sometimes, during the day, she did have certain thoughts, certain fantasies of which she was quite ashamed, picturing in her mind some ideal child that she might have borne and raised—a daughter, surely—who would now be a grown woman, of course, someone to chat with about the news, or the neighbors . . . or even the soap operas! It wouldn't really matter, what they talked about; what mattered was her daughter's presence, this child of her dreams—her idle, frivolous daydreams, Rayford might have said, if he'd ever guessed—and maybe a grandchild or two underfoot. But yes, she felt ashamed of these foolish ideas. Whenever Emma spoke fancifully at all, on any subject, Rayford would make some grinning retort that implied a mental imbalance on Emma's part, which didn't make her mad but made her wonder: did other women in her situation have such thoughts, or had she truly lost touch with reality somewhere along the way? Or was it something in her own nature—she'd always been a stay-at-home, and always said that Rayford was the only friend she needed—some hesitation, or shyness, or outright weakness of character that kept her secretly daydreaming about what might have been, instead of contenting herself with her life as it had actually unfolded? But then again, Emma told herself, she *was* content, and like the lady psychologist had said on *Phil Donahue* one morning, fantasies never hurt a soul and probably helped some people, especially lonely people.

Yet Emma shrank from the idea that she was lonely, and that might have been why she said to Janine Whitehead, this blunt-mannered young woman who now sat at her kitchen table, gulping lemonade like she'd just come off the Sahara, "Do you know, sometimes I do *imagine* that I have a child. I guess that's an awful thing to admit."

There, she thought, I've said it; sharing it with someone, even a stranger, made the idea seem less strange to herself. She watched the young woman's face.

"Is that a fact?" Janine said slowly, taking a last gulp and swirling the lemonade in her mouth, like mouthwash. She parted her chubby lips and said "Aah" in a way that Emma decided was a compliment, but then she focused her flat, unreadable gaze past Emma's shoulder. She said, "Well, what kind is it? What kind of child?"

Emma looked down, embarrassed. She rubbed one hand with the fingers of the other, an old habit of hers: when they were courting, Rayford would sometimes reach across and say gently, "Here, little girl, let me do that." Now her hands were brittle, and sprinkled with liver spots. She thought: Lordy, I haven't blushed in thirty years.

"Oh, I don't know—a daughter, I suppose," she said. "Someone with a beautiful family, a nice husband and some kids of her own. Probably they'd live in Atlanta, where her husband works, but they'd drive over on weekends. Or I'd go there, and babysit when they wanted to go someplace."

"If it's babysitting you're after, I could help you out," Janine Whitehead said shortly. But then, in a confiding tone: "I reckon you're after more than that, am I right?"

"Oh yes, that's right," Emma said, feeling suddenly breathless.

She'd been thinking how much time had passed, since that stillbirth that had begun the worst suffering of her life. Almost forty years, she thought vaguely, and in all that time how many bleak winter mornings, how many long and formless summer afternoons had she spent thinking about that child, buying her school clothes and brushing her pigtails and teaching her how to bake—how to crimp the pie-crust, how to separate egg whites with a deft turn of the hand. How many times had Rayford risen at three or four in the morning to find her in the living room, her eyes fixed blankly on nothing, or rearranging her knick-knacks in the kitchen as though performing some urgent work. C'mon baby, c'mon back to bed, he'd say, murmuring as one does to a child, and in the bedroom he'd rub her back or talk idly about inconsequential things until she drifted

93

off. Forty years, she thought. Forty years of shopping trips and game shows and sitting across from Rayford at supper, her mind turned numb. But had she been unhappy, really? Or maybe she had, and hadn't quite known?

Over the noise of the window unit Emma heard something from the living room, and she thought vaguely of Templeton—they really should get back to him. She ought to bring him a glass of lemonade, and refill Janine Whitehead's glass, and stop talking this nonsense that couldn't possibly interest anybody. Stop thinking the nonsense, too. She thought again of the heat, so intense for this early in the year: that was it, she teased herself. The heat had gotten to her.

Janine Whitehead turned in her seat, adjusting her great bulk. She put her elbows on the table, chin to her upraised knuckles in a thoughtful pose. Like most of the country people Emma had known, she took her time before speaking, her shiny skin and colorless hard eyes looking shrewd and a little mean.

"Well, before I can picture your baby," Janine said, "I need to picture *you*. As a mother, is what I'm saying. Now after the baby's born, for instance, just what do you plan to feed it?"

"What?" Emma said, startled. "I don't understand—"

"Just try to imagine," the woman said, shutting her tiny eyes as though to demonstrate. "I mean, you've got to feed the thang, don't you? Bathe it, burp it, rock it to sleep? And them's the easy parts."

The eyes snapped open, glaring.

Nail-heads, Emma thought. The woman's little gray eyes reminded her of nail-heads, they were that flat and that hard.

"Well, it would be quite a job—I'm aware of that," Emma said, hoping this would satisfy Janine Whitehead. But really, did the woman think Emma was stupid? She knew what was involved in raising a baby.

"Well then," Janine said, her lips curling with satisfaction, "just times that by eight and see how it goes. Shut your eyes and imagine *that*, and see how much time's left over for daydreams."

"I understand you," Emma began, "but—"

"Why, most of the girls I know, they'd be right jealous of you," Janine said, looking around again, tapping her empty glass on the table. "They'd trade half their kids, I guarantee you, for that set of china out in the living room yonder. Or for what you've got in that drawer—that silver drawer of yours."

"I doubt that," Emma said primly. Really, country or not, this young woman was unbelievably rude and presumptuous. "I'd offer you some more lemonade," she added, rising, "but I guess you're wanting to see the house—"

"Yep, the lemonade was right good," Janine said, tapping the glass once more. "Don't mind if I do."

"But what about your—what about Templeton?" Emma asked.

"Him? He's good at amusing hisself," Janine said, and now she leaned forward with such an intense, sharp-eyed look that Emma felt her heart jump. The woman added, "They're good at that, ain't they. Amusing their*selves.*" She pointed to her stomach and gave a loud, ribald laugh.

Emma smiled feebly. "Oh, is he the father?" she asked. "He looked so young, I guess, to be the father of eight children, so I wasn't sure—" As she stammered along, she took the two lemonade glasses and refilled them and sat back down, one hand rubbing the other in her lap.

"Yeah, he's young," Janine said between swallows.

More noise from the living room: a heavy, thudding sound, followed by a series of grunts. Over her upraised glass Janine's eyes shot in that direction, then toward Emma.

"We're both young, for that matter," she added. "Anyhow, Templeton's only the daddy of the last two. Before that—"

"But what is your friend doing?" Emma said, her neck stiffened in a pose of intent listening. "It sounded like—"

"Push-ups," Janine said abruptly. "He likes to do that, when I keep him waiting. He don't get much exercise, except for one kind." She patted her stomach, giving Emma a lewd wink.

Emma had had enough. She took her lemonade to the sink and poured it out. Then she turned and faced Janine, folding her arms to keep them from trembling. "Well, Mrs. Whitehead, this has been a delightful visit," she said, "but I really need to get back to my—my housecleaning," and her voice wavered on that last, dishonest note. Rayford had always said she wasn't capable of fibbing; something in her eyes—a little, childish gleam, he said fondly—always gave her away. Now she heard the front door slamming shut and she thought, with a small surge of hope: Rayford?

"Looks pretty clean to me," Janine said. She pushed back from the table, then struggled to her feet. "A good bit cleaner than when we lived here, that's for sure."

"And when was that?" Emma asked, feeling suddenly very brave although she knew it wasn't Rayford, who almost never came home for lunch. "Exactly when?"

95

Standing in Emma's tiny kitchen, the woman looked taller and bigger. She folded her fleshy bare arms as though mimicking Emma.

"Okay, let's just relax," Janine said, with a dry smile. "I reckon you're not quite as dumb as I thought."

Emma took a step backward, panicked. Opposite this big red-haired perspiring woman she felt useless, like a tiny child. Her courage shriveled to nothing. Over the grinding of the window unit she heard more grunting, then the front door opening and slamming shut again. She kept picturing Rayford, longing for Rayford, and her eyes darted to the strip of wall-space next to the refrigerator where the aqua trimline hung in its cradle. It looked distant as any dream.

The front door opened again, slammed again.

"What—what do you people want," Emma said hoarsely.

But the truth had hit her, like a smack to the forehead: newsprint swam before her eyes, and then the blow-dried head of their local newscaster, Kip Kendall, his eyes crinkling happily as he told about the rash of daytime robberies in the area, how the couple got entry with one flimsy excuse or another, selling Bibles or offering free "security checks" (these folks had a sense of humor, Kip chuckled) or just talking their way inside, usually choosing older people and sometimes completing a robbery without the victim even knowing what had happened. . . . Old people, Emma thought. Stupid people, she thought fiercely. *Mrs. Sands! The real estate lady said.* . . . And Emma had smiled, had flung the door wide open!—not thinking that her name graced the silver-painted mailbox out front for all to see, in gold day-glo letters three inches high! Remember, Rayford had told her, weeks ago, don't let anybody in the house while I'm at work . . . his voice slow, patient like he was talking to a child. Or a mental defective, maybe. If she'd bothered to make friends in the neighborhood, she thought, they'd probably talk about the robberies day and night, and it would all be fresh in her mind; or if she'd really concentrated on the newspaper, the way responsible folks did; or if she did have a child, a lovely young daughter who might call periodically just to see how she was, laughing, apologetic—*Just checking, Mama!* But not one of these simple things was true.

Suddenly Emma thought, *I deserve this,* but now that it loomed so close she wasn't sure. Janine had stepped forward, unfolding her arms and leaning sideways against the sink. Emma could smell her warm, perspiring body; she thought of the woman's swollen breasts and stomach, heaving with life beneath that flowery blue top.

"You know," Janine said, jutting her head forward and narrowing her eyes to slits, "folks like you make me sick, just plumb *sick*. If it were any choice in the matter, I'd just as soon pass you by—you and all your fancy things—people like *you.*"

Janine looked as if she might spit; in disgust her lips had made a little *o.*

"But—but we're not fancy people," Emma stammered, both hands gripping the counter behind her. "My husband's a working man, he always has been, and I—my father was a druggist, down in Macon, anybody will tell you that. Why, we didn't have anything. It's just that when you get older, you begin to accumulate things, you know? Rayford will get me a piece of silver for my birthday, or just something to set around the house—a little knick-knack or something—and the furniture isn't expensive because I redecorate so often. . . . Why, those lamps in the living room are from J. C. Penney, and we haven't replaced the carpet since '79, and—"

Babble, babble!—but she couldn't stop. What did this woman want? she thought wildly. Why did she stand there with her plump hands flexing at her sides, as if she'd like nothing more than to wring Emma's neck? Oh, if only she hadn't closed the window and turned on that blasted air conditioner, then she could at least lunge toward the screen and scream bloody murder, maybe a neighbor or the mailman would hear, but now there was no one, only Janine herself and, in the next room, that odd-looking little man. . . . And now, as if responding to her thought, Templeton appeared at the kitchen door. His face was flushed and his hair had fallen down across one side of his forehead, pasted with sweat. He stared dully at Janine.

"Well, what now?" he said.

Janine didn't bother to turn around. She still had Emma fixed in place with her little nail-heads, her lips twisted in contempt. But she did reach down, patting the drawer just behind her. Said in a flat, bossy voice: "Silver."

Templeton disappeared for a moment, then returned with a big cardboard box and began unloading the drawer.

"No, that ain't what I meant," Janine said to Emma, untwisting her lips just long enough to speak. "You know that ain't what I meant."

"What?" Emma cried. "For heaven's sake, I don't understand you! You're stealing me blind, aren't you—what more could you possibly want?"

Hunkered down over his box, Templeton snickered.

"Shut up," Janine Whitehead said over her shoulder. Then, to Emma: "You're just the kind we're always running into, in our line of work," she said. "Seems like every other house around here's got an old lady like you in it, all wrapped up in herself and her bunch of gew-gaws and her big pile of daydreams, sorry daydreams about what did and didn't happen forty years ago. The men are getting some work done, at least, if their wives ain't already sent them to the graveyard, but not the women, hell no. They hang on forever, like leeches—they don't never give up!"

Frightened as she was, Emma took offense at the phrase *old lady*—she was sixty-three, but that wasn't exactly *old*, was it? The way Janine Whitehead spoke, it sounded like her life was over.

"That's—that's not a very nice thing to say—" Emma stammered.

Janine came a step closer and rasped out, "No, it *ain't* very nice, is it?"

The way her lips bunched together put Emma in mind of big fleshy worms—live worms! The closer she came, the harder Emma pressed back against the counter; it seemed that the room had grown smaller each minute, no longer a compact kitchen but now the size of an elevator—a closet—her own coffin! Try to stay calm, she told herself. These people are evil but all they want is money, or things they can sell for money. Emma had already glanced at Templeton's pants, and sure enough there was a gun-shaped bulge in them—not that he'd bother to take it out, probably, with just one *old lady* in the house. Emma didn't think they were murderers, never mind the fierce glinting of Janine's nail-heads as she stood there, hands on her hips, as if trying to decide if Emma was worth killing.

"You—you can have whatever you want," Emma managed, in what she hoped was a cooperative tone. "Back in the master bedroom, you'll find my purse sitting out on the dresser—it's got a few dollars in it, I think. Not much, but a few dollars. I—I can understand," she said, her smile wobbling, "how hard it must be, raising so many kids and all, and trying to make ends meet—"

Janine Whitehead turned sideways, her cheeks bunched in a grim smile. "Hear that, Templeton? We're charity cases now, thanks to the nice old lady here. She don't even think of us as crooks."

"No, I didn't mean—" Emma began.

"Who the hell cares what you mean!" Janine cried. "What do you know about life, sitting up in this house all day long drinking lemonade, and watching your crappy programs on TV! I tell you, lately I been making a science of it, what with all the old biddies Templeton and I come acrost—I'm too far gone with this young-un to do any hauling, so Templeton does that, but lately I've taken to studying. I swear, they ought to teach about you in school—freaks of nature like you! You ain't done a dad-blamed thang since the day you got married, you ain't earned your way, you ain't done a lick of real work your whole life long—now ain't that right? Like I said, I been making a science of it, this past little while—every time we come acrost a dried-up old lady like you, I study her like she was some kind of bug, some kind of freak of nature! Don't I, Templeton, don't I make a science of it?"

Templeton, finished with the silver, had begun opening and closing the other drawers. "You done made a science of it, I reckon."

"Damn right," Janine said importantly. "I'm getting to the age where I like to think about things, pondering where I've been and where I'm going next. That's something *my* momma never did, you can bet your sweet fanny. She never thought about nothing and never *did* nothing, neither. Except talk about when she was a young girl, and some man with a funny accent came up to her and said she was wasting herself down South, said she ought to be an actress. Oh, she was pretty, I reckon—in her little shriveled-up way. So Daddy'd bring home gew-gaws and fancy dresses, and spew baby talk to keep her happy, and she hardly looked at him, she'd spend all her time grinning at the mirror. Pfaw!" Janine Whitehead cried, her lips moving again as though to spit. "But she had a husband, didn't she, and so then she had me, and I reckon that scared the life right out of her. Reckon *I* got it all! You should have seen her and me walking the streets together, me just about straining out of the dresses she forced over my head, my feet about to bust out of those little strapped shoes—Lord, was I miserable. But when anybody'd look, what did Momma do but step aside, pretend to be interested in a window display, pretend like I wasn't there at all!—her only child! Oh yeah, she was pretty all right, but a freak all the same—a freak of nature! On the day they laid her in the coffin, looking like a china doll with her cheeks painted pink and white, I made myself a promise or two, you hear? Now I may have ended up poor—Daddy followed Momma a year later, and she'd kept him broke his whole life long—but at least I'll know I did for my kids, got em fed and schooled and brought up right. I don't let a man hang around the house," she went on, rambling, her eyes glassy, "that beats up women and kids, and that's why the ones before Templeton here done hit the road—and Templeton will too, if he starts acting up. I don't take nothing from nobody, not men and not the government and not the people in the stores, either, if we show up to spend our perfectly good money and they try to turn up their noses! I tell you, I don't care what they think. Whatever I want, I get. Whatever I need, I take. That's my principle of life, lady, and you can't deny that I'm alive, now can you? Can you deny it?"

"What?—oh, no. No," Emma said faintly.

"Damn right," Janine said. "I'm more alive in one day, lady, than you have been in your whole sorry life, a freak of nature like you! Why, you was next door to dead on the day you was born, far as I'm concerned!"

Slowly the blood had drained from Emma's head; the woman's words were so ugly, her voice so hateful, that Emma's eyes and cheeks had gone numb. Maybe she was dying, after all?—right in front of this big flushed pregnant woman, her stomach pushed out so proudly? And now the woman was doing something, something with her dress, Emma didn't think she could bear to look—

"See here? Here's the proof if you need it!" Janine Whitehead shouted. She had lifted her maternity top and exposed her huge white belly, jutting it toward Emma, so that Emma had no choice but to stare at the distended navel, the pale blue veins snaking along the taut milky flesh. . . . "Templeton had a part in this," she said, gloating, "but now it's all me, just look at it! I tell you, I wouldn't trade nothing in the world for this!"

"I feel—I feel sick—" Emma gasped, and she felt her knees buckling, her hands losing their grip on the counter. Her eyes burned, seared by the whiteness of Janine's flesh, that huge tight drumlike mound of flesh: like nothing she had ever seen or imagined. Now Janine let her maternity top fall back and she turned around to Templeton, hurrying him along, saying they'd had enough of this place, but Emma could no longer grasp what was happening, she felt sick and hopeless, she felt a great void opening inside her that wasn't a whit smaller than that baby Janine Whitehead carried.

Now she heard Janine say, "Get on back in the bedroom, see about that purse. I'll meet you out in the truck." The woman had turned to Emma, but Emma couldn't look up. Her eyes were seared, blinded. All her energy had gone into that hunger, that aching black void—she felt herself sucked inward, drawn down inside her emptiness like so much water swirling down a drain. She was afraid Janine would start yelling again, but instead the woman just stood there, waiting. When Emma managed to focus, Janine shook her head and gave her a detached, almost pitying look.

"Think about it like this," the woman said. "What if you *had* gotten that baby of yours, and it turned out to be me?"

Rayford had been his usual self—patient, long-suffering. "Just pretend it never happened," he told her, sitting on the edge of the bed. He'd dimmed the white ruffled lamp on the night table; he'd turned the ceiling fan on LO. There would be no insurance claims, he promised. No police, no reporters, no Kip Kendall reading her name on the air. He moistened a washcloth and arranged it on her forehead. He rubbed her limp, unresisting hands.

Try to accept things as they are, he'd told her once, though in her foggy condition she couldn't recall if he was talking about the baby or the living room furniture. Otherwise you'll make yourself crazy, he'd said, sternly. Otherwise you'll make yourself *sick*.

"We'll replace everything," he promised, sitting above his wife's motionless body, "you'll be able to walk through the house and not know that anything was ever missing. All right, baby? Does that sound all right?"

From a great distance, she heard him. Heard the love and worry in his voice, though she saw nothing but that woman's face on the ceiling above her—crowded with flesh, smirking. *Knowing*.

"I'm not a freak, am I?" she whispered. "A bad person, an evil person . . . ?"

"I told you, baby, nothing has changed," Rayford said patiently. "Just pretend like it was a bad dream, won't you? Just pretend like nothing ever happened."

And so later—after a brief, hellish while—Emma did exactly that.

Him

H E WAS tall, unlovely, perhaps even homely, and from the
first he had ignored her. Then she found that he wasn't
homely: he was beautiful. She pursued him. Considering
her intelligence, her social standing, and her high self-esteem, she
pursued him quite shamelessly. Usually he was polite, if rather
oblique—he seldom met her eyes. After a few minutes' conversation
he would find some reason to walk away, spotting a friend across the
room or deciding to refill his drink. He would leave her standing
alone, perplexed and humiliated and intrigued. Openly, she gazed
after him. Having spoken to the friend or refilled the drink he did not
return to her. The party, the reception, whatever it was—they were
always running into each other—would continue as if their paths had
not crossed. At some point she would discover that he had departed.
Always he left before she did. She came to hate him.

The perplexity was understandable, for why should she care for
him? (She did not hate him, of course; she wanted and therefore loved
him.) The humiliation, too, for she had everything, was envied, was
considered beautiful in the sleek, slender-boned way of career women
in their thirties, and had inherited from her parents unusual quan-
tities of pride and independence. Twice she had been on the brink of
marriage, both times to handsome and socially prominent men, but
had discovered in each some lurking flaw—in one a barely percep-
tible effeteness that made her flesh crawl, in another the simple
habit, made worse because it was so good-natured, of taking her for
granted. She had been pulled one way, then the other. Afterward she
let herself be drawn into work (she was a successful account execu-
tive in her father's company), into preoccupations with clothing,
travel, and interior decoration, and into an intense and ceaseless
sociability. She was invited everywhere. With her large bracelets and
slender throat, her shining honey-colored hair, her habit of easing
back her head for a metallic yet oddly pleasant laugh, she'd found
herself much in demand. People seldom forgot her name. Men were
forever phoning. She felt confident, she was seldom exhilarated or

depressed, she wrote to old college friends that she had reached an "emotional plateau." Five years had passed in this way, and then she sighted him.

He was homely, yes. Hair that was long and straggly, as if in contempt for his host; eyes too small and a mouth too large, too sensual, so that when he smiled the effect seemed unnatural; rather rough, pitted skin; clothes that were well-made but styleless, saying nothing about him. His manner was self-possessed, perhaps subtly arrogant. He was too thin, so that the styleless clothes hung poorly, and something in his coloring made her think that he ate the wrong foods. It seemed that he knew everyone. He drifted from one knot of people to the next, always quiet, unobtrusive, utterly at ease. Out of pride she asked none of her acquaintances about him. She had seen him first at a large reception following the opening of an art gallery, and though they'd been introduced she'd forgotten his name. In their few brief, disjointed conversations since then, he'd never spoken her name or given any sign that he remembered it, nor had she asked again for his. They were strangers.

It was absurd, really, the way she pursued him. It was undignified. One evening, at a small cocktail party given by a close friend (that afternoon, bathing, she'd thought to herself that tonight, at least, she would be safe from him), she had done something bizarre: she blushed. She could not recall having ever blushed before, not in boarding school or in college, not in conversation with men she had befriended, not even when certain malicious acquaintances would ask her, usually in public, about one of her broken-off engagements. She was unflappable, always. Friends envied her self-possession, her consistent high spirits. She had, at first, merely stood there, experiencing the upward slow relentless crawl of blood with utter dismay, her hand tentatively brushing her crimson cheek, her eyes stinging. Then she looked at him, her heart pounding with fury. She had turned her head just for a moment, adjusting a diamond starburst clasp—it had been her grandmother's—that held back her hair on one side, and suddenly there he was. His back to her, absorbed in conversation with several people she knew very well. Her lips parted in shock. She blushed fiercely. He wore a navy suit, his straggly black hair curled over his collar in a way some women might consider charmingly unkempt (though she did not) and when she glimpsed his profile she saw that even his nose was ugly—slender but hooked, with flaring nostrils—and felt again how desperately she wanted him. She fiddled with the clasp, waiting until the blush had died away. She turned back to her friends, shaken but relieved. No one had seen.

103

That same evening they spoke briefly, and she was so guarded, so inwardly tense, that he sensed the change in her. He asked if anything was wrong. She said no, but it was so warm in here, so stuffy, and something she'd eaten—the liver pâté, perhaps—hadn't quite agreed with her. She didn't feel well, really. She hoped, then, that he wouldn't mind if she . . . And she turned away, expecting he would try to stop her; would express his concern, offer her a lift. So shameless, what she was doing—! But he did not stop her. He said nothing. She had turned, and for a moment she felt off-balance, not knowing where she was. What had been done with her coat? What if everyone made a fuss when she tried to leave, since it was still so early? She never left early. She could not claim illness to her friends, for they knew she was never ill. She ended by simply walking out the door, hurrying downstairs where she waited, shivering—the night was clear and frigid—for the doorman to summon a taxi. She would retrieve the coat tomorrow, she thought. In the cab she blushed again to think what he had done to her, and how unforgivably she had behaved. Yet there was nothing she could do. How she wanted him, and how senseless it was! How ashamed, how furious he made her! By the time the cab reached her building she was no longer shivering. Her blood kept her warm.

Weeks passed. It was a somber, still, frigid New York winter. Though she declined many invitations, she was determined not to avoid him. She was determined that her life would not be changed. At work she was completely herself, and rarely thought of him. Over a business lunch one day she spotted him, passing outside the window as she sat with two of her associates, and a chill seized her heart to see how unremarkable he was, passing alone down the sidewalk, head bent as if lost in thought, wearing a heavy coat of black wool and a lilac-colored muffler. Is something wrong? one of her friends asked and she looked back, alarmed. She had only glimpsed him, of course, but long after he was gone she had kept staring out the window, her chilled heart tapping weakly. What?—oh I'm sorry, she said, I thought it was someone I knew. But you look pale, you don't look *well*, said her other friend, but in response she threw back her head, she laughed, she returned to the conversation as if nothing had happened. Already she had forgotten him.

She had not forgotten him. At night, having dinner or attending parties with other men, she felt a shiver of distaste whenever they came near her, touched her, whispered something in her ear. She could not distinguish one man from another, somehow. They were bland and featureless, and did not exist for her. There was only *him*. At home, sitting before the mirror in her dressing-gown, she asked herself why this should be so. Not accustomed to such thought, or to the fine bitter lines that had appeared along her brow, she found herself staring into the glass with a sense of terror. What was happening? Whom had she become? She could no longer summon her anger, her hatred of him—she could no longer tell herself, calm and pragmatic and bemused, that he was a perfect stranger and her behavior made no sense—she could no longer even blush, or cringe at the idea of her friends perceiving the change in her. By now, she supposed everyone had noticed. She had paled, she had lost weight, and her hair—though she sat here every morning, like this, faithfully brushing it—no longer shone. Somehow she appeared taller when she stood before the mirror. Her eyes had mysteriously enlarged.

Over the past few weeks she had found out, mostly by accident, a few things about him—he was a journalist for a fashionable left-wing magazine, he was recently divorced, his familiarity with many of her friends dated back to his college days at Princeton—but somehow these facts were not important. Even his name, which she had discovered again, was not important. When they ran into each other, and it still happened frequently, she did not even listen to his words, which were forgettable enough. (Though her appearance and demeanor had changed, his attitude had not: he remained polite, distant, perfunctory; as though, like the men she dated, she did not truly exist.) Rather she let her eyes roam across his rough, longish, sensual face, his large capable hands, his nondescript clothing beneath which she imagined, without shame, a body that was lanky yet strong, a lover's body, impatient and deft and thorough. He had become impersonal, nameless, and so had her own identity been stripped away, leaving this large-eyed woman staring dolefully into a mirror. One morning she understood, though without dismay, that she had become as ugly as he.

By the end of winter, she had begun to skip days at work, sometimes only one but often three or four at a stretch. Her friends telephoned, and worried, and continued to extend invitations, but she accepted very few; it embarrassed her that she had so little to say, that she had stopped paying attention to her clothes (they no longer fit well, and the idea of shopping brought an inexplicable dread), and most of all she wanted to avoid her friends themselves, who were always exchanging glances, always giving her pained sympathetic stares. To the men who called she made some feeble excuse—a friend of hers was ill, she already had plans, no it wouldn't be a good idea to call back in a few days but she hoped they understood. They claimed to understand, always, though of course she did not care. They did not exist for her.

She spent long hours doing nothing, simply thinking of him. Lying naked on her bed, unsmiling, staring upward. Stretched out in her bath, the water gone tepid. Gazing sightlessly at the blaring television set, her slender hand wrapped around a snifter of brandy. She did not understand herself. She did not understand *him*. All that existed in her was this fierce, strangely impersonal desire that was nonetheless for him and only him, a lust that literally burned inside her loins, drained her skin of all color, dried her throat and mouth with its terrible thirst. More often than not, she let the telephone ring until it stopped. She wept large, painless tears. She was afraid to look out the window, or even to focus on the television screen in the absurd fear that she might see him. He was an infection, she thought weakly, that must be allowed to pass out of her. She must cloister herself like a nun, seeing no one, not until this white-hot passion had died away. Yet day followed day, and still she wanted him. She had concluded that, if nothing else, she must at least allow herself to die.

To her surprise, the thought of death gave her strength and purpose. In the first week of March, obeying a dark and whimsical impulse she returned to work, smiling vaguely, and accepted the good wishes of her associates, their hopes that her recovery was complete. But, unknown to them, she carried death in her heart. It was only a matter of time, she thought. During these days she took a grim pleasure in everything—the stupid conversation of people around her, the murky unpredictable weather of early spring, her own murderous thinking. She walked down the crowded streets in a daze, but no longer afraid. She stared insolently into anyone's face, man or woman. Her friends had received her back into the fold but now, uncertain, they handled her gingerly, they stuck to safe topics, they made vague hopeful comments about the future. Because of them, she tried to improve: she wanted to appear normal. She did not want them to guess that she would die, or that she no longer cared anything for them, or that a frantic and pitiable desire for a man, a mere man, had rendered her senseless. Gradually, she began accepting invitations once again; she began going out with men. She bought herself some jewelry. She bought a new spring outfit, then returned the next day and bought several more. At a party she overheard: Thank God it's gone away, whatever it was. We think someone jilted her, but no one really knows.

She smiled, hearing this. When she smiled her lips parted thinly, showing a minuscule line of darkness between them. A death-crack. Yet her appearance had improved. She did not look like a woman about to die. Her hair shone again, her new clothes were quite becoming, her skin seemed to have benefited from the long weeks of fasting and despair. It was taut, unlined, impeccably clear. In conversation, her eyes glistened with pleasure as if she were really listening. Her ringing laugh had returned, though her friends did not perceive that it was shaded with contempt. Soon she was going out nearly every night, as she had always done. The awareness that she no longer saw him, as it turned out, came very gradually. Her lack of fear had caused her not to think about it, but soon she found herself glancing around the crowded rooms, her eyes brushing one man and then another in her curious search for him. She would like to be able to give him her insolent stare, to show him that she was no longer pursuing him and no longer gave even a thought to him. She had a new lover, and that lover was death, and soon he would claim her. So she hadn't any use for *him*. Out of malice, she wanted to tell him.

Yet he was gone. Week upon week she searched for him, idle curiosity turning to impatience and finally to a bitter sense of wrong. How dare he abandon her now, when she no longer cared for him!—how dare he try to humiliate her again! One night, on the arm of a suave career diplomat in his sixties—he was silver-haired, almost relentlessly gracious—she attended a large charity ball and saw, standing near a bar, the group of friends with whom he'd been talking the night she had blushed and run away. Excusing herself, she boldly approached them, her heart tensed with malice. She had become aware in recent days that the hold of death upon her had lessened, that perhaps she would not die, and in this knowledge her heart had blackened. It was irremediable, her sense of evil; it was pure. They warmly welcomed her, of course, and only casually, craftily—she had waited for the right moment—did she mention his name. The reaction was quick, his name giving them obvious pleasure. They liked him, it seemed. She remembered how everyone had liked him. But she had never known him. She had only wanted him, she thought wildly, and had not wanted to like him. . . .

Yes, they said, he'd left the city—the offer of a new job, quite an exciting position really, but she did not listen any further. They had mentioned California. San Francisco. She had visited there on several occasions, and she pictured him walking the steep, colorful streets, she saw him mixing comfortably inside the city's best houses, welcomed by everyone, she saw him sitting alone at Fisherman's Wharf, staring quietly out to sea. Never again would she enter his life, or even his thoughts. He had forgotten her. . . . And how have *you* been, her friends asked, we'd heard you were ill for a while. The flu, was it? The one that's been going around? Oh yes, she said, the flu, and she rolled her eyes in the old way, even throwing back her head to laugh. It was impossible, surely—wasn't it impossible?—that these people recognized her, that she was herself, that her every gesture and re- mark had this odd air of familiarity? Impossible, surely, that she felt no bitterness, no sorrow, no apprehensions over what might happen tomorrow, or five minutes from now? And that she was herself, really, quite healthy and strong? Oh yes, she said, kindly, for she loved her friends and would always love them, always. Yes, it was the flu, she said, and really quite a bad case.

Getting Through

FROWNING, Graham maneuvered their car through the heavy noontime traffic. He changed lanes frequently, responding to the honks of other cars with an ominous muttering under his breath, followed by several quick, combative honks of his own. He squinted at the harsh winter sunlight, at the surrounding sea of cars, at the weakened, mournful voice of the woman beside him. During these past few weeks, his wife's conversation had evolved into a whining, predictable monologue that Graham tried to keep at the fringes of his awareness. Today he pretended that the driving took all his attention. His face, surprisingly youthful for a man of sixty-one, had a smooth, opalescent hardness, the skin of a man feeling obstinate and guilty in approximately equal measures. His eyes were a patient, lucid gray, but now they had narrowed, hardened as if turned to tiny pieces of flint. Resolute, he inched the car forward. It was a few minutes past twelve, and Ruth's appointment was not until twelve-thirty. The doctors' building was only a few blocks ahead.

Now a metallic-blue sports car crowded him on the right side, and Graham pressed his horn for several long seconds. His anger was a reflex, thoughtless and pure.

The crisis passed. Ruth did not seem to notice her husband's grim, aggressive handling of the car, and this pleased him. It meant she would not give him the indifferent stare that implied she was seeing through Graham, finding him once again dishonest, or frivolous, or obtuse; somehow worthy of contempt. This mild disgust sat strangely upon her petite, blond features, and it had chilled him often, throughout their long and placid marriage, to think that some lack of his could so decisively mar her still-girlish beauty, even for a moment. Now, in his knowledge that he might never suffer that look again—that his wife had lost something, irrevocably—Graham had a guilty thrill of satisfaction. The thrill eased his anger, his sense of strain. The guilt made him turn toward Ruth, smiling hopefully.

She had fallen silent, not from anything he did but in response to some new turn in the pained, ill-lit labyrinth of her thinking.

"Only another minute, dear," Graham said. They were stopped at a red light; the buff-colored doctors' building loomed in the next block.

"I've changed my mind," Ruth said in an even, nearly toneless voice. Startled, Graham stared at her; his face went pale. Still a large, healthy man—despite his thinning silver hair, his few pounds of unnecessary flesh—Graham felt helpless before his wife's eerie poise, her taut, collected power. He saw that she had lost nothing, after all. "I've decided that he really didn't hate you," she said. She did not glance aside; her pale green eyes, less resolute than merely fixed somewhere in the distance, did not even flicker.

"I hope not," Graham said humbly.

"No, he couldn't have. You're not to blame."

His wife was apologizing, and he wanted to respond generously. Yet he was put off by her toneless, mechanical voice. She might have been speaking into a microphone, recording this not only for him but for posterity.

From behind them came the brief, polite encouragement of someone's horn: the light had changed to green. Graham glanced into the rear-view, but did not sound his own horn. He moved the car forward, obedient. He felt that his anger, his struggle to force air inside his lungs against all constraining odds, to continue breathing whether he deserved it or not—this angry battle had left him, dispossessed him. Now he breathed calmly, normally. He did not understand why he should feel so frightened.

"I don't know what to say." He felt that his words expressed confusion but also gratitude. Nevertheless he let them stand.

"You don't need to say anything," she said flatly. Her voice conveyed a soulless pragmatism, an awareness that her charity, her fair-mindedness, lacked meaning. But her gesture was a good sign, Graham thought, under the circumstances. *Under the circumstances,* he repeated to himself, mimicking the sympathetic wellwishers who had written, phoned, and visited these past sixty days. He realized, now, that she hadn't really apologized. It was only that some new turn in the labyrinth had somehow included him.

Graham turned left into the driveway marked ENTER, and began steering them up the spiraling concrete ramp. On the third or fourth level, he found a parking spot and removed the keys from the ignition. But his wife's small, gloved hand had touched his forearm.

"Don't bother," she said. "I'll go alone."

"But I always walk you inside," Graham said, hurt.

His wife sighed. She was still staring forward rather than at him, though there was nothing ahead but a concrete wall marked with arrows, painted a glaring yellow, and luminescent signs.

"It's time I stopped being so dependent," she said. "Dr. Goode agreed with me about that."

Absurdly, Graham would miss leading his wife inside the building, their arms linked, then up the elevator and into Dr. Goode's office, where he finally released her. Solemn as a messenger, delivering priceless, exquisitely fragile goods to the care of another man. He would miss the brief, sympathetic smile of the glassed-in receptionist, and even his own resentment, standing alone in the elevator down, of that man he had never seen, the faceless Dr. Goode, his rival.

"You're punishing me," he said softly.

And his wife got out of the car.

For several minutes he merely sat there, like a man who has lost his bearings. At such times his mind seemed the prey of any random, desperate terror, and he thought again that it was he, Graham Hough, who should be visiting a psychiatrist. Twice a week he drove Ruth to her appointment with the venerable Dr. Goode, whom a friend had recommended as a "grief therapist," a man who helped people get through the most shattering experiences, and Graham was always left wondering why she never suggested their seeing him together, or why her husband struck her, evidently, as someone not in need of healing. It was only in the past few days that Graham had begun to see the doctor as a rival, the three of them forming a triangle—exactly, he thought, as if they were acting in a play—in which Graham had a mild, subordinate role. He was merely the husband—"the husband"—and remained a shadow, without much substance or character; he was kept apart from the drama, the airings of grief and pain taking place behind Dr. Goode's thick, sealed doors. But the thought always followed, as it did now, that perhaps they were treating him kindly, their condescension merely a way of avoiding the unspeakable. If he sat with them, behind those doors, perhaps he would learn explicitly what his wife had only hinted thus far, through a hundred gestures and signs: that this triangle had formed around a heinous, quite obvious crime, and that he was the guilty party.

Moments like these Graham accepted as flickerings of insanity, and they always ended with his trying to assume that imaginary burden of guilt, so vivid and palpable in the minds of others. In truth, Graham did not feel guilty, and now he started the engine, backed carefully and sanely out of the parking space, and began proceeding

111

back down the concrete ramp. Inside this expensive, well-built car, he must appear perfectly normal to strangers: an aging, solid citizen, probably a businessman. He had sold his lucrative imports company only the year before, at the urging of his wife, and he had yet to feel the uselessness or boredom his acquaintances had warned him against. He still rose early, still dressed in expensive, dark, conservative suits, and now applied his considerable energies to whatever small events his day could offer: visits to the offices of his broker, a kindly, balding Jew who was probably Graham's closest friend; or long lunches with his former associates, who pretended to envy Graham his new "life of leisure," a phrase they always used; or these drives with Ruth to visit Dr. Goode. Even in retirement he seemed busy, but this was part of a self-image he had evolved through the years. A patient, dutiful husband; a man concerned with the development of the community (a small but rapidly growing industrial city in the Southwest); someone who could be called upon when it was time to help the underprivileged, the orphaned, the handicapped. Several years ago, some of Graham's associates had suggested that he run for mayor (the present mayor was a young black, whose fiscal policies were far too liberal for these bleak times), but the idea had openly horrified his wife, though no less than it had secretly horrified Graham. Politely, he said no. With his diffident smile; with his mild, self-deprecating laugh that his friends and family—and in former years, his wife—had often pronounced the most charming thing about him.

Driving along the city's main street, relieved that the traffic seemed lighter now, Graham found himself picking out faces on the sidewalk—businessmen, shoppers. Ordinary people. *Graham Hough is a pillar of the community, a model citizen, businessman, husband. Model father of a gaunt, unusual son, recently deceased.* Did they really know him, these people? Had they any idea what he was living through, or what his wife, *Ruth Hough, née Allesandro, reticent but charming asset to the community, frequent participant in community projects, model wife, bitterly grieving mother,* was living through? They knew what they had read in the city newspapers, perhaps. They had pondered the Houghs' tragedy over their morning coffee, had glanced at the ten-year-old photograph of Graham and Ruth and Peter Hough, a unique aggregation of tiny black and white dots covering a certain amount of newsprint, all three of them wearing the same vague, hopeful smile. A model family. A cliché. The nineteen-year-old son looking a little anemic, as those artistic types often will, but the affluent solidity of the parents making up for this, creating a kind of balance. Graham stared out at the passers-by, aware that this image had stuck forever in their minds, indelible; instantly forgotten, yet recalled whenever Graham Hough was mentioned, or whenever they drove by Hough Imports, such a famous institution in the city that the new owners had retained its original name. He resisted the urge to roll down his window and yell at the people out there, all of them seeming to proceed down the sidewalk in a kind of mist, a hectic but frivolous dream. They might know his name, he thought, but they did not know him. Whether they thought of him as the model father or as the guilty party, they did not know him at all. Reluctantly he forced his gaze back to the road. Only after a few minutes, after he had calmed himself, did he realize that he did not know where he was going. The car was headed nowhere.

Alarmed, Graham pulled immediately to the side of the street, and fortunately there was a parking space. *Good. A good sign.* This was the outskirts of the business area, a stretch of road dominated by car dealerships and fast food chains that had sprung up in this city only during the past several years, like enormous mushrooms sprouting overnight. Graham got out of his car and began walking along the sidewalk, aimlessly. Headed nowhere. When Ruth was at the doctor's he always had this problem, not knowing what to do with himself. . . . All his life Graham's days had been filled to bursting with events, people, a constant hum of activity that energized him, that did not allow for much thinking. He made decisions swiftly, and if something turned out badly he accepted the responsibility without hesitation and moved on, refusing to feel weakened or even momentarily defeated. He did not look back. He had never been a reflective man, and he disliked these small, gaping holes in his day, open spaces in which anything might happen; he hated the sensation of his life slipping away from him, even for an hour. Ordinarily he waited for Ruth in a coffee shop two floors down from Dr. Goode's office, reading *Fortune* or *The Wall Street Journal*, sipping at a diet soft drink. He yearned to be there now, complacent and safe, absorbed in his reading, even though risking that disgusted look his wife sometimes gave him from the door of the coffee shop, jerking her head to indicate that it was time to go.

He kept his eyes trained downward, avoiding the faces of the people hurtling past him. There was always a certain moment, when someone was approaching but still several feet away, when Graham had the nearly irresistible urge to look up, throwing a sharp glance directly into the person's eyes; and, perhaps, that person would glance up at exactly the same moment. Again and again, Graham let this moment pass. He forced it to pass, without his participation, and then he felt, at his back, the unglimpsed person hurrying away from him just as Graham now hurried away from his own car, his own thoughts, the distance widening immeasurably between himself and them. He did not think of his wife, hurting openly (*shamelessly*, he thought, and then felt his own shame) in the presence of another man. He did not think of that night eight weeks before, in his other life, when he had innocently approached the shrilling telephone, not knowing it signaled his doom—his absolute doom, blunt and irreversible. He did not think of this. Instead he walked quickly, hands jammed into the pockets of his handsome, dark-plaid overcoat, his head ducked, avoiding even the momentary glance of another human being. An anonymous, well-dressed businessman, hurrying along. He might have been pondering some important business decision, or the latest market quotations. He was certainly not a man about to cry; in fact, he was not a man who had ever cried.

Though this had almost happened, a few days earlier. He'd run into Jerry Markus—his broker, and also his friend. Perhaps his best friend. It was noontime, and they'd decided to stop inside a popular downtown cafeteria for lunch; and during their meal, after half an hour of small talk, Graham had suddenly asked: "Jerry, do you consider yourself a good father?—you know, when the kids were younger?"

Jerry had looked down, embarrassed. Graham felt his own embarrassment, but an unexplained urgency pushed him forward. He forced himself to use a coaxing, reasonable tone, feeling another voice—radical, unfamiliar—rising inside him like a shriek.

"That would probably help me, more than anything," Graham said. "If you could talk about that."

Jerry's plump, florid face had reddened. He was shaking his head. "You shouldn't think of it that way, Graham. It'll only drive you crazy. How one behaves as a father, bringing up a son—there aren't any set rules, you know." Jerry paused, as if aware that Graham might take this as an affront. But he did not look up. He said gently, "Graham, I think you know that your son was probably a genius. Marsha said that to me, the first time we went to one of his recitals—that boy will be a great pianist, she told me. Now I'm very ignorant about music, but I knew it was true. He was only twelve or thirteen, but he had that tremendous poise, that *authority*. . . . What I'm saying, Graham, is that I don't know. *I don't know.* How does a father relate to a son like that? There's no simple answer. But you shouldn't go around thinking of yourself as a failure, as having failed. You shouldn't be too hard on yourself."

A note of apology had crept into Jerry's voice, and now he sat nervously turning a coffee cup between his hands, his face flushed. Graham wanted to comfort him, but a stone-like immobility had overtaken his own face; it seemed to be spreading downward, through his entire body. He had been embarrassed to ask that question about fatherhood, about being a good father, but he had never guessed that the question had no answer. Weren't there any rules, any guideposts a man could follow? Was there nothing he might have done? These questions haunted him still. The irony of his asking them now, two months after Peter's suicide, did not escape him, nor had it helped, lately, that he'd begun to think obsessively of his own father, who had died when Graham was four, and all his life had been only a hazy memory—a large pair of hands, a gruff voice. When Graham tried to focus, looking up from his father's khaki-colored knee, the image blurred further. Yet he did not remember that he missed his father. Nor did he miss his mother, a fretful, melancholy woman who had never remarried. She had died only last year, and Ruth's parents had both died in the same year. One heart attack, two cancers. The end.

Like Graham's father, Peter was already little more than an image. A pale, quiet, pleasant-faced boy who had grown into a moody adolescent and then into a silent, morose young man, always looking sickly and uncared-for, seldom even talking to Graham during his infrequent visits home. Ruth, herself complacent at the time, had insisted that this was merely the behavior of a genius—they were moody, they were temperamental. Sometimes they forgot to eat. As if to corroborate this theory, clippings arrived home at regular intervals, detailing the success of Peter's latest recital, often accompanied by copies of letters from famous conductors and composers, or from Peter's former teachers at Juilliard, all of them predicting greatness. The word "genius" was used again and again, so that over the years Graham had become accustomed to this idea, and the thought did not even faze him: his son was a genius. He had seldom, if ever, stopped to ponder what that meant. Since neither he nor Ruth had much interest in music, it had largely come to mean that their son was a remote, difficult presence in the house, often bursting into a rage when his mother questioned him about his music (her questions, Peter told her, were "ill-informed") or rushing out of the room whenever Graham entered, wanting to start a friendly conversation with his son. Over the years, they had become inured to all of this. They were no longer hurt when Peter neglected to call or write for months at a time—he had lived in New York for over nine years, having entered music school immediately following high school graduation; later he had decided to remain there, giving private lessons and performing at countless recitals—and they no longer expressed their unwelcome curiosity about Peter's private life, about which they knew absolutely nothing. Although Graham had not dared tell his wife, he was actually relieved that Peter's visits home were so short, and that invitations had stopped coming after their first few trips to New York. It was simply true that they had nothing in common, father and son. It was no one's fault. It was not particularly tragic. Oddly, Graham had come to feel a certain satisfaction in their relationship, aware that he had fathered a "genius" and that this reflected well on him, and that the other side of his son—the dark, uncommunicative side—was something for which he could not be held responsible.

They'd had no idea, Graham and Ruth, that their son had any great unhappiness in his life, and now their lack of understanding had become a source of torment. If only they *knew,* Ruth often said. Then she could accept it, perhaps. Then she could begin to put it behind her. But they knew nothing. The phone call had been from another young man, supposedly a musician-friend of Peter's, and in a curt, almost businesslike voice he had conveyed the facts to Graham: a single bullet to the temple, no suicide note, no hints to any of his friends or students, nothing. Would they please come to New York at once, to see about disposal of the body. No, he would not care to meet with them, or even give his name: it was impossible. Very sorry, Mr. Hough. Good-bye. And the line had gone dead. At first Graham thought that someone was playing a joke.

Now he had reached an intersection, and he stood waiting patiently for the WALK sign to appear on the opposite side of the street. His car waited in the next block. To his right, half a block down the intersecting street, was the large, ultra-modern shopping mall that had been completed only a few years ago, and he realized now that this accounted for the heavy traffic around here, and the extraordinary number of pedestrians seemingly walking in all directions, with the self-absorbed busyness of ants. Unlike Graham, many of the people ignored the traffic lights and scurried across the street, glancing quickly in both directions. Several people had just left the curb—while Graham remained there, feeling foolish for adhering to the law—and one in particular caught his attention. He was a tall, slender young man, wearing a beige trench coat which he held wrapped tightly around him. As he hurried across the street he had a peculiar, hobbled walk, like that of a much older man. Exactly like Peter's walk, Graham thought: defensive, hurrying, his head ducked. Forcing his way through. Even the trench coat seemed the one Peter had worn the last time they had seen their son alive: that visit, six months before, had been particularly difficult, long and grueling and tedious, punctuated with small pockets of tension that had filled Graham with an eerie restlessness. Peter hadn't lost his temper, not that time, but Graham had felt him simmering—or believed he had felt it, later—and had not shared his wife's surprise during the good-byes at the airport, when their son looked at them after the ritual, perfunctory hugs and kisses, shook his head mysteriously, a little sadly, and said: "Take a good look. Take a good, long look." "What?" Ruth had said, alarmed. "What did you say?" But Peter had not replied. His face was pale and creased, as if he needed sleep. He had not bothered to comb his hair—it was dry and almost colorless, flying in all directions. Even his skin seemed dry, flaky. He shook his head. "Nothing," he said. "Never mind." His tone had seemed faintly apologetic. And then he had glanced at Graham, who merely stood there, solid and unsurprised. For a moment their eyes met, soullessly.

The young man, Peter's double, reached the other side of the street just as the green letters flashed on: WALK. Graham stared at the sign, blinking. The young man had turned and begun walking down the sidewalk in his careening, haphazard way: he was headed toward the entrance of the shopping mall. Graham could see, because of the overcoat held close around his body, that the young man was extremely thin, emaciated. In his walk there was the restless, lean desperation of the perpetually hungry. Graham felt something happening in his face: the skin seemed to flush, as if with embarrassment, and then become deathly pale. From across the street, Graham could not see the young man's profile clearly—but his bony, anemic-looking features seemed fixed into a scowl, the head staying ducked as he rushed combatively toward the mall. . . . Graham knew, suddenly, that he was not seeing Peter's double—it was Peter himself. His own son, just across the street but hurrying away, fleeing Graham on his brittle legs.

Graham rushed into the street, holding up his arm and calling out to the boy: "Wait! Please—please wait!" His son did not turn around. A few of the passers-by stared at Graham with brief, curious interest. Now his son had reached the mall entrance and disappeared inside.

Graham followed him. His chest had filled with a pure, childish delight, a nearly ungovernable elation. But, reaching the entrance to the shopping mall, he faced a disheartening sight: an enormous tide of people, hundreds of people moving in all directions, in and out of the brightly-lit stores lining the walkway on each side and stretching, it seemed to Graham, to infinity. . . . In here the people moved at a more leisurely pace; there was the soft drone of Muzak in the background, and the small, faint roar of countless voices. Graham stood at the mall entrance, gazing soberly at all this; he felt dizzy. Somewhere in all that chaos was his son, a young/old man with pale, creased features and an air of perpetual bewilderment. Graham would find him. Graham Hough would not give up, he thought, until he had found him. His eyes began to dart among the shoppers, searching for that beige overcoat, that hobbled, careening walk. . . . He was considering the idea of approaching the mall's manager and having his son paged in all the stores—*an emergency,* he would tell the man; *a matter of life and death*—when suddenly, only twenty yards ahead, he caught a glimpse of the beige overcoat. His son had just emerged from a small record shop, a specialty store that kept a large stock of classical records. This had always been Peter's favorite store, and Graham winced at his own stupidity: why hadn't he remembered? Why hadn't he rushed in there at once? Now the boy was continuing down the mall, walking quickly. Graham followed. He felt the urge to cry out—in excitement, in exasperation—but he managed to restrain himself. This was a kind of test, he thought wildly, that he must get through—but then it would be over. This perplexing day would come to its logical end.

So they hurried down the mall, father and son. Graham could hardly keep up with his son's quick, furtive walk. He was not accustomed to walking this quickly, he rarely took exercise of any kind, and he could feel a thin layer of sweat breaking out on his forehead, and beneath his expensive clothes. . . . Faces bobbed in the near distance, indistinguishable to Graham because his gaze remained fixed far ahead of him, thirty or forty yards ahead; the distance was increasing, he knew, between him and his son. On either side of him, store after store passed by. Brightly colored signs, blue and green and red . . . boutiques, clothing stores, restaurants, pet shops . . . all this he kept in his peripheral vision, a blur of passing lights. His eyes ached. He kept his gaze fixed ahead, into the darkness. At the end of the mall was a large department store, and it occurred to Graham that his son was probably headed there. The music department, or the men's department. It pleased Graham that he was able to think so clearly. Yes, he would find his son in that department store, just now coming into full view, the darkness giving way to its mammoth entrance lined with tiny, blinking white lights, growing larger and more real as Graham approached.

And there was Peter's overcoat, headed into the store. Graham felt his chest swelling again, in jubilation. But now, suddenly, there was a large group of shoppers in his path, standing still and talking together in loud, hilarious voices. Accidentally Graham collided with a small, blond-haired woman, knocking a package from her arm. "Hey, watch where you're going!" Graham did not even pause. He had scarcely glanced at the woman, and he ignored her voice shouting after him; it faded quickly. He was not far from the department store entrance, but in that moment of confusion something had happened: he had lost the beige overcoat. The entrance was well-lit and he could make out the smallest details of those walking inside—a woman's dress printed with small magenta flowers, the shining flaxen hair of a young girl—but he had lost the overcoat. He had lost his son. He broke into a run, and when he arrived at the entrance to the store he stopped, panting, and let his eye roam among the tinseled labyrinth of departments and walkways and escalators. Graham did not know what to do. If he started in one direction, his son might emerge a few moments later from another. Yet it was probable, also, that Peter would not come back through this entrance and out again into the mall. He would leave the store by one of the outside exits and go directly to his car. But which exit? He could not remember if there was an exit near the music department. He did not dare go forward, losing himself in that maze, and yet it was profitless to remain standing here. A leaden, despairing sensation suddenly weighed on him, centered at the pit of his stomach. His eye moved desperately among the hundreds of shoppers, but somehow he could not make himself go forward. He stood there for several minutes, hesitating.

Then, as if by a miracle, Graham spotted him. He had just appeared from behind a rack of sport jackets, in the men's department, and was now headed toward a large display of dress shirts, evidently on sale. Graham rushed forward, his arm raised.

"Peter!" he called. Several people near Graham, including a salesgirl, looked up. But now his son had disappeared again. Graham blinked, incredulous, but there was no one even near the bin of dress shirts.

Graham stopped about ten feet away from the bin, dismayed. His arm was still raised in the air, senselessly.

Then, something teased one corner of his vision: a light-colored flash, quick as a moth's wing. Graham turned, confused, and there was his son, standing quietly on the escalator going up to the next level, his back to Graham.

"Peter!" Graham shouted. "Wait at the top of the— Please wait—"

His son did not turn around. Graham turned toward the escalator, his heart pounding. He could not wait, the escalator moved too slowly, so he began running up the moving stairway, two steps at a time. He had to force his way past several shoppers, all of them holding packages. A man said to Graham, "Hey, be careful! I almost lost my—" but Graham ignored him. When he reached the second floor, he looked quickly in all directions.

His son had disappeared.

But no, there he was—beside a counter in the jewelry department. His son was bent over one of the glass cases, squinting; Graham remembered that Peter was very near-sighted, yet refused to wear glasses. This time, Graham would not take his own eyes off the boy. Again he rushed forward. A heavy-set woman pushed a child's carriage directly into Graham's path; he wanted to cry out with vexation. "Peter! Peter!" Again he raised his arm, imploring.

Take a good look. Take a good, long look. . . .

By the time he reached the jewelry counter, his son had vanished.

Graham stood there, exactly where his son had stood. He felt that he might begin to whimper, like a child. Looking down into the glass counter, exactly as Peter had done, he saw nothing but the bright reflection of the fluorescent lights overhead and his own blank, terrified features, staring wide-eyed up at him.

Graham closed his eyes. Very slowly, he straightened. He felt humiliated. He felt abused. All around him was a large space, remarkably free of other shoppers. There was nowhere his son could have gone—unless he had gone behind the counter itself. Perhaps he was hiding back there, playing some childish game? Crouched down behind the counter, to avoid his father's searching gaze . . . ? Graham moved around the counter and behind it, a slight fascinated smile playing on his mouth. "Peter? Are you back here, hiding from me—?" It was clever of his son, playing this little game. Clever, but perhaps rather cruel. Children played such games, he thought. Hiding. Seeking. "Peter, are you here? Peter . . . ?" Graham would find him; he would play along. Children were rather cruel, yes, but still they were lovable, adorable, and they meant no harm. Graham didn't mind.

Finally someone approached him—a middle-aged woman, redhaired, with a pencil behind her ear.

"Sir, can I help you? Customers aren't allowed back here."

Graham stared, but he could not bring her into focus. She hovered in his eyesight, detached and mysteriously floating.

"Sir? Are you all right?"

"What—oh, oh yes. Yes, of course." Then, in a lowered voice: "The way out? . . . which way . . . ?"

The woman smiled indulgently, then pointed. Somehow Graham

got out from behind the counter, walking uncertainly in the direction she had indicated. A moment later he had found the escalator and had gotten on, ignoring the sign above his head, in huge black letters: DOWN.

When Graham arrived at the doctors' building, his wife was already waiting outside, on the sidewalk. She stood there stiffly, her thin shoulders hunched. When he pulled the car up alongside her, she hesitated a moment before getting inside.

He kept the car in Park, staring at his wife—he wanted to apologize, since he was more than an hour late, but something blocked his voice. He could not even form the words in his mind. So he merely sat there, his mouth slightly opened.

There were tears in her eyes. Tears of rage, glistening.

"Where have you been?" she said fiercely. "*Where!*"

Graham stared back at her, eyes widened with horror. He shook his head slowly, as if dumbfounded.

"I don't know," he whispered.

He turned to the steering wheel, to the business of driving the car. His wife looked out her own window, disgusted. Twenty minutes later the Houghs arrived home.

Intensive Care

WHEN Vince arrived at the hospital, no one but his brother was there. And his brother was sleeping.

When Lisa did come he picked a fight. What if something had happened? What if Kenny had cried out, or needed something?

"You can't be here every minute," she said, not patiently but with a hollowed-out look.

As they stood in the hall outside their brother's room Lisa hugged herself as if chilled. She wore an old grayish-green sweater, maybe a man's sweater. Vince saw that she'd mis-buttoned it, so it hung lopsided, goofy.

"You haven't been here," she said. "You don't know what it's like."

Down the hall Lisa's two boys played shoot-'em-up, they were making too much noise—but their mother didn't glance at them.

"You have no way of knowing," she said again.

They wandered the halls for a while, Vince trying to keep the kids quiet in a friendly, nice-uncle way. Lisa kept hugging herself, her face pale and severe, but she agreed with his idea that they alternate eight-hour shifts during the day. At night, Vince promised, he'd get Kenny settled and then stop by their mother's place to make sure she was OK.

He was staying at a Holiday Inn, just down the street. He hadn't anything else to do, and clearly Lisa's kids and husband needed her. Clearly she'd gotten stressed out, these past few weeks.

Lisa said that Mother was more trouble than Kenny was, lately. She said that Vince could really have no idea.

For the next few days it was mostly just Vince and his brother. The doctor, a brisk bald-pated man in his fifties, said that Kenny had stabilized, that he might go home in a few days, but Vince could scarcely believe this. His brother's face which he remembered as fleshy, ruddy, grinning, had become skeletal and pale. Points of bone at his chin, his cheek tops. That glaring plate of bone above his sunken dark eyes.

The lesions on Kenny's legs had bothered him most, at first, but now he scarcely noticed them. The terrible thinness was a worse effect, especially the gaunt face which haunted him nights as he lay in the motel room, the churning air conditioner like the noise of acids in his stomach. He kept thinking of those newsreels made in the '40s, the gaping stares of the concentration camp victims. Liberated, maybe, but really too late to matter.

Had he come to liberate his little brother? He'd been the heroic older one, in fact nine years older so that they'd seldom been playmates or friends. Occasionally they'd played cards together, or Vince would take his little brother to the movies. Vince had been the good-natured high school and college athlete, the up-and-comer; Kenny had adored him.

Vince had loved his little brother but had seldom thought about him. Hadn't thought much about his having a private life, not when they were kids and certainly not later, what with Vince's three stormy marriages and the up-and-down construction business he'd established so far from home.

When Lisa finally called with the news, last week, he'd stood there befuddled for a while, willing his brother's face into his mind's eye. Why hadn't he known? Why hadn't he wondered?

Lisa had said she couldn't handle Mother any more, Vince *had* to come. She knew that family wasn't important to him, she said bitterly, she knew he hadn't been to Georgia in six or seven years and probably had no intention of coming, but she had no one else to call, it was all too much, she had the kids and Roy wasn't all that sympathetic and—

He said okay, fine. Of course.

Anything to cut off the shrill blast of his sister's voice.

He'd had to get some business details in order and explain the situation to his current lady friend. Leukemia, he said quickly—very near the end. He didn't feel guilt but only a rising sense of urgency, a fear that Kenny might die before he arrived. He couldn't analyze the fear but as the plane neared Atlanta his stomach had begun roiling and, embarrassed, he handed the flight attendant his half-drunk Scotch on the rocks and asked for a carton of milk.

She said that cabin service had been discontinued but then she saw his eyes. He downed the milk in a few desperate gulps.

Visiting with Kenny at mealtimes Vince would drink his brother's untouched milk, as he'd often done behind his mother's back when they all lived at home. Kenny hated milk and the brothers would wink at each other, grinning. He hadn't thought of this in years.

But he urged Kenny to eat, especially the green vegetables. He had the vague idea they helped the immune system, and the doctor had said that Kenny must keep up his strength.

To please his brother, Kenny picked at his applesauce or peas. He seemed happy that Vince was there, though he didn't say much. At first Vince thought Kenny was embarrassed—about his condition, about all the unspoken past that lay between them—but soon he understood that Kenny was far beyond such a feeling and Vince felt embarrassed, himself. He remembered the fluent lies he'd told Alicia, back in San Diego, and blushed to the roots of his hair.

Kenny's hair was thin, wispy, colorless, but on Vince's third day, a Saturday, Kenny asked him to comb it. The request seemed odd but Vince complied. He'd noticed that the nurses and orderlies from both shifts avoided the room, and were grateful when Vince met them at the door and took the meal trays, the tiny containers of pills. When they took Kenny's temperature they wore plastic gloves and face masks; they made the smallest imaginable talk about the flowers in Kenny's room, or about the weather.

The doctor had suggested that Vince wear a mask and gloves, too, though the doctor himself did not. Vince declined. He hadn't come this far to talk to his brother through layers of plastic.

"You don't have to worry about it, you know," Kenny had whispered, that first day. "Even I know that much."

Half an hour after Kenny asked to have his hair combed, a friend of Kenny's named Malcolm arrived, looking furtive and ill-at-ease. He wore a fresh-smelling leather jacket and brought a fistful of chrysanthemums. These various odors assaulted Vince's nostrils. Already he was accustomed to the unchanging stale air in his brother's room.

Vince left the men alone and wandered the halls for a while, as he often did. He was amazed that this place had so quickly become an alternate reality for him, his life in San Diego seeming distant and long past. He knew the layout of the hospital's main floors, he knew what was edible in the basement cafeteria, he made small talk with nurses and security guards. Vince was forty-four, stocky, handsome in a small-town way. He made an impression. Clearly the staff was surprised by such a man taking all this time and effort for his younger brother.

Often Vince stopped in the men's room and rinsed his face with cold water. He saw that his eyes were threaded with blood. He hadn't slept much since arriving but, for some reason, didn't feel tired at all.

Just a bit light-headed, occasionally. Just that odd floating sense of unreality, having to look out windows to recall whether it was day or night.

Only his stomach bothered him. In the men's room he downed the small white pills Kenny's doctor had prescribed. Stopping by his mother's late at night, he would hear about her stomach cramps, her diarrhea, but she refused to take one of the pills. God forbid you should accidentally feel better, Vince thought.

Angry at his mother, very angry—though he knew the anger was pointless. Now that his mother lived in the city he felt that she'd become another person, much weaker, even hateful at times. In Vince's childhood they'd lived on a small farm, in an area east of Atlanta, but now in its place was another tacky suburb, overrun with cheap housing developments and fast food joints. The fresh air, the cows, the wet morning clover of his boyhood seemed to Vince a pipe dream, a sentimental fantasy.

His mother had sold the farm and moved when Vince's father died, wanting to be nearer Lisa and Kenny, suddenly afraid of being "alone"—he remembered the first time she'd used that word, how foreign it sounded, and his own reaction of astonishment and scorn. Whenever he mentioned the farm his mother would quickly change the subject, and that angered him, too. Yet he knew better. So he downed the pills for his stomach and kept his mouth shut.

When Vince returned to the room Kenny's visitor had left. His brother looked drained.

"That's my lover," he said, and Vince nodded quickly.

"He's got a real demanding job, he can only come on Saturdays," Kenny said.

Vince remembered that what he'd always liked most about Kenny was his lack of malice, and what he'd disliked most was his willingness to let others take advantage.

For the rest of that afternoon the brothers played cards. Gin rummy, five-card draw, blackjack. Their boyhood games. Sitting beside the bed, Vince would occasionally glance to the window and see a smudge of city skyline, a whitish overcast sky. The mums looked cartoonish and hideous on the sill.

Vince and Kenny talked back and forth, idly. Almost all their talk had been idle. On the plane Vince's stomach had clenched with dread at the thought of messy emotions, the melodrama of fatal illness, but he should have known better. His family wasn't like that.

Though his father had been a drunk, sometimes a mean one, and had died eight years ago of cirrhosis of the liver, Vince couldn't recall a single conversation with his mother or siblings about the problem. His mother complained incessantly about small things, but never about anything important. Both Lisa and Kenny had large streaks of resignation, or was it fatalism, in their essentially gentle natures, and Vince himself had never been one to make scenes. Oddly he had gotten involved, one by one, with tempestuous women, and one by one he'd left them.

He already knew that he wouldn't leave Kenny, no matter what.

"Gin," his brother said, with a smile almost rueful.

"You were always smarter than me," said Vince.

"I guess that's why I'm in this fix. I'm so smart."

"Don't blame yourself. Don't listen to the propaganda."

"Mama blames me, and Lisa—they're madder than hell, though they won't admit it."

"Give them time," Vince said.

Kenny's laugh brought a fit of coughing. "Time's what I don't have," he said. "And anyhow, why're you any different?"

His brother was asking, What are you doing here, exactly?

"I don't know," Vince said. He dealt out the cards.

That night Kenny's doctor called Vince, about an hour after Vince had gone to bed. He couldn't sleep because he'd had an argument with his mother, who didn't understand why Vince wouldn't take the guest room. Her querulous, whining voice had pestered Vince's consciousness as he lay there. The ancient motel air conditioner churned and hissed. When the phone rang Vince was almost grateful.

Yet the doctor's news shocked him. Kenny had developed pneumonia and was being transferred to Intensive Care. The doctor had placed him on oxygen, had begun a new course of treatment, but the situation was nonetheless grave. Vince might want to phone the other members of his family.

Instead Vince got dressed and went to the hospital alone. It had been several days since Lisa had done her shift, and that evening his mother hadn't even mentioned Kenny. When he reached Intensive Care, a nurse stopped him. In here, the mask and gloves were mandatory, along with a disposable paper gown. Hurriedly donning them, Vince glanced inside the glass-walled cubicle assigned to his brother. There were tubes going into Kenny's nose, attaching him to a couple of ominous-looking machines. His brother appeared to be sleeping.

Inside, he held Kenny's hands and occasionally spoke to him in a low murmur. Once, toward morning, Kenny woke, gave Vince an intense long look, and motioned as if he wanted to write. Vince got paper and pencil from the nurse and waited while Kenny scribbled a few words: "Tube choking me. Ask doctor remove."

Later that morning, Vince pleaded Kenny's case with the doctor.

"It's uncomfortable for him, I know," the doctor said. "But if I remove that tube, he'll be gone within minutes."

Vince went back to tell Kenny the news, but his brother had drifted off.

During the next few days, Vince was Kenny's only visitor. Their mother and Lisa came to the hospital, but they stayed in a small waiting room just outside of Intensive Care. Lisa said she couldn't take it any more, seeing him like that, and Vince said he understood. Their mother had stationed herself on one side of the vinyl sofa, a hospital blanket over her legs. She no longer complained, which Vince took as a bad sign. A pale, heavy-set woman, she seldom spoke and her skin now had a grayish tone. She kept removing her glasses and rubbing the bridge of her nose. Whenever Vince asked if she wanted anything, she shook her head vaguely. Once or twice she said, "My baby," and wept soundlessly.

Kenny slept most of the time. When he did wake, Vince reported whatever positive news he could—a rise in Kenny's blood oxygen, for instance—and if there was no good news, he made some up. Kenny kept writing messages, but they had become very difficult to read. Late in his fourth afternoon in Intensive Care he motioned urgently for the pad and made a few scribbles. Vince stared down, but the message was illegible. They seemed the random scrawls of a small child, Vince thought, or words in a foreign language. Hieroglyphs.

But he nodded, quickly. "Okay," he told Kenny. "Right away." A moment later Kenny's eyes were closed.

Days passed. Vince talked to the doctor and nurses about things that might be done. A woman doctor, who took Dr. Bradley's place on weekends, was always more blunt and pessimistic. To Vince's hopeful queries she would only answer, "Your brother is gravely ill. Be with him. Comfort him."

There were other visitors, or would-be visitors. The general policy of Intensive Care was to allow immediate family inside the room, though the family could approve other friends. Significant others, for example. When Malcolm asked, Vince said that Kenny could not receive any more visitors. Other nameless young men—some who seemed to know Malcolm, others from the accounting firm where Kenny had worked—milled in the hallway outside the swinging doors of Intensive Care. Patiently Vince told them how Kenny was doing, conveyed the doctors' reports. Then he would go inside the waiting room and sit with his mother and sister.

One day, from out in the hall, he overheard a conversation about his brother's clothing. Did he own a black suit? one man asked. I don't remember, said the other, I'll have to ask Malcolm. If not, should we buy him one? the first man said. Or should we ask—

Vince got up, quickly. He closed the waiting room door.

Sometimes he and Lisa and his mother reminisced, talking in soft murmurs. The time Kenny got bit by a water moccasin, during a family picnic at the lake. The clinic doctors had told Mrs. Acton that in another hour he'd have been dead. A couple of years later he'd climbed up on the roof, which he'd been forbidden to do, and a kid from the next farm had knocked the ladder away and then run off. Rather than face his father's hiding Kenny had jumped, and had sprained his ankle. His father waited until the ankle was completely healed, and then hided him.

Vince's mother managed to laugh. "We always said he had nine lives," she said. Almost at once she started to cry.

Lisa looked at Vince.

"We've got to stay hopeful," Vince said. "He's young. He's fighting hard."

Lisa took kleenex out of her purse and moved closer to her mother.

His words were a lie, Vince thought. Several days had passed since his brother scrawled those unreadable words and closed his eyes. He'd lapsed into a coma, the doctor told him, though Vince hadn't reported this to the others. The doctor said they were giving his brother maximum oxygen and could do no more.

Every couple of hours Vince got up and wandered the halls. His stomach no longer hurt but now he felt an eerie panic that brought a tingling sensation to his head and chest, even to his groin. In the men's room he stood before the mirror, breathing hard as if trying to work up the tears. But his pink-stained eyes were expressionless and dry. He opened his mouth to yell but no sound came out.

In the area just beyond Intensive Care, near the waiting room, more and more people milled about. Some of them had virtually camped in the hallway for days now, eating junk food from the vending machines, talking in ordinary voices, even laughing and joking at times. Once when Vince was returning from the men's room a blond-haired boy, nineteen or twenty, approached him and asked in a polite voice if Vince had any boyhood pictures of Kenny, if maybe some of the negatives still existed so he could—

No, Vince said rudely. Absolutely not.

He returned to his waiting room chair and stared straight ahead at nothing.

"Vince?" Lisa said. "You want to take a break or something? Roy is home with the kids today, so if you want to—"

"We're taking you away from your business," his mother said guiltily. "If you need to get back, nobody would blame you."

"No," Vince said.

Not for the first time he had to ponder the idea that he was using Kenny's illness to bring together his random, drifting life, which others perceived as "successful" but which seemed a mere jumble to him. He'd lived in San Diego for years, but now his life there seemed unreal, a long and somewhat lurid daydream. . . . And he understood his family's anger: the ordeal had challenged his mother's vision of herself as the one who suffered most, had worn out Lisa's high spirits and energy which before had seemed almost ferocious, without limits. Vince too felt that he could not care for his brother, not really, and that he'd been shoved out of the bluff good-natured daytime self that he'd evolved since his boyhood days. He fought down the urge to get up and return to the men's room mirror. Instead he looked at his mother and sister and saw himself in the bleak look they returned to him, which day or night remained cruelly the same underneath these harsh fluorescent lights.

By late the next day his mother had broken down. Dr. Bradley made his evening visit to the waiting room to report in a hushed voice, his eyes downcast, that Kenny almost certainly would not wake from his coma. Renal failure had begun, he said softly, and Vince held his breath as he remembered the yellowish cast to his brother's face that afternoon. "You're going to make it," he'd said, stroking his brother's hand. "Just hang on and you'll be fine." One of the nurses had said that comatose people, some researchers felt, heard you on some level and responded to positive reinforcement. So Vince had begun talking and stroking during each of his visits, even telling a joke or two. Now as he asked the doctor, leaning forward, "Are you sure?" he heard Lisa's brief stifled cry and looked over just as his mother slumped forward, her glasses unlatched from one ear and hanging askew. Quickly Dr. Bradley took charge, and told Vince an hour later that his mother was suffering from "shock and exhaustion" and would need to spend a night or two in the hospital. Vince agreed at once. Together they had convinced Lisa to go home to her family. Nothing more could be done tonight.

Even Vince decided he had to get away. He went into Kenny's room and said he'd only be gone for a while, he needed a few hours of sleep. His brother lay still, his flesh heavy and chill to the touch. Vince glanced behind him, saw that none of the nurses were watching through the glass partition, then bent to kiss his brother's cheek. His first instinct was to avoid the large plum-colored lesion near Kenny's right ear, but at the last moment he placed his kiss directly on the lesion; on Kenny's shoulder was another, larger lesion and Vince kissed that one, too, and another on his brother's breast-bone, and another just above his knee. Breathing jaggedly, his eyes stinging, Vince drew back, only vaguely aware of what he'd done, and wiping his eyes he said, "I'm sorry, Kenny boy, we're so sorry. . . ." Kenny's eyelids hadn't flickered.

In his motel room Vince lay fully dressed on the bed, knowing he would not sleep. He fiddled with the TV remote control, but it was very late and there were only round-the-clock news reports, religious programs, and sex programs. He flipped the channels mindlessly for a while, his mind accosted by the series of images, bright colors, flashes. Like a kaleidoscope, he thought, only there was no logic to what he was seeing, no logic or pattern or beauty.

When he returned to the hospital about five A.M. he went to his brother's cubicle and by rote began donning the paper gown and gloves. Only after a moment did he focus through the glass partition and see the two black orderlies inside, working busily. One of the men was mopping the floor, the other was spraying the room with an aerosol can. Vince's eyes shot to the bed, which was empty.

Vince barreled into the room. "What the hell!" he shouted. He could feel his brain tingling. The orderlies had stopped; they watched Vince fearfully. The one with the mop said, "Sir? Would you like to—" He motioned to the door.

"Where's my brother?" Vince whispered fiercely.

"Sir?" the orderly said.

From behind came a nurse's voice. "Mr. Acton?" she said. Vince whirled around. He hadn't seen this woman before. She was youthful and foreign, maybe Indian or Pakistani. Long fine black hair that reached to her waist. The two orderlies had left quickly. The nurse stood there with her doleful gaze, one hand extended in Vince's direction.

"Sir, we're sorry, but your brother is gone," she said. "We phoned your sister, and—"

"Why didn't you phone *me*?"

"Your sister said that she would—"

"Where is he," Vince said roughly. "I want to see him."

Another nurse entered the room, an older woman he remembered. The kindly but efficient type. No nonsense.

"We're sorry, Mr. Acton," she said, "but we had to send him down right away. In these cases, they insist we do that."

"Send him down? I want to see him," Vince said. His hands had become fists at his sides. "I want—"

The nurses exchanged glances. "I'm afraid that's impossible, Mr. Acton," the older one said. "We had to send him down right away. They insist on it."

"Send him down where? What the hell are you talking about!"

The nurses stood side by side, slump-shouldered. The older one spoke again. "To pathology, sir. We have to send them. You see, it's important because—"

Vince came at them, shouting. "Get the fuck out!" he cried. "Get out of my brother's room!" Quickly the nurses retreated, and Vince shut the door. He walked to the center of the room and stood there, disoriented. Outside the glass partition he could see several nurses, all looking inside at him, aghast. He could hear the dark-complected one, that foreigner, speaking in a heightened voice—into a telephone, probably—and he heard his own name being spoken, and beyond that he heard the random humming noises of the hospital and of the city itself and of the world. He ignored them. He willed himself to turn and confront his brother's empty bed, but he could not.

He knew that he wouldn't leave Kenny, no matter what. . . . The words skittered through his mind, mocking him. He opened the door and went out, passing the nurses without a glance. It wasn't going to happen this way, he thought. He'd imagined his mother and Lisa out in the waiting room, huddled on one end of the sofa, and Vince entering the room sadly, stoically, to comfort them as best he could. Instead he'd been the last to know, and his family was not even here. Where were they? It wasn't Kenny who was alone, now; it wasn't his mother or sister. He walked blindly to the elevator and entered, heard its doors shudder closed a final time. He was relieved that no one else was inside, but then he wondered: how could it matter, really? He stood and pondered this question, descending.

131

A Dry Season

"NO, you're not a failure," Eleanor says. "That's nonsense."

She sounds exasperated, downright angry, but then she laughs. A loud, ribald laugh that Nora, after fifteen years, knows not to take personally. The laugh is Eleanor's typical response to human problems: it clears the air, puts the situation in perspective.

For that, Eleanor says, is what Nora has gotten herself trapped inside. A "situation."

Nora says, caustically, "You mean I've even failed at that? Being a failure?"

Eleanor makes a gesture with her hands—fingers outspread, held clutched above her ears. Pulling out her hair.

Go ahead, Nora thinks.

"It's just that you're so intense, so damned *serious*," Eleanor says. She laughs again, though less convincingly. "You've always been that way, you know. Ever since college."

"Have I," Nora says.

Eleanor smokes thoughtfully, staring past Nora's shoulder to the parched, bumpy lawn. The lawn leads down to the lake, not quite visible through the massive ridge of trees, and throughout this stale, restless conversation with her oldest friend, her college roommate Eleanor Jenks, Nora has let her thoughts wander down to the lake, the rippling cool water. Only eleven A.M., it's already ninety in the shade. It's August, the dog days. A thick, settled heat—a murderous heat, really—has hugged the lake and its environs ever since Nora's arrival the previous week. The heat, the three of them have decided, is beyond remedy. Neil takes a cold shower after work, but ten minutes later, he says, he's covered in sweat. While he's at work, Eleanor and Nora sit out on the redwood deck, as they're doing now, sipping iced tea or margaritas in the morning shade of an enormous elm, wearing practically nothing. Short shorts, halter tops. Their hair pulled back, tied carelessly with rubber bands. But still the heat is stifling, and occasionally Nora has trouble getting her breath: last night she'd sat up suddenly in bed, gasping for air, her throat and tongue feeling unnaturally dry, parched. For Nora, only a swim in the lake brings relief, a luxurious total immersion with her limbs outspread, her head leaned back until the water laps over her calm face, her closed mouth and eyes.

"I think it's the weather," Eleanor says at last. "It's affected Neil, too, have you noticed how anxious he seems about work? He's not that way, normally. Does Mr. so-and-so really appreciate him, will the dastardly so-and-so get promoted instead, that kind of thing. He's usually good about leaving his work at the office, but lately he's been coming home with that grim look around his mouth, full of doom and gloom. And now you—"

As she talks, the ash on Eleanor's cigarette grows impossibly long—nearly an inch, Nora guesses. She has watched it obsessively, scarcely listening, yet knowing that Eleanor is the type who'll notice the ash at the last possible moment—just in time—and then flick it into the ashtray as if nothing had happened. As if there'd been no suspense, no danger. And then she'll keep talking.

"Nora, are you all right?" Eleanor says, interrupting herself. "Listen, kid," she begins, in a gentler tone, "you really shouldn't worry—" But then she follows Nora's wide-eyed gaze down to the cigarette and quickly moves her hand toward the large Mexican ashtray, already heaped with Eleanor's butts. As they sit watching in silence, the ash falls.

There's nothing worse, Nora resolves, than a boring houseguest. That evening, before Neil gets home, she changes into a white sun dress she hasn't yet worn during this trip. It's the only good dress she has brought, and half-consciously she's been saving it for some special occasion; but they seldom go out, and in any case the lake people never dress for anything. Twice they have gone to a nearby tavern for ribs and draft beer; occasionally Nora and Eleanor go shopping in town, but like everyone else they wear as little as possible. Appraising herself in the mirror, she wonders if the dress looks inappropriate. Neil plans to make tacos, Eleanor will mix the margaritas, and the three of them will sit on the deck, as usual. It's true, Nora thinks, that lately the conversation has centered on Neil and Nora—their problems, their confusion. She understands why Eleanor has gotten restive. Hearing Neil's car crunching the gravel out front, Nora decides that the dress looks all right. Impulsively she removes the rubber band, then brushes out her tawny-blond hair in a few quick strokes. She hurries out to greet Neil.

In the kitchen, Neil has already removed his tie, draped his jacket over a chair. The grocery sack contains ground beef, peppers, taco shells; peering inside, Nora feels childish in her bare feet and white dress.

"Hungry?" Neil asks. He stands with the refrigerator door open. It's a tic of his, she has noticed, that he opens the refrigerator door when he gets home, whether he wants anything or not. He looks inside for a minute or two, sometimes takes out a beer or the iced tea pitcher, sometimes nothing. He greets the food, Eleanor says cheerfully, before he greets his wife. Now he takes out a diet soft drink and slowly lifts the metal ring.

"Starved," Nora says, watching him. She wants something to drink, too, but suddenly she's shy before Neil. Vaguely she's aware of Eleanor out beside the deck table, clinking knives and forks together. "How was the office?" she asks. "Any better?"

He turns around with a swift, sudden grin. Neil is tall and well-built, with only a small ridge of flesh around his middle; Eleanor claims that he's lazy, that he dislikes sports and yard work, but Nora can tell he's the type who knocks himself out at the office. He underwrites marine insurance, and frequently travels the coasts of Georgia, the Carolinas, Florida. He's tanned and light-haired, with a full, open face capable of subtleties Nora finds startling. He's six years younger than Eleanor and Nora, and ever since receiving their wedding picture a decade ago (Neil had been nineteen at the time, his hair reaching nearly to the shoulders of his tuxedo jacket) Nora hasn't stopped thinking of Neil as a boy.

"I'm not good," Neil says slowly, "at office politics. I'm only good at my job."

"That should be enough," Nora says.

"Hardly," and the grin disappears. He looks tired.

"I'm sorry," Nora says, feeling inane.

"How about you? Any progress?"

"I'm fine," she says quickly. "I've burdened you enough with my problems—both of you," she adds, hearing the glass door sliding open behind her.

Holding a half-finished margarita in one hand and a cigarette in the other, Eleanor looks startled for a moment, slightly off-balance. She's still wearing her shorts and halter from this morning, and her eyes pause briefly on Nora's dress. Then she looks at Neil, who lifts his eyebrows at her.

"Come on, you two," she says, going past Nora toward the kitchen and giving Neil a friendly poke in the stomach. "Let's cheer up, let's get this show on the road," she says, and she begins taking cooking utensils out of the cabinet. At the same moment, Nora and Neil hurry forward to help.

Again that night, Nora wakes suddenly. At the very moment of waking, she'd glimpsed a dark figure—mere shadows, resolved vaguely into the shape of a man—towering over the bed, as though bending down to embrace her. She connects this figure with her breathlessness, her sudden, raging thirst. Now fully awake, she rises quickly. Putting on her light robe, she goes to the glass-paned door that leads from her room onto the redwood deck. One hand on the door knob, she pauses. Out on the deck, sitting on the round table with both feet resting inside one of the chairs, there's a dark figure, barely discernible in the scant moonlight. He wears a pair of short pajama bottoms, and sits gazing down toward the lake. Every few seconds he lifts a cigarette to his mouth; Nora watches the tiny reddish glow, magnified several times in the circle of glass doors giving onto the deck. Nora turns the knob of her own door, slowly.

Startled, Neil glances around. "Nora? I hope I didn't wake you."

"No," she says, in a low whisper. "I just woke up, I—I was thirsty, that's all."

He nods, taking a loud, hissing draw on the cigarette, which he holds tightly between his forefinger and thumb.

"There's no relief, is there?" he says. "Even now, it must be close to ninety."

"What time is it?" Nora says, faintly.

"Around three," he says.

Nora feels like a wraith, as though her dream-self hasn't yet taken bodily form. She places a chair beside Neil; he looks impossibly large, sitting on the table above her. She's forced to crane her neck, which instantly begins to ache.

"I haven't been sleeping well," she says. "Not for days."

Silently he brings the glowing cigarette down to her, and she sees that it's marijuana. The sweetish, ashen smell threatens to choke her. She shakes her head.

"We should ask Eleanor how she does it," he says, laughing gently. He draws on the cigarette again. Nora feels her eyes drawn helplessly toward its glowing tip, red-hot and dazzling in the viscous dark. "She sleeps like a load of bricks, from the moment her head hits the pillow."

"She's lucky," Nora says.

For a moment they sit together, silent. After Neil flicks the glowing butt out into the lawn, they sit watching as a few strands of parched glass flame up, then quickly die. Neil reaches down, idly, and begins kneading the back of Nora's neck with his right hand.

"It might have been a mistake," he says at last, "moving down here. We thought of it as a great escape, you know, a kind of permanent vacation. It's only a half-hour's drive into the city, but they're such different worlds. Somehow the contrast is too great, at least for me. When I'm at work, none of this seems real. Once or twice lately I've stopped at a bar before leaving downtown, as though I dreaded coming home. But then when I'm here, the office seems unreal. And unbelievably depressing."

Startled more by Neil's frankness than by his hand on her neck and shoulders, massaging her gently, Nora says nothing for a long moment. Then: "What about Eleanor? She seems to like it." To Nora's ears her voice sounds hoarse, not quite her own.

"I think she feels isolated," Neil says. "She doesn't like the weekend people, by and large. And she seldom goes near the lake."

"Then, why . . . ?" Nora sits remembering the large, sunny condominium Neil and Eleanor had bought in Atlanta, shortly after their marriage, and how happy Eleanor had seemed.

"I think," Neil says, softly, "that Eleanor believed it would help. That it might save our marriage."

Now and then Nora glimpses the barest suggestion of water, glimmering through the distant trees. Suddenly she yearns to bound toward the lake, running like any natural creature, and immerse herself in a single abandoned gesture, unthinking. The imagined coolness of the water sends a shiver along her back and arms. In a single movement she gently removes Neil's hand, rises until she stands with her face only inches from his, and gives him a dry, cool kiss on the cheek.

"I'm sorry you're unhappy," she says. "It seems to be a bad time for all of us."

She sees the astonished whites of his eyes.

"Nora?" he says.

"I'm going into the kitchen, get some ice water," she says. "Then maybe I can sleep."

When she gets back to her bedroom, she flicks on the lights for an instant, as though to dispel any lingering shadows. In her stomach she feels the nearly painful cold of the two tumblers of ice water, drunk down in a matter of seconds. A minute or two later, getting drowsy, she spreads her limbs and feels herself adrift upon a fathomless dark, floating.

A week later, Eleanor and Nora go shopping in town. It's the last Monday in August and still very hot, though less humid. Several times recently Nora's face has felt mask-like, tightened by the dry heat; she feels that it could break easily into fragments, like pieces of crockery. Eleanor, on the other hand, looks plump and rosy. On their way down a steep hill near the center of town, they have stopped to peer inside a gallery window, their two reflections in the glass—Nora's willowy and ghost-like, Eleanor's more solid, firmly planted in her open-toed shoes—forming a contrast that Nora finds mildly comical.

"They're not bad, I suppose," Eleanor is saying, looking at the pictures inside, not herself in the glass. "But they have an air of sameness, don't you think?"

"Yes, but that's rather sweet," Nora says. "And comforting, somehow."

"It's disturbing," Eleanor says with finality, and gives a little shiver. From behind them, the noon sun beats on their exposed shoulders, browned and freckled from long afternoons out on the deck.

"Why disturbing?" Nora says, lightly, but they aren't really arguing. Often they disagree with each other, rhetorically. Lately they've been putting more effort into their conversation, Nora has noticed, as though each woman fears becoming tiresome to the other. The half-dozen landscapes in the window, each studiously executed and neatly framed, are by a group of local artists, all of them retired and over seventy. The paintings depict various small corners of this lakeside town, a resort area nestled into the wooded hills north of Atlanta, and it's true they might have been painted by the same artist. All show a fastidious eye for detail, a disarming earnestness; and they convey a great placid certainty—perhaps, Nora thinks, complacency. She finds the pictures quite appealing.

"I don't know," Eleanor says, stepping back. "They're not very original, are they?"

Now she does see their reflections in the glass, Nora hovering several inches taller, each woman staring briefly at the other. Then they continue down the sidewalk.

"What about you? Have you given up painting?" Eleanor asks, once they're seated for lunch and Eleanor has gotten her first margarita. "I remember the portraits you used to do, back in college. They were so lovely, so haunting. . . ."

"Self-portraits," Nora says. "Yes, I've stopped." She laughs, briefly. "I've turned into a hack."

"Oh, come on," Eleanor says. She's lighting a cigarette, glancing around.

Nora often adopts a pretended cynicism when referring to herself, but perhaps it's a technique, she thinks, of holding to the truth. It's true that both her illustrating jobs in New York—one for six years, the next for three—had dulled her interest in her own work. There had been a crucial point, soon after she began the second job, when she felt the fatal dullness settling over her like a mantle, slowing her mind and imagination and even, it seemed, her physical being: she seemed to move through a thickening element, like water. She no longer saw very sharply; she no longer thought very deeply about what she saw. At this time she'd also begun to consider marriage. At thirty-two, she'd had a history of broken-off engagements, relationships that her lovers initiated and pursued with Nora following along, grateful but rather listless, until she reached the inevitable moment of severance. Always she'd felt apologetic and chagrined, and she had, she knew, hurt two or three people quite badly. Everyone had a personal crime, usually repeated throughout life, and this was hers. But after beginning a new job Nora had met another artist, Martin, and for the first time felt her allegiance subtly shifting from herself—her own perceptions, her own art—to this other, rather mysterious and powerful person, who seemed a force field gradually pulling her out of an outworn life into something startling and new. In short, she fell in love, and really for the first time. Martin was an abrupt, dark-haired man in his late thirties, an Irish Catholic with an explosive temper and an inexhaustible passion for Nora. After their lovemaking, he would often say that she was a passionate woman, the first he'd ever known who could equal him, who had the same hunger for life. Lying there, listening, she did feel her heart still pounding in her chest, dully, hungrily. She'd recognized the truth of Martin's words, but each time, nonetheless, the idea startled Nora. The word itself, "passion," had sounded foreign to her.

Unlike Nora, Martin had not lost interest in his work. After spending all day at the office, working impatiently alongside Nora on illustrations of living room furniture or ladies' undergarments, he would paint for six or eight hours after dinner, standing before his huge abstract oils like a god before his universe, looking utterly serious and sometimes—to Nora's eyes—slightly bombastic. She would come into the room late at night, slipping her arms around his waist, and urge him to bed. Usually she did not look at the painting. She found his work enormous, intimate, and violent, and the contrast with her own tame, smallish pictures—still-lifes, ghostly and rather attenuated portraits of herself—was too painful. But Martin never resented her interruptions. He would turn to her and give a quick smile, his eyes softening, his presence returning quickly to human scale. How grateful she had felt, witnessing this. What had she done to deserve him, after all? Hadn't she lived as a selfish, rather cold woman, absorbed in her own thoughts and aspirations? Hadn't she done harm to other people and then simply walked away, unscathed? Martin said that she was too hard on herself, that she was no more selfish than anyone else. Whether she agreed or not, what mattered to Nora was Martin's believing this, his curious faith in her, his acceptance. His love was both casual and profound—exactly what Nora needed. During their two years together, Nora gradually learned to use Martin's vocabulary of love—words like *completion, passion, fate*—without self-consciousness.

When Martin died by his own hand, four months ago, and only a few weeks before they'd planned to marry, Nora's response had not been, technically speaking, grief: rather she had been like a fish out of water, thrown back inside herself as into a foreign element that had only a dreamlike familiarity. From Martin there had been no note, no personal hint of any kind, only the tiny spare bedroom he used as his studio that had been stripped of everything, his dozens of stacked canvases, his sketches, even his books and supplies. Thrown out, evidently. Everything. Having no formal connection to him, Nora had backed off when the family arrived. She had not attended the funeral. Dull-brained again, she had left New York, had spent a month or two simply traveling around, visiting old friends without telling them what had happened, finally reaching her parents' home in Atlanta, where she had grown up. An only child, she had always felt a sense of panic and claustrophobia when visiting her parents, even during those first college vacations. She'd felt stifled by her father's determined drinking, her mother's determined sorrow; and little had changed over the years. She did not, of course, tell her parents about Martin, either. Then she remembered the letter she'd received early in the summer from Eleanor, her college roommate and still, she supposed, her best friend, who had moved out of the city, she wrote, to a place that's "lovely, peaceful, but hot as hell in the summertime. Come visit," she had added, "it's about time you met Neil!"

By now, after two weeks, she has stopped worrying about overstaying her welcome; she has become a familiar part of her friends' routine, especially Eleanor's, and more than once she has wondered how Eleanor coped before her arrival. The loneliness must have been stifling.

"But *those* things," Eleanor is saying, wrinkling her nose as she sips the margarita. "I'm really surprised, Nora."

"Surprised?" Nora says, embarrassed. She hasn't been listening. "Sorry, what did you . . ."

"Those pictures," Eleanor says, giggling, "by the local geriatrics. *I* might be expected to like them, Nora. But not you."

"Stop putting yourself down," Nora says, sharply. This habit, she has noticed, has become frequent with Eleanor, who had been all bubbling self-confidence in college.

Suddenly, Eleanor looks wistful. "You're right, I think I'm catching it from Neil. Or vice versa."

When the meal arrives, Nora eats very slowly, taking small bites. She doesn't really like Mexican food, which is Eleanor's favorite. After each bite she takes a long swallow of water.

She says, "You're lucky, you know, to have Neil—" But then she stops. Eleanor hasn't glanced up. "I mean, you're lucky to have each other. Especially during the difficult times."

"Yeah, but we have our problems," Eleanor says, talking between bites.

"For instance?" Nora says casually, knowing that Eleanor wants to talk.

"For instance, although Neil has conflicts at the office, I'm stuck out by the lake, where everything is so peaceful and there *are* no conflicts. Which becomes a conflict in itself."

"But you chose that, didn't you? Moving out here?"

"Yeah, we chose it," Eleanor says, pushing her plate aside and reaching for her cigarettes. "But the freedom we were choosing, or the fresh start, or whatever—it was just an illusion. I see that now." She lights the cigarette, nods vaguely as the waiter brings a fresh drink. "You know," she adds, giving Nora a sudden, penetrating look, "it's really been sad and moving, hearing what's happened lately in your life, but in a way I've envied you, I really have. I've envied the way your life moves along so dramatically, from one crisis to the next, while mine just stays the same. Right now, for instance, you have a whole new set of possibilities. A new life, really. At the moment you're looking back, of course, you're still grieving over Martin, but you do have a future, and that's enviable. I hope that doesn't offend you."

"It doesn't offend me," Nora says quickly.

"As for Neil, he's a wonderful guy, but—" Eleanor pauses, her cigarette poised inches from her mouth. Nora sees that her lips have begun to tremble.

"It's all right, Eleanor."

Eleanor's eyes have filled. "Everything went stale, somehow, it just happened. I know it wasn't my fault, but still I *feel* that it was, you know? Like I failed to hold him, keep his interest. That I failed as a woman, some sick cliché like that." She shakes her head, pawing away the two or three tears. "I know better, though."

"I hope so," Nora says. And then, smiling: "Besides, I'm the one who's a failure, remember? You're stealing my thunder."

Eleanor laughs her abrupt, careless laugh, then lifts the margarita in a little salute and drinks greedily. This gives Nora the excuse to push her uneaten food away, casually laying her napkin over it, and to take another long swallow from her water glass. When Eleanor puts down her drink, there's a dab of salt perched on the tip of her nose.

"Sure you don't want one of these?" Eleanor asks, her gaze a bit fuzzy as she searches out the waiter. "This place makes the *best* margaritas."

"No thanks," says Nora, disappointed that their conversation, their genuine talk, has ended so quickly. "I think I'll just have some more water."

When Nora announces her plans, she notices an abrupt change in both Eleanor and Neil. Eleanor becomes bouncy, enthusiastic—her old self. What a wonderful idea!—she hadn't known Nora was considering settling back in Atlanta; she had assumed, frankly, that Nora wanted to live at some distance from her parents. . . . But now she and Neil will see a lot of Nora, Eleanor says; there are several attractive men they know in Atlanta, they'll be glad to arrange the introductions when Nora feels ready; and she'll have no trouble, of course, in finding a job, no trouble at all. . . . But Neil turns shy, boyish. Does she know where she wants to live? Does she have any real prospects, job-wise? He'll be glad to help her, in any way he can. He'll be glad to make use of his connections, such as they are.

It's Sunday afternoon, and as usual the three of them have gathered out on the deck, where Neil plans to grill hamburgers for dinner. For the second time Nora has put on her white sun dress, sensing that today marks a special occasion, a turning point. She feels suddenly grateful for her friends.

"Thanks," Nora says, smiling. "I went through today's paper, the want ads. If you don't mind, Neil, I need a ride into the city tomorrow morning. I might as well start pounding the pavements."

"That's terrific!" Eleanor says, lifting her glass of iced tea. The other evening, she'd made an announcement of her own: she planned to cut down on her drinking. At first, she would drink only every other day, and after a month she would stop altogether. Today is one of her "off" days, and thus far she seems to have no trouble abstaining—though she smokes even more, Nora has noticed, and her behavior seems more hectic, as though she's trying to distract herself. Both Nora and Neil have said, repeatedly, that they're very proud of her.

"Of course," Neil says. "And you may as well keep the car during the day. Just pick me up at five, and we'll drive back together."

Nora waits for a moment, feeling her way. She says, "No, I think I'll stay in town for a while. It'll be easier, really, to use Mom and Dad's spare room, and I'm sure it won't take me long to find a place."

Both Eleanor and Neil look at her, startled.

"My goodness!" Eleanor says, slapping her forehead. "Then this is your last night. Come on, Neil, we'll have a farewell party, we've got to celebrate Nora's decision, her new life. . . . Break out the champagne, honey. Then I'll have two off days in a row. It won't matter."

"That's not necessary," Nora says, alarmed. "Really."

Neil sits quietly, his blond head perfectly still. He gives her a sad, admiring look. "No, Eleanor's right," he says. "If you're leaving us, we've got to send you off in style."

For the next few hours, Nora feels herself inside a kind of haven, not needing to think, pampered by these two people who have both, in quite separate ways, come to love her. The champagne combines wonderfully with Neil's excellent burgers, and halfway through the meal Eleanor sneaks off to the kitchen, wearing a mischievous expression, to put a second bottle in the freezer. Neil and Nora laugh, shaking their heads. Despite themselves, they have taken on Eleanor's jaunty, devil-may-care mood, and Nora realizes how seldom in the past few weeks Neil has actually laughed. Tonight he's wearing a white knit shirt and khaki shorts; beneath these clothes his body is tanned and strong, the kind of manly physique on which clothes look a bit awkward and out of place, but at the same time he's a blond, grinning, overgrown boy, indulging in forbidden pleasures. Though both Nora and Neil are sparing drinkers, tonight they keep pace easily with Eleanor.

They open the second bottle immediately after dinner.

"But it hasn't chilled yet," Nora protests, laughing.

"Come on, don't be a party pooper," Neil says, sampling the first glass. "Umm," he says. "Delicious."

"'Yep, it's cool enough," Eleanor says, tasting. She laughs brightly. Then they begin proposing toasts.

"To Nora's new job," Neil says, his pale-blond eyelashes quivering for a moment. Nora doesn't know if he's still shy with her, or if he's simply getting drunk. "Long may Nora prevail!" he adds with a grin.

Nora lifts her own glass, which feels weightless in her hand. Her entire body feels light, buoyant. "To Neil, future company president," she says. Sipping, she peers at him over her glass.

"President?" Eleanor says, facetiously. "Hell, why not chairman of the board?" She gestures toward the center of the table, drains her glass and immediately pours another.

"Well? What else?" Eleanor asks.

Neil and Nora share a long, embarrassed moment: they don't know how to toast Eleanor. Stealing a quick glance at him, Nora sees the faint blush climbing into Neil's cheeks. And she looks away, keeping her eyes downcast.

"Wait, I know," Eleanor cries. "To friendship!"

When she wakes, much later that night, there are no shadows above her bed, no uneasy dreams trailing off behind her. Her heart beats steadily. Calmly. As a small girl, hearing her father mount the stairs late at night, muttering to himself and stumbling into the banister, into the walls, Nora's mother trying to shush him until she'd gotten him inside the bedroom and discreetly closed the door, Nora would lie still for a long time, hearing nothing but her frail, stubborn heart- beat. What kept it beating, exactly?—what gave it such a brave, re- lentless life of its own, so that Nora lay cringing in terror, only nine or ten years old, dreading the unholy persistence of her own heart? How long, she thinks now, that memory had stayed buried; how many times she had lain beside Martin, feeling both terrified and exultant, without recalling herself as a child, lying in bed alone, in utter incomprehension. . . . After lovemaking Martin would fall asleep, almost immediately, leaving Nora alone, her heart still pound- ing madly, convulsed and sore after the violence of their passion. She remembers, suddenly, the acute loneliness of those moments, and how she longed to wake him, and how her lust seemed to arise again, so quickly, her mouth and throat turning dry, patchy, her thirst be- coming so urgent, so relentless. . . . Now, shaking her head as though to dispel this memory, she finds her sun dress (looking ghostly but familiar, draped over a chair drenched in moonlight) and lets it glide down along her body, then rakes her hair backward with the splayed fingers of both hands. She walks quickly to the glass door and steps out onto the deck, and of course there is Neil, sitting there quietly, smoking.

This time, he doesn't turn around.

143

"Neil?" she says, and then, thinking she spoke too softly, "Hello, Neil? Couldn't you sleep?"

When he rises, she sees that he's wearing a bathing suit: white, with a small insignia on one side. The trunks, like his hair and his bare chest and shoulders, glimmer faintly in the moonlight.

"Come on," he says, holding out one hand. He doesn't look at her.

Gingerly, they move down the grassy slope toward the trees, the water. Their feet bare, they pick their way among rocks, small bumps and ridges in the earth, sudden hollows. Nora thinks they must look like children, a pair of blond children holding hands, dressed in white, moving down toward the lake. . . . Now Neil makes a casual, quick gesture: throwing down the cigarette. Isn't that dangerous? she wants to ask. Out here where the grass seems so parched, the trees so desiccated and forlorn? It's so hot and dry, such a dry season. . . . But she says nothing. Now they are coming out of the trees and there is the water, seeming limitless as it stretches before them, winking in the moonlight. From somewhere out in the water—perhaps it's the water itself, Nora thinks—comes a dull but persistent roaring, like the crashing of waves but much subtler, more sinister. Like something strong but muffled, Nora thinks; like the crashing of a distant wave, a distant heartbeat.

They stand at the edge of the water, their hands linked.

"Neil?" she says, looking up at him. She should feel alarmed, she reasons, and yet she doesn't. She senses a dangerous peace, flooding her. "Neil, are you all right . . . ?"

Now he does something surprising: he laughs. He drops her hand and suddenly rubs his eyes, laughing. A child's gesture, Nora thinks; a gesture of dismay.

"Oh yes," he says. "I'm wonderful."

She doesn't understand his mood: only a few hours ago he'd been so jaunty, so cheerful. The three of them had sat toasting one another until the second bottle of champagne was gone, and then Eleanor had made up a batch of margaritas. Though the liquor and salt made her tongue contract, made her thirstier the more she drank, Nora had kept drinking right along with her friends. She was glad to see them so happy, so carefree. . . . Perhaps her visit had been good for them, Nora thought. For once, perhaps she'd been at the right place at the right time. Then, around ten o'clock, something happened that disconcerted Nora: Eleanor began to complain of being tired, and suddenly she asked Neil to massage her shoulders. Neil rose instantly, and stood for five or ten minutes behind his wife's chair, massaging her gently. What disconcerted Nora was the quick, undeniable pang of jealousy that rose in her. She felt relieved when Eleanor reached back and stilled her husband's hands. "Shall we continue this indoors?" she'd said, slyly. "I don't think I can sit upright another minute." And Nora had risen quickly, saying she had to get to bed, herself; tomorrow would be a tiring day, after all. So it had ended. The farewell party. The celebration. Somehow Nora had known, as she prepared for bed, that her sleep would not last through the night.

"You're being sarcastic," Nora says, lightly, "but you *are* rather wonderful, you know. Eleanor thinks so," she adds, hating herself.

"Eleanor would think so," Neil says, "no matter what I did."

"Don't underestimate her," Nora says quickly. She's said the same thing, she remembers, to Eleanor herself.

"I won't," Neil says, in the hoarse, half-desperate tone Nora recognizes very well. When he turns to her, reaching out his arms, she steps back neatly. The moment is more than difficult, somehow; it's impossible. She turns and walks to the edge of the lake. Then, not knowing what else to do, she wades out a few yards, feeling the water begin to drag at the hem of the sun dress.

"Nora?" he calls after her, bewildered.

She keeps wading, quickly, till she reaches a depth of three feet or more, and then she turns back toward shore and lets her legs collapse beneath her. The skirt balloons around her shoulders and suddenly she thinks, giddily, *Ophelia*. But she isn't drowning. The water feels wonderfully cool at her throat, her shoulders and breasts, and is actually quite cold around her legs. She has parted her knees and feels the cold water moving deliciously between her thighs, a quick, cold, friendly current; she moves her legs and arms slowly, dog-paddling, enjoying this sensation in its fullness, its purity. Then she hears a loud splashing, which stops as abruptly as it began. "Nora? What are you—?" But she can't see: her eyelids have fallen shut, and in a graceful, arcing motion she leans backward and lets her head sink beneath the surface of the water. When she lifts up again, she pushes her hair back with both hands, smiling. She spurts out a mouthful of water and lets her eyes blink open.

For a moment she sees the woods beyond Neil, beyond the shore, suffused in terrible flames. She remembers the cigarette Neil had thrown down, and sees Eleanor come running down toward the water, waving her arms. Eleanor screams "Fire!" and then comes to a stop near Neil, who ignores her, and begins jumping up and down comically, stamping her feet. "Look what you've done, you two! You've destroyed everything! That's just what you wanted, isn't it?" Nora smiles at this vision, which quickly vanishes. Now she sees the

145

shoreline during the day, in springtime: the massed gatherings of elm, oak, and white pine, the swaying grasses, the darkish-red glintings of the earth beneath. A landscape that Nora herself might paint, perhaps, trying to accentuate its packed, overabundant life, its look of quiet foreboding. She hasn't painted, hasn't *really* painted, in years, how odd she should think of that now. . . . She cups a handful of water and splashes her face, smiling, blinking her eyes as the water rushes along her cheekbones, the sides of her parted mouth, her aching tongue, and she thinks: Yes, how clearly she sees. She sees everything.

Neil has waded only a few feet into the water and now stands bewildered, dull-looking. Moonlight gleams along his hair, his shoulders. He's quiet, muscular, and beautiful, but what's wrong with him? Why doesn't he come running wildly into the water, why doesn't he save himself?

"Neil, I love you!" she cries. She splashes at the water with both hands, like a child.

Neil stands with his feet in the lake, staring.

Escalators

MY Aunt Dinah has a crippling fear of escalators. She has many fears, both rational and irrational, and at fifty-two has decided to begin conquering them, one by one. She is afraid of crowds, she is afraid of people dressed in costumes (even Santa Claus, even small children on Halloween), she is afraid of loud and startling noises—firecrackers, especially. On the Fourth of July she stays indoors and plays Handel's *Water Music* while running the dishwasher and vacuuming the rugs. We laugh about these things, which doesn't mean that her fears aren't genuine or that her suffering isn't acute. For some years she has been seeing a therapist, who prescribes nerve and sleep medications (which she once said, with her low trilling laugh, were her "dearest friends—except for you, Gary"), but I was the one who suggested she begin working on her phobias. Despite everything Dinah is a strong woman and I wasn't surprised when she agreed at once.

But we should be realistic, she said. We should begin with the small ones first.

So we go to the mall one weekday morning, arriving early enough so that the mall corridors are open but the stores are not. We are not so much avoiding crowds—our city's single mall is seldom crowded on weekdays, even now in midsummer when the teenagers are roaming free—as we are hoping there will be no one to witness our attempts to ride the escalators. Whether our efforts would appear comical or pathetic to a stranger I don't know, but wanting an objective opinion about Dinah's phobias, I phoned an old college friend over in Atlanta who has a thriving hypnotherapy practice. After I explained the situation, he said he thought Dinah would probably resist hypnotic suggestion, but he did think an outing to the mall was a good idea, and he offered some pointers. Try to appear relaxed and comfortable, he said, and indulge her whims in every way not directly related to the object of phobia. Be supportive and patient. Don't rush. Take breaks. Above all, don't indulge in censorious or punishing behavior if she fails. And he said a good deal more. There are so many instructions to remember that by the time we reach the mall I'm at least as nervous as Dinah.

"Dinah, are you OK?" I ask while we're still in the car. "Do you still feel good about this?"

Close-mouthed, she nods. She has dressed up for the occasion, which I find touching: a sleek luncheon dress of navy silk, a crocodile handbag with long straps, girlish white cotton gloves with pearlized fasteners. Her erect posture and careful makeup and chic new hairstyle—short in the back, elaborately fluffed about her forehead and ears—add to the impression of formality blended with terror.

"Because you don't have to," I say, by now hoping she'll change her mind. (What am I trying to accomplish today? I'm wondering. Have I really been thinking of Dinah?)

"No, I'm fine," she says, expelling the words like a gasp. "Let's go, honey."

Already the heat is stifling. As we escape sunlight into the dimmed lower-floor entrance to the mall, I have a brief impression of cavelike unreality that makes this outing seem both less perilous and less significant. Evidently Dinah shares this perception, for she touches my elbow and chats amiably while we drift toward the escalators, as if we were an ordinary pair of shoppers. Usually people assume that we're mother and son, and today I must seem her inevitable offspring in my beige linen jacket and Bass Weejuns, my stalwart but still vaguely boyish appearance. I even have my aunt's rosy coloring, her light-blue eyes, her willingness to raise her top lip at an instant's notice in an affable smile. Dinah's the envy of all the other little old ladies, she jokes, whenever we go out for dinner or a concert. Though she plays bridge on alternate Saturdays and belongs to a Great Books club, she goes out of her way to avoid introducing me to her friends. "I'm not *that* addlepated," she laughed once, with a little twitch of her mouth. "There's not one of those girls who wouldn't love to whisk you away," she said, "even the ones who have sons. Especially the ones who have sons."

She laughed again and I laughed with her, not quite sure what she meant. Dinah's son, Avery, had died when he was ten, killed when he tried to cross an old two-lane highway on his bike. I'd been waiting on the other side of the highway, safely across, and in his hurry to catch up Avery hadn't seen the farm-livestock truck barreling toward him; he'd been killed instantly. I didn't think Dinah was really referring to Avery, whom she hadn't mentioned in so long people might have assumed she'd forgotten him. But I knew that Dinah dreaded her past, her memories, far more than she feared loud noises or moving stairs.

Soon enough, we're standing at the base of the escalators, Dinah gazing up toward the second floor while I stare at Dinah.

"It's so early," she says, "I thought maybe they wouldn't have turned them on yet. I thought maybe I could practice—you know, when they're not moving." She speaks slowly as if trying to stall.

"That'd be fine," I tell her. I point behind us. "You could practice on the regular stairs."

Already she's shaking her head. "Nope," she says. "I came here to ride these stupid things, and I'm going to ride them."

I'm startled by this sudden resolve. Driving over, I'd deliberately talked about other things but had tried to remember when her specific fear of escalators really began. It had always been one of the phobias she joked about most freely, describing her futile attempts as a young woman to ride the escalators in the old Rich's department store in downtown Atlanta. "I'd stand off to the side for awhile," she'd say, "and watch how other people did it. I knew the trick was that you paused, chose your step, and hopped on. But with me, I'd always lose my footing, and by the time I settled on one step, my back foot was lost out behind me somewhere, and then my knees would buckle, and I'd try to get back off. If I couldn't do that, I'd just freeze with one foot in the air, hanging on for dear life." She'd laugh brightly, even standing to act out the fiasco, crooking her dainty elbows and knees. "And *then* there was the matter of getting off. I'd try to hop off like everybody else, but I was either a beat too slow or too fast, and I'd think I was off but still be on, still moving, or else I *was* off but would hit the floor at a strange angle and twist my foot or lose my balance or think I was falling when I wasn't. I'd have that strange feeling you have when you're half asleep, that the floor is about to slam you in the face."

And besides getting on and off, she said, there was the possibility of getting your shoe stuck in the gears, wasn't there? Or what if that darned moving banister caught onto your sleeve? Or your bracelet? You could lose an arm or a leg quick as that, she was sure—you could lose your life! She told this story often and everyone would laugh, including Dinah, though a hollowness settled in her eyes that only I could see.

So I flattered myself, anyway. Since Dinah and I are each other's sole surviving relative, we've become accustomed to the idea that we have some exclusive, blood-deep understanding of one another.

149

Dinah's infrequent beaux—those hardy enough to pierce her cheerful but outright indifference to romantic attachments—have never lasted more than a month or two, quickly becoming the objects, poor men, of our after-dinner hilarity, as Dinah describes some instance of coarseness or self-importance or otiose presumption that destroyed any chance of intimacy or, for that matter, friendship. For my part, my longstanding relationship with a woman named Karen Reynolds, a colleague at the investment firm where I've worked for the past eight years, depends on her understanding that some slight need of Dinah's might call me out of town at any moment, possibly for a protracted length of time. I've clung to the idea that I'm indispensable to Dinah, though probably it's the other way around. Often I make the hundred-mile drive to Dinah's for no reason, exchanging my striving, sharp-angled city life for Dinah's unchanging quirks and obsessions—her definite fears, her inchoate longings. Is she more than a fixed point, a reference point? After some time in Dinah's company the mental image of my cluttered office or Karen's attractive, impatient face brings a sudden *frisson* of denial, an amnesiac's puzzlement at the thought of some other, established life.

So I'm thinking, guiltily, that I have encouraged this adventure of Dinah's out of some base need to justify myself, to provide the fiction of some forward—or upward—motion in her life. I clasp her elbow gently, whisper temptation in her ear.

"You don't have to, Dinah. You really don't."

Despite her last words, Dinah looks far from resolute. We've stood here for five or six minutes and twice have stepped aside to let someone pass. Dinah watches the gently rising backs of these other people—these normal people, she must be thinking—with a child's dark wistfulness. She takes an audible breath, then sinks back into the arm I've drawn firmly around her shoulder.

"Maybe in a minute, Gary," she says. "Let me rest a minute."

"That's fine," I say. "We've got plenty of time."

I follow Dinah's mesmerized gaze back to the escalators, to those bottom few steps rising implacably out of the floor as if bearing an opposing, fateful message: there isn't much time, it's now or never. Dinah seems to ignore this message, her shoulders limp beneath my arm. She removes a scented handkerchief from her purse and pats her cheek, then replaces the handkerchief, sighing.

"You know, Gary," she says, in a tired voice I don't recall hearing before. "These outings probably aren't a good idea. I hate to say this, but—"

She hesitates, and I offer no encouragement; surely she feels the stiffening of my arm. I'm pondering her phrase, *These outings*, fearing that she means more than our plans to work on her phobias.

"I remember how Lucy used to go on and on," she says, "about your future. Gary would do this, Gary would do that—he'd be a baseball star, he'd be President of the United States!" She laughs, vaguely. I keep my arm around her shoulder although I want nothing more than to withdraw it. Dinah's younger sister Lucy, my mother, died the year before Avery's accident out on the highway. She died by her own hand, taking an overdose of pills one Sunday morning after Dinah had taken us boys to church and Sunday school. My father had abandoned us long before, in much the same way Dinah's husband, Uncle Winston, had left town (as I'd gathered from stray, overheard conversations between my parents) before Avery was even born. No farewells, no warning of any kind. Not even a note. So, in what seemed a natural arrangement at the time, my mother and I had moved in with Dinah and Avery. All around us, people clucked about the shame of those darling Barrett girls, the prettiest girls in town when they were young, having suffered such a fate. The idea developed that their beauty—a vulnerable, almost sickly beauty, people said—was the kind that seemed destined to be disappointed, blighted after a short time of splendor. But they had their daddy's money, at least. They had those darling little boys, at least, who would eventually grow up to take care of their mothers. . . . Until this moment, watching the escalators rise into some darksome rarefied sphere, some higher stage of being it almost seemed, I hadn't considered that over the years Dinah and I had formed a pact, unspoken but virtually sacred: that neither of us would recall, either by direct or oblique reference, the ghosts of the dead. I couldn't remember the last time Dinah had spoken my mother's name, and only now did I understand how foolhardy was this morning's venture, what a wayward and unreasonable longing had brought us to this juncture in our lives.

"Dinah, let's go home," I tell her.

She hasn't lost her thought, however; she has only been gathering strength.

"It's not fair to you, Gary," she says, her voice steady, lacking its customary lilt. "I've held you back, I know that—but you're still a young man, after all. You and Sharon should get married, you should have children—"

I give a quick, barking laugh that resonates strangely in the mall's open dark spaces. "It's Karen," I say. "Her name is Karen."

Though they've met several times, it isn't so odd that Dinah should mistake my friend's name; whenever my aunt and I are together, it could be said that Karen joins, temporarily, the company of Avery and Lucy and the others. We seldom refer to her.

Dinah takes out the handkerchief again and this time wipes her brow.

"I'm sorry, honey. I guess that proves my point."

"And we don't want children," I say, almost curtly. "Neither of us wants that."

Dinah squeezes my arm. "Don't be mad, honey," she says. "We've needed to have this talk, you know. For a long time."

We still haven't looked at each other. My vision has blotched, watching the endless rise of the escalator steps—each made to hold a human form, each empty this morning. I suppose Dinah is watching the escalators, too, her blue eyes gone watery with bewilderment, or some dismal recognition.

"I started thinking about this—about all of this—on the day we first began talking about my phobias. You know, about getting rid of them. Then I talked to Dr. Shields about it. I hadn't mentioned you very often before, and he asked a lot of questions. Anyhow, it all came tumbling out, and that's when I knew—I knew—"

"Aunt Dinah," I say calmly, "you shouldn't get upset."

She pauses, taking deep breaths. Again that impression of recouping, gathering strength. Has the doctor taught her that? Will she report back to him, during their next session? *Dr. Shields, I did try to talk with Gary. He wasn't too receptive, but I think we've made a start. . . .*

"I'm not upset, Gary," she says, with a hint of condescension. "Not at all."

My heart tenses. "All right, then, why don't we get this over with? Why don't you hop on?"

I gesture with cruel nonchalance toward the escalators.

Aunt Dinah seems to know that the moment has come. She steps out of the restraining circle of my arm and approaches the base of the escalators. She removes one of the white gloves and reaches her brown-spotted hand toward the ascending banister, touching it once or twice, lightly. She starts to turn around, to glance at me, but she doesn't. Watching her fluffy dark head, the curve of her pale neck that still looks fragile and lovely, I feel my heart begin tightening, contracting. I'm aware that my fists are clenched and that I'm holding my breath.

One hand touching the banister, Dinah watches her feet and after a beat, or two beats, steps onto the escalators.

Almost at the same moment, there is a whooping noise from somewhere above. Near the top of the escalators, descending out of the shadowy second floor, I see a boy in glasses carrying a waxed cup filled with Karmel Korn. He's about ten, wearing blue jeans and a horizontally striped red-and-white T-shirt, and at first I'm sure that I'm hallucinating. The boy is smiling, munching the candy, as he sidesteps quickly down the same set of escalators that Aunt Dinah, clutching the banister, is bravely ascending. He seems to be playing a game, seeing how fast he can descend against the implacable upward current of the stairs. Moving nimbly, monkey-like, he is chuckling to himself and does not seem to notice Dinah, though they are on a direct collision course and though Dinah has summoned the temerity to release one of her pale quivering arms and begin gesturing wildly, trying to get the boy's attention. I'm still convinced that I'm seeing things until I hear, from the second floor, a woman's voice: "Do you hear me, Jeffrey? I said *no*, you'll get yourself killed, you'll—" But her voice breaks off, hopeless; her son is already halfway down the "up" escalators, moving rapidly. When it seems certain that he will crash into Dinah and send her sprawling, the boy hops agilely to the other side and goes past her, still chuckling, still sidestepping with uncanny skill. He has almost reached the bottom when I think to glance upward again, where I just have time to see Dinah's diminished form—head slightly bowed, shoulders slumped—move safely off the top of the escalators, onto the second floor and out of sight.

"Hey Mister," the boy says, tugging at my sleeve. "I came down the wrong way, did you see that? Pretty good, huh?"

I am thinking, bitterly, that she didn't once look back.

II

When I leave home for the first time, a few weeks shy of my twentieth birthday, I am not afraid, exactly. But I am concerned. Apprehensive. Though I "took a year off," as the jaunty phrase goes, after high school, and helped Aunt Dinah sort out her tangled financial and personal affairs, I did not feel good about leaving her. Deciding against a prestigious northeastern school, I enrolled in the state university in Atlanta, only a two-hour drive away.

During those first weeks of school I am not homesick, exactly, but I feel oppressed with a vague sense of guilt. All during the summer my Aunt Dinah's nervous problems—insomnia, night fears, fainting spells, abrupt mood swings—had worsened, but when I suggested postponing college another year, Dinah quickly brushed her own wor-ries aside. She invoked my excellent test scores, my sparkling future. She became cheerful and forward-looking, exactly the opposite of the way I feel during September and most of October.

When I call home each night, using the battered pay phone down the hall from my dorm room, I have trouble believing her brave assurances that she's fine, perfectly fine. The medication is helping, she says. Dr. Shields is a wonderful man, and Father Hopkins calls or visits several times each week. Listening, I shift my weight uneasily. Her voice sounds timid and far away. As the weeks pass, I find it more and more difficult to concentrate on my freshman courses.

When Father Hopkins telephones, one Thursday afternoon in late October, I'm almost relieved. I pack an overnight bag, but during the drive home I decide against continuing with college, at least for this year. Since my mother's suicide, eleven years ago, and the death of my cousin Avery so cruelly soon after that, Dinah and I have devel-oped a close and mutually supportive bond. My only reason for at-tending college (though I haven't said this to Dinah, not in so many words) is to study business, so I can do a better job of handling Dinah's investments. When I reach twenty-one, there will also be the stock and bank accounts my mother left in trust. These are respon-sibilities which I take very seriously, as I suppose I take most things seriously. (During my six weeks on campus, I've gathered that I'm not your typical college student. I've grown accustomed to the kidding of my dorm-mates, who insist that I think and brood too much. They've coaxed me out a few times—to get some pizza, to drink a few beers—and though they're pleasant company, I have trouble paying attention to their friendly banter, their endless jokes. As I drive home their laughter rings in my ears, brittle and unreal.)

I'm startled by the number of cars parked outside Aunt Dinah's house. Helplessly I recall the days after Avery's funeral, when the cars of family friends and hangers-on clogged the circular driveway. Bearing flowers or covered dishes into the high-ceilinged parlor, the ladies hugged and wept over Dinah, while their embarrassed hus-bands chucked me under the chin and mumbled that I was "the man of the house" now, that they hoped I'd be good and strong and brave. (This was, of course, our family's second funeral in less than a year, but when my mother died there had been no such outpouring. Father Hopkins had officiated at her service, too, but it had been extremely brief and attended by only five or six people. In the ensuing weeks he had leaked out the news gradually, discreetly, prompting Aunt Dinah to remark how much tact Father Hopkins possessed, how much foresight and wisdom. At school, eventually, I endured a few cruel jokes and blunt queries, but in general my mother's suicide was a non-event.)

When I come inside, everyone rises except Dinah herself. My eyes dart immediately to her overstuffed easy chair, where she sits looking blurry and distraught. I say "blurry" because her hair is mussed, her makeup uneven, her eyelids and lips trembling—the opposite of her usual well-groomed, focused demeanor. Father Hopkins comes forward and pumps my hand, expressing hearty thanks. "We've had quite a time of it," he says, in the jovial manner he uses for crisis situations. He's a burly, big-chested man, with a head of silver-gray curls; his skin is coarse and flushed. Although Aunt Dinah secretly dislikes the Episcopalian service and seldom goes any more, Father Hopkins visits often, as though she were his most faithful parishioner; suddenly I wonder if he's in love with her, either knowingly or not. It's not a bizarre thought, really. Also seated in the room are Dr. Shields, who has twice proposed to Dinah, and a "beau," as she always calls them, whose name is Martin, or perhaps Morton—I can't remember. It probably doesn't matter. He's thin, dapper, and sad-eyed, perched in a straight-backed chair nearest Dinah. Dr. Shields is about Dinah's age, blond, handsome, but weak-looking. He sits on the antique brocaded love seat, cracking his knuckles. These two men stare at me, with a kind of dull envy, as Father Hopkins leads me over to Dinah's chair.

"What happened?" I say, pleased by the sound of my cool, clipped voice, which cuts through the muggy emotional atmosphere in the room.

"Oh, honey," Aunt Dinah says ruefully, reaching out a white fluttering hand. For a moment we simply clasp hands, while the others look on, slack-mouthed.

Even in a somewhat disheveled state, Dinah's beauty is nothing short of spectacular. Her glamour has always been a matter of small but heartrending details—the fragile jaw bone, the just-exposed tips of her ear lobes, the deliberately arched and penciled brows above her dark, quick-moving eyes. Speaking softly, she lifts the brows into tiny, V-shaped peaks.

"Oh, honey, your auntie did a stupid thing."

Her eyes fill, and at the same moment she gives an inconsequent laugh.

"Dinah?" I say, worried.

"I've given her a sedative," Dr. Shields says, from the love seat. "She's much calmer than she was."

"I'm not sure about sedatives," Father Hopkins says, frowning. "I'm not sure they're good for her."

"Poor Dinah," says Martin, or Morton, clucking his tongue and shifting his body sympathetically in the chair. "She went upstairs this morning—up into the attic, I mean—and she—"

Dinah flutters her hand once more.

"Let *me* tell Gary," she says, her eyes roving about my face quickly, hungrily. I know what she is feeling, for I feel the same: we have missed each other tremendously. Despite her edict against weekend visits until Thanksgiving—she didn't want to "depend" on me, she wanted me to plunge fully into my exciting college life—there hasn't been a Friday when I haven't wanted to come home, for my sake as much as hers.

"Go ahead," I say gently. "Tell me."

She laughs briefly, trying to settle herself, and takes a deep breath. Behind me, I can sense the sharpened attention of the other three men. There's a tension, a general anguish in the room.

Dinah says, haltingly, that she'd gone up into the attic that morning. Wanting for something to do, she had boxed up some things of mine—old sweaters and scarves, a pile of high school memorabilia gathering dust in the back of my closet—and had taken the boxes, one at a time, up the rickety wooden stairs from the second-floor landing. In the attic, she says, the air was incredibly musty and overheated. Somehow, up there, it was like another world. Once she had gotten the last box upstairs, she felt how drastically her mood had changed. Whereas she'd felt "at loose ends" earlier that morning, and a bit melancholy, now she felt energetic and spry, as though her physical labor had helped her break through the lassitude of recent weeks. Having stowed the boxes away, she obeyed a sudden impulse and went over by the attic's tiny window, whose thick piece of glass—octagon-shaped, tinted a pale amber—allowed only a dimmed, hazy vision of the yard and street below. Dinah says, hesitating, that she felt a chill enwrapping her shoulders at that moment, despite the intense heat and her own sense of energy and power. She'd been thinking how her view out the attic window resembled one of those old, sepia-toned photographs from her grandparents' days, and at that moment she noticed, beneath the window ledge, an old beechwood crate whose contents—the lid was open—snagged her attention at once. Before she quite knew what was happening, she had reached into the crate and removed several bulky envelopes filled with photographs—some of my mother and myself, but mostly pictures of Avery. She says anxiously that she shouldn't have looked at them, she *should* have

156

dropped them as though they were burning coals, but soon enough she was going through the pictures one by one, greedily, the yellowish glare from the window tinting the photographs so that *they* appeared sepia-toned, much older than they were and somehow absolved of harm. There was Avery at his fifth birthday party, wearing his first pair of glasses and smiling from behind a lighted birthday cake. There was Avery standing next to me, a year or two later, after a neighborhood baseball game. Avery looked slight and exhausted, she says, his glasses askew, a smear of dirt along his cheek, while I looked tall and athletic and smug—Dinah uses that odd word, "smug," without glancing at me—as I stood with my chest pushed out, my arm around Avery. She found a picture of my mother—"Lucy was so lovely, so young-looking!" Dinah cries—with Avery and me perched side by side on her knees. And there was a shot of Avery out in the back yard; he was holding a butterfly net, she whispers, so it must have been taken after his tenth birthday, not long before he died.

Dinah says that she put the pictures away, after that one. She knew that in another box to her left, marked "Toys," was the butterfly net itself, and his coin collection, and his coloring books. One of the coloring books, I suddenly recall, had Bozo the Clown on the cover, and I remember how Dinah would shudder whenever she saw it, and how Avery would laugh. I can imagine Dinah opening the box and seeing that coloring book and literally dying of fright, but fortunately this did not happen. By this time, Dinah explains, the chill she'd felt had intensified and she'd begun trembling. At some point she had also started weeping. She backed away from the window and went awkwardly down the stairs, stumbling once or twice, getting to the bottom in a state that she ought to call, she supposes, "outright hysteria." On the second-floor landing, the door to the attic stairs closed, it was her ordinary surroundings that seemed unreal. She was shivering uncontrollably, she was sobbing, she knew that she'd made a terrible mistake and that she needed help at once. So she called Martin—she says the word distinctly, "Martin"—and Martin called Dr. Shields and Father Hopkins. Though she begged Father Hopkins not to bother me, the priest had insisted. All three men told her that she didn't look well, she'd suffered a tremendous shock and needed all the support she could get.

"Anyhow," Dinah says, her eyes watery again, apologetic, "that's what happened. Your auntie made a stupid mistake, and it's everyone else who pays."

"Don't be ridiculous," Martin says at once, from behind me. "Don't say such things."

He sounds angry, but no one pays much attention.

"We're glad you're here, Gary," Father Hopkins says.

"Your being here, plus the sedative," Dr. Shields says, "ought to make her good as new."

Aunt Dinah is looking at me, as though alarmed that I haven't said anything.

I lean across and kiss her cheek, whispering in the same breath, "I'm home. Please don't worry." Then, feeling self-conscious, I excuse myself by saying that I want to shower and change my clothes. There's a murmur of agreement—of course, of course. Dinah says to take my time—she's fine now, really she is. As I move slowly up the stairs, feeling deathly tired, Father Hopkins calls out something cheerful and encouraging, but I can't make out the words and I don't bother to turn around.

Upstairs I take a long, hot shower; then I change into slacks and a soft cotton shirt. Still feeling tired, I decide to lie down for a while, but for some reason I leave my room and go across the hall, to the seldom-used bedroom next to Dinah's. When we were boys, Avery and I had shared this room, which is still furnished with twin "youth" beds and identical pinewood chests of drawers. I drift toward my old bed and lie down, raising dust and an odor of disuse from the tan chenille spread. Lying on my side, I gaze across at Avery's empty bed. When we were very young, our mothers would often send us upstairs for afternoon naps, and we would lie here fully clothed, not even removing our shoes. We talked idly but doggedly, refusing to fall asleep. An hour or two later we would reappear downstairs, ostentatiously yawning and stretching our arms. At that age, the temperamental differences between us were not so pronounced, and there must have been a particular fondness between myself and Avery. Our mothers, at that time, looked so much alike that they were often mistaken for twins. Gazing across at the empty bed, idly remembering, I become drowsy despite myself, and feel gently suffused in a gauze of memory, desire, and longing; then, opening my eyes, I have that abrupt, plunging sensation, as of a helpless fall through space. My limbs jerk, my heart races, but when I land I'm still on the bed, still lying on my side.

Then, for a brief moment, I do glimpse Avery in the other bed. He's lying on his side, too, and staring across at me. He's nineteen now, neatly dressed, still wearing thick glasses, and he stares expressionlessly with his slightly magnified eyes. I think how peaceful he looks, how white and untouched and whole.

I rise from the bed and drift out to the top of the stairs. From the parlor below, I hear conversation, laughter; Dinah's high trilling laugh cuts through the muddled deeper voices. Looking down at my bare feet, feeling detached and emotionless, I begin descending the stairs. As I move downward, the heads and chair backs of Dinah's guests are visible beyond the curve of the banister. Straining, I can now make out what Dinah is saying. With clever, charming self-mockery, she is talking about her lifelong fear of escalators. By now the story must be familiar to all three men, but nonetheless their laughter sounds genuine, filled with masculine delight. I can't quite see Dinah, but I can picture her antics as she stands with her arms flailing, one leg bent in mid-air, her eyes widened in exaggerated fright.

Imagining this, I now have the thought that it's not myself descending the stairs; rather it's my cousin, Avery. That's why he's moving with such quietness and stealth, awaiting the moment when he reaches the parlor door and catches Dinah in this mood of hilarity, her limbs distorted, her male audience held in thrall. Then Dinah's eyes will bulge, her cheeks sag unbecomingly, as her make-believe fear turns to stunned disbelief and then to outright horror.

As I come off the stairway, this unbidden fantasy vanishes as quickly as it came. I'm shaken by the experience, of course, especially by its suggestion of hostility toward Dinah, but I don't feel particularly surprised or even displeased. When I come into the parlor, Dinah continues her antic monologue and none of the others glance around. Taking my seat I feel weightless and happy, insubstantial as any ghost.

III

One Saturday morning when I am twelve years old and my cousin Avery is ten, we decide to take our bikes and go out riding. Though Aunt Dinah has forbidden us to go past the circular driveway, it's fairly early and Dinah is still sleeping—"getting her beauty rest," as she likes to say, with a wink at us boys. I use this same wink on Avery when he pauses at the edge of the driveway, one foot on the ground, and says he doesn't like disobeying his mother. Aah, I tell him, what she doesn't know won't hurt her, we'll be back before she's even awake—and with a whoop I start pedaling down the street, yelling for Avery to hurry up, come on! After a moment's hesitation, he does.

We pedal slowly through the residential streets, where most of the houses, like Dinah's, are set far back from the road, with curving snakelike driveways and huge porches. One day last summer Avery had tumbled off our own porch and gashed his forehead on the bottom step; the cut took eleven stitches, one for each of the brick steps leading down from the porch. The day after Avery's accident, wanting for something to do, I had counted the steps and had examined the bottom step for traces of Avery's blood—but there was nothing. Aunt Dinah or our part-time maid, Flora, must have already washed the blood away.

At school the kids taunt Avery for being so clumsy, and I always take up for him. Several times I've gotten in fights with bullies from Avery's class, and I've won every fight. As we're riding along through the neighborhood, though, I can't help teasing Avery and showing off—lifting my hands from the handlebars and folding them nonchalantly across my chest, zigzagging the bike at dangerous angles along the pavement. "Hey, try this!" I call out to Avery, riding circles around him, laughing. "See if you can do *this*," I cry, not quite understanding the savage joy that's coursing through my chest and limbs.

"Cut it out," Avery says. He rides with his thin shoulders slumped above the handlebars, steering cautiously, frowning. He wears thick black-framed glasses, and at school some of the kids call him "four eyes." I wish I could keep Avery from acting like a sissy, becoming an object of ridicule, but if anything he gets paler and skinnier, and becomes more of a Mama's boy, with each passing year. The kids tease him about our family situation, too, and even about what happened to *my* mother—though they wouldn't dare say a thing when I'm around. I inherited the strong build and bony, sharp-looking features of my father, Jimmy, who left town several years ago, on one of his "sales" trips, but never came back. Avery's father had left Aunt Dinah before Avery was born, so neither of us kids remembers him, but in pictures Dinah keeps in her lingerie drawer he looks like a grown-up version of Avery, his face smooth and girlish-looking, his hair and even his eyelashes a delicate pale blond. So I've always felt a bit superior to Avery because of our different fathers, and it's clear that others sense the difference, too. Even Aunt Dinah has remarked that Avery and I don't look like blood relatives, that we don't favor each other or share any traits or behavior whatsoever.

Now that I've turned twelve and will be transferring out to the junior high school next year, leaving Avery to fend for himself in the fifth grade, I know I shouldn't egg him on—but this particular morning I can't help it, somehow; I'm too cheerful and full of energy. When we cross Main Street and start riding along the little-used oil road that runs parallel to the highway, I call out again, "Come on,

Avery, pedal faster, try riding with no hands—look here at me, look how easy!"

Avery glances over, mistrustfully. "Cut it out, Gary," he says. And then, after we've crossed the railroad tracks—Avery getting off his bike and walking it across, while I jolt over the tracks at high speed, bouncing and laughing—he comes to a stop and just stands there, with his usual woebegone expression. He waits for me to ride back and then says, "Come on, Gary, we'd better go home."

"What for?" I ask, riding around him in small neat circles, so that he never knows quite which way to turn. I'm wiping my forehead with the back of my hand (even this early in the morning, it's fiercely hot in mid-August), feeling irritated that Avery hasn't even broken a sweat. He stands there with his white knuckles gripping the handlebars, looking pale and sullen.

"What's the matter?" I ask him. "You afraid of something—afraid to go riding, get too far away from Mommy?"

"Cut it out," he says again, but he looks away and I can tell he's really bugged. Another nickname they have for him at school: bug-eyes. Avery's glasses make his eyes look bigger than they are.

"Come on," I say, in a friendlier tone, clapping him on the shoulder, "let's cross over the highway and go out the farm road a bit. There's some great hills out there, you can get going really fast."

"We're not supposed to be *this* far," he says, his lip curling downward a little, which means he's about to cry.

"OK, how about this," I tell him. "There's a big pecan tree up on that hill," and I point across the highway. "You can sit under the tree, in the shade, and I'll go zooming up and down the hills. I'll do every trick in the book, all for you—you can just watch. I'll even show you how to do a couple of things—you know, the easier ones. Come on, Avery, it's too soon to go home."

There's a sudden urgency in my voice, combined with the persuasive salesmanship I've inherited from my charming but long-gone father. Despite everything, I know that Avery looks up to me; even "worships" me, as Aunt Dinah claims. So I know already—as I keep circling Avery, and cajoling him, and making promises in a buoyant, cheerful voice—that I'm going to get my way.

IV

In her rare moments of pique, that's what my mother would say about her sister—that Dinah "always got her way." Though the Barrett girls had been equally pretty, and were sometimes mistaken for twins, their temperaments were dramatically opposite: Lucy had been a quiet, withdrawn girl who never made a fuss and disliked attention of any kind, while Dinah had been the perverse but lively "belle," flirting at some point with every available man in a fifty-mile radius of town, and with some who weren't so available. Despite their beauty and the fortune each inherited at the death of their father, no one was surprised that both girls had married unwisely. Lucy accepted that grinning charmer, Jimmy Wheeler, after only two dates, falling in love precipitously and madly in the usual way of melancholy girls, but within months had resigned herself not only to his endless "sales" trips but to a considerable amount of philandering right in her own hometown. It was to Lucy's scandalous victimization, in fact, that Dinah would later ascribe her own ostracism from the polite Southern social circles into which the girls had been born. From what I've been able to gather (Dinah being much less forthcoming about her own emotional history than about my mother's), it appears that Avery's father, far from having abandoned his wife and son, might actually have been banished from their presence; certainly his photographs suggest a dependent, besotted admirer of the kind Dinah still keeps about her—albeit at a safe distance—to this day. I've often distrusted, in short, her melancholy references to the time when Uncle Winston "took off," or her patient explanations to Avery that his father was a romantic wanderer, the type who couldn't be held down. This description, of course, fit my own father rather than Avery's.

By the time I learned with some degree of certainty what had really happened, our lives were already set: my mother and I had moved in with Dinah and Avery, where the four of us lived in relative isolation, getting few visitors except for unshakable admirers of Dinah like Father Hopkins and Dr. Shields. Once her divorce came through Dinah did occasionally have a "beau," as she'd already begun calling them, but when these men began phoning too persistently Dinah would no longer encourage them, and if we boys were present in the room would even make faces into the phone, keeping the receiver covered with one palm to cover the sound of our laughter. (Even Avery would laugh, looking from his mother to me as if trying to discover what was so funny.) As for Lucy, she disliked her sister's coquetry but seldom objected, and she actually seemed to approve my growing closeness to my aunt, gladly retreating to her room and allowing Dinah to run the house and the daily lives of us boys. By the time we were both in school, my mother spent almost all her time sequestered, showing up only for mealtimes and an occasional visit to church. It did not strike me, at the time, that my mother was desperately unhappy. Dinah had explained to both Avery and me that some people were merely "reserved," liking to keep to themselves and read a great deal and think their private thoughts. I had noticed how Avery's pale, big-eyed face had seemed to brighten in my mother's presence, and how he would sometimes accompany her back up the stairs, the two of them talking in quick, confiding voices. So I had assumed that, by some quirk of nature, Avery took after my mother, while I took after his. It didn't seem to matter, somehow. Our daily routine was stable, predictable; we had all settled comfortably into our separate lives.

At about this same time—a year or two, I suppose before my mother's death—Dinah began developing, or at least began talking about, her various phobias. One Halloween when Avery and I presented ourselves for her inspection (one of us dressed as Bozo the Clown, the other wearing a crimson devil's suit, complete with pitchfork and horned mask) she had taken two or three steps backward, truly alarmed. "Gary? Avery? Who are— Which one is—?" Her skin had gone white, and even her pupils had shrunk to tiny points inside the whites of her eyes. Since I was already a couple of inches taller than Avery, I had trouble believing she couldn't tell us apart. Nonetheless I'd grabbed Avery's arm and dragged him out the back door, and I made sure we removed our masks before returning that evening from trick or treat. Only a couple of months before that, Dinah had displayed in spectacular fashion her fear of escalators. She had driven us boys into Atlanta to buy school clothes at Rich's, and while the three of us were ascending the escalators toward the boys' department, Dinah had suddenly lost her nerve: her knees buckled, her purse dangled off her wrist at an awkward angle, she somehow had her feet on two different steps and her face, wide-eyed, wore a look of abject terror. When we reached the top Dinah stumbled off, and stood panting for a few moments, her shoulders bent, while Avery and I watched helplessly. This turned out to be Dinah's last attempt to ride the escalators. That evening, in our bedroom, I remember how angry and bothered Avery seemed. "Why is Mama so afraid of things, what's *wrong* with her?" he asked, his eyes bulging behind his glasses. I remember feeling queasy and empty, and to cover this I threw a pillow at my cousin, trying to distract his attention. I knew I couldn't explain.

It often seemed, in fact, that Avery could perceive things the rest of us couldn't. In the ten-month interval between my mother's death

163

and Avery's own, Dinah had often remarked on this, bewailing the fact that we hadn't listened to Avery, had discounted his anxiety as the whining of a sickly eight-year-old. For that morning, as the three of us were getting ready for church, Avery had kept saying that someone should check on Aunt Lucy. Although she hadn't shown up for breakfast, this wasn't really unusual: my mother had begun using sleeping pills, which sometimes kept her unconscious throughout the morning. Avery insisted that Aunt Lucy had wanted to go to church this morning, she'd attended the previous few Sundays and wanted to become a regular churchgoer again, but both Dinah and I had brushed him off. "Honey, let your Aunt Lucy sleep," Dinah had said, adjusting her hat and gloves in the hall mirror. That morning, I believe, she had never been more beautiful: her dark hair dramatically upswept, her skin taut and glowing, her figure trim, compact, but sensual in her close-fitting spring dress of yellow linen. Behind her, dressed in my navy blue suit from last Easter, I said quickly, "She had trouble sleeping all last week, so she's probably just catching up. It would be stupid to wake her, Avery, just when she's getting some rest." "That's right, Gary," Dinah said, but I noticed how Avery kept glancing toward the stairway, as if he would suddenly break away and go flying up the steps. So I went over to him, clamping a hand on each shoulder. "Race you to the car," I said. "Last one there's a little turd!" I added, laughing. Avery had no choice but to run off behind me, as Dinah called after us, "Gary, what awful language!—and on a Sunday!"

It's possible that, almost a year later, when I taunt and tease my cousin about riding our bikes out past the highway, I am recalling that Sunday morning. For who understands, finally, the sudden warps and sinister promptings of memory? Certainly I am visited, at the oddest times, with a procession of images rising into my awareness slowly, implacably, with the mechanical certainty of fate itself: once we'd returned from church, Avery rushing downstairs with a white, wrenched expression, saying wildly that Aunt Lucy would not wake up, would *not* wake up; the arrival of Dr. Shields, then the ambulance; the covered stretcher borne carefully down the stairs by a pair of black paramedics, who looked rueful and embarrassed; the visit of Father Hopkins to discuss the funeral services; and then the funeral itself, so meager and quickly accomplished that afterward it seemed, eerily, that Lucy Barrett Wheeler might never have existed. Yes, when Avery and I do pause beside the highway, each resting on one leg as we await a break in the traffic, I am remembering clearly Avery's pinched, woebegone look during the funeral service and in the days

164

that followed, a look of diminished hope that suggested the extremes of both innocence and fear.

"Now we can go," I tell him, raising my foot to the pedal. "Right after this station wagon passes."

"Wait, Gary," Avery calls after me, in his thin whining voice. "There's too much traffic, it's too dangerous—"

But I don't listen; I push hard on the pedal, and the moment the wood-paneled station wagon is past I shoot across the highway, letting out a wild whoop, crossing easily before the next car, its horn honking and brakes squealing, rushes by.

Across all this noise, Avery is mouthing words from his side of the highway, clearly angry and offended, but rather comical at this distance. I fold my hands together and lift them above my head, in the sign of victory. Then I yell: "Come on, Avery, you can make it! Let's go!"

Now Avery looks doubtful, fearful; cars and trucks are whizzing past, and it seems there's never enough of a clear opening for him to cross the highway safely. Nonetheless I stand waiting, resting my weight on one leg, feeling strong and confident and even, somehow, exultant. I can feel the blood coursing swiftly through my legs, my heart, I can feel the pulsebeat at my throat keeping time to my words: "Come on, Avery, don't be a little chicken-shit! Look, there's plenty of time between cars if you hurry, so come on, will you? Come on!"

His expression changes again; he looks across at me, gloomily, his eyes the fixed dark points I remember still from last October, the night before my mother's death. It was past midnight, I suppose, when the telephone rang, and we were all upstairs except Dinah, who had just gotten home from a date. By the time she answered, in the downstairs hall, I had risen from bed and drifted to the top of the stairway, where I could see only the hem of her red silk dress, her shapely ankle, her black patent stiletto heels. But her voice wafted clearly up the stairs, and within seconds I knew that the caller was my father. "But why now, why now?" Dinah said, in a kind of soft wail. I remember only snatches of the conversation. At one point Dinah said, sarcastically, "Aren't you calling for Lucy, really, but you're afraid to admit it?" And a bit later, low and wounded: "It's not in my nature, you know that, I've always *told* you that. You want too much, Jimmy, you always wanted too damn much. . . ." It was then I felt, beside me, the ghostly apparition of my cousin Avery, wearing his thin cotton night shirt, giving me his dark fixed immutable gaze that achieved a spectral power in the scant light cast up along the stairs. Even as I heard, from behind me, my mother's door softly

165

closing—I hadn't known, until that moment, that it had stood ajar the whole time—I felt a paralysis in my limbs that prevented my calling down to Aunt Dinah, pleading for her to rush up the stairs in all her dazzling light and beauty, and that likewise kept me from fleeing downstairs to her. I felt immobile, frozen in place. Between us there was not a mere flight of stairs but an irreparable distance, a gulf between two worlds, and my cousin's innocent dark eyes seemed the bearers of this knowledge and of my own perdition. He turned back to his bedroom just as Dinah, downstairs, angrily slammed down the phone, and from that moment a deeper silence reigned in the house, suggesting the loss of all human connections.

V

Am I remembering this—any of this—at the moment Avery, his eyes fixed on mine, lifts his small body and begins pedaling across the highway? He has time, of course; that ancient wheezing farm truck is at least a quarter-mile distant, there's no other vehicle in sight, so naturally I'm gesturing him forward, of course I'm yelling out friendly taunts and boyish encouragement as Avery, his bike wobbling, starts across the highway. What I hadn't predicted, of course, is the dreamlike slowness with which Avery weaves across, not even glancing aside at the oncoming truck, his enlarged eyes in all their innocent dark fury fixed upon me. It's then I raise my hand, a half-completed gesture, to cry out, "Wait, Avery, go back!—there isn't time, look out for that truck, *look out!*" But he continues forward with perverse slowness, wobbling from side to side, not even reacting to the truck's blaring horn and its dramatic noisy skid as the driver, trying to avoid Avery, spins the truck over sideways and buries my cousin beneath several tons of braying livestock and crashing metal. From under the shuddering mess something flies out and lands near my sneakers—Avery's glasses, crushed and blood-spattered. It's then that a horrified cry tears from my throat and I mount the bike and begin pedaling wildly, madly. In less than ten minutes I'm back at Aunt Dinah's.

It turns out that my behavior will be excused as the result of panic, understandable in one so young. Even the truck driver, emerging shaken but unhurt from the wreck, will report to police how I had motioned wildly for my cousin to get back, how I had appeared to be shrieking in horror as Avery continued—obstinately, perversely— into the truck's path. At the time, of course, the opinions of these others mean nothing. During that desperate ten-minute ride, all my thought and energy are focused upon Aunt Dinah, whom I want to reach before all the fuss begins, before she has even heard the news. This is so important. This is so crucial. Once I hit the driveway I begin shrieking her name at the top of my voice, and by the time I throw my bike underneath the old water oak and turn toward the porch she is there, opening the screen door, blinking curiously as she squints out at the sunlight and at me. "Gary, honey?" she says, a tremulous catch in her throat. She comes out onto the porch, to the topmost edge of the steps. She looks youthful but worried, her dark hair gleaming in the sunlight, her hands splayed down the front of her pale-yellow dress. She leans out, fondly. "Honey, is something—" she begins, but doesn't finish. I see her face sag, her eyes darken, but already I am bounding up the porch steps, panting, weeping, ready to be enfolded in her arms.

ACKNOWLEDGMENTS

Stories in this collection appeared in slightly different form in the following periodicals, to which the author and the publisher extend their thanks: *Antigonish Review,* "Him"; *Carolina Quarterly,* "Escalators"; *Crosscurrents,* "Child of My Dreams"; *Missouri Review,* "A Dry Season"; *Shenandoah,* "A Friendly Deceit"; *Southern Humanities Review,* "Private Jokes," "A & P Revisited," and "Getting Through"; and *The Southern Review,* "The Boarder."

"The Boarder" was reprinted in *New Stories from the South: The Year's Best, 1990* (Chapel Hill, N.C.: Algonquin Books, 1990). "Fever" was included in the PEN Syndicated Fiction Project, 1991. "Nickels and Dimes" first appeared in *You Haven't To Deserve: A Gift for the Homeless* (Atlanta: Longstreet Press, 1991).

Greg Johnson is the author of one previous collection of short stories, *Distant Friends*, for which he was named 1990 Georgia Author of the Year. He has also published two volumes of literary criticism, and in 1993 he will publish his first novel and his first collection of poems. Johnson's fiction has been included in such anthologies as *Prize Stories: The O. Henry Awards* and *New Stories from the South: The Year's Best*; his book reviews appear widely. He lives in Atlanta, where he earned a Ph.D. in English from Emory University, and is currently an associate professor of English at Kennesaw State College.

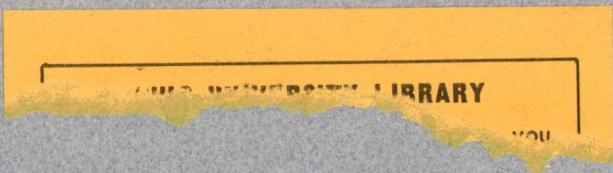

FA